THE DARLING DAHLIAS AND THE UNLUCKY CLOVER

This Large Print Book carries the
Seal of Approval of N.A.V.H.

THE DARLING DAHLIAS AND THE UNLUCKY CLOVER

SUSAN WITTIG ALBERT

THORNDIKE PRESS
A part of Gale, a Cengage Company

Farmington Hills, Mich • San Francisco • New York • Waterville, Maine
Meriden, Conn • Mason, Ohio • Chicago

DEER PARK PUBLIC LIBRARY
44 LAKE AVENUE
DEER PARK, NY 11729

LIBRARY OF CONGRESS CIP DATA ON FILE.
CATALOGUING IN PUBLICATION FOR THIS BOOK
IS AVAILABLE FROM THE LIBRARY OF CONGRESS.

ISBN-13: 978-1-4328-4902-3 (hardcover)

Published in 2018 by arrangement with Levine Greenberg Literary Agency, Inc.

Printed in the United States of America
1 2 3 4 5 6 7 22 21 20 19 18

To the many friends of the Dahlias
who urged me to return to
the little town of Darling.
This book is yours.
Thank you.

October 1934
The Darling Dahlias Clubhouse and
  Gardens
302 Camellia Street
Darling, Alabama

Dear Reader,
Well, here we are again! Are you surprised? We'll bet dollars to doughnuts that you thought we wouldn't be back — and we were thinking along those same lines as well. Life in our little town has been pretty uneventful lately, which is exactly the way most of our folks like it, but it's not very interesting if you're looking for headlines.

But then things took a turn for the worse. One of the men in Darling's wonderful Lucky Four Clovers barbershop quartet met with an unlucky accident not long before Darling played host to the Dixie Regional Barbershop

Quartet Competition! This tragic event threw a monkey wrench into the Clovers' hopes of winning the competition. While Sheriff Buddy Norris was able to get to the bottom of the situation, there are still some unanswered questions hanging on. We hope he gets those loose ends tied up soon.

Mrs. Albert told us that she hadn't planned to write another book about us, but she changed her mind when she heard about the tragic mishap and its unfortunate aftermath. We're sorry to say, however, that not everybody in Darling is pleased to hear that she's added another book to our collection. Far be it from us to name names, but there are those who are afraid that her books may tarnish the reputation of our wonderful town, the way Miss Agatha Christie did with St. Mary Mead, which will forever be remembered as the unluckiest village in all England. Our Darling people are good as good can be, so don't you go thinking we aren't. We hope that Mrs. Albert will clear up this little problem somewhere in her story.

In case this is the first time you've read a book about the Dahlias, we would like to tell you that our garden club is named for Mrs. Dahlia Blackstone, who generously gave us her beautiful house and gardens on Camellia Street, along with a vacant lot where we've planted a big vegetable garden. We know that flowers nourish the heart and soul, but a big plate of stewed okra with tomatoes, buttered corn on the cob, and potato salad go a long way to comfort a body, especially these days, when jobs don't grow on trees and money is scarce as hen's teeth. Every Dahlia agrees: If you've got a garden, you'll have all the wealth you need — and good health to boot.

Now, let's see. Before you start reading, we have several messages to pass along. First, Mrs. Albert wants us to tell you that the title of her book refers to the four-leaf clover as well as to that misfortunate member of Darling's famous barbershop quartet. But she asked us not to tell you which one, since that would spoil the story.

Second, Miss Rogers (our Darling librarian, who wants everybody to use the correct names for plants) asks us to tell you that the Latin name of the four-leaf clover is *Trifolium.* But some of us are very confused, since *trifolium* means three leaves, and the four-leaf clover has

9

four. (And sometimes five or six or even more!) Anyway, in case Miss Rogers asks, please say we told you. *Trifolium.*

And third, Aunt Hetty Little has asked us to pass along these heartening words from that well-known gardener and plant breeder, Luther Burbank. He said, "Flowers always make people better, happier, and more helpful; they are sunshine, food and medicine to the mind." Mr. Burbank ought to know what he's talking about, since he invented the Shasta daisy. (Which Miss Rogers says should properly be called the *Leucanthemum x superbum.*) When times get hard and days get dark, a few *Leucanthemum x superbum* will go a long way toward making things better and happier and luckier for everybody, and especially for you.

Well, you're probably anxious to start reading, so we won't hold you up any longer. But if you get tired of sitting with a book in your hand and want to get up and move around, you can go in the kitchen and bake a pie — Mrs. Albert says she has included a few recipes for you. And of course, you have an invitation to join us in our garden. We can

always find you some weeds to pull or a
row to hoe.

                          Sincerely yours,
                 The Darling Dahlias

THE DARLING DAHLIAS
CLUB ROSTER

Autumn 1934

Club Officers

Elizabeth Lacy, president. Secretary to Mr. Benton Moseley, attorney-at-law, and garden columnist for the Darling *Dispatch.*

Ophelia Snow, vice president and secretary. Reporter, Linotype operator, and advertising manager at the Darling *Dispatch;* also works part-time at the CCC Camp. Wife of Darling's mayor, Jed Snow.

Verna Tidwell, treasurer. Cypress County treasurer and probate clerk. Verna, a widow, lives with her beloved Scotty, Clyde. She is in an on-again-off-again relationship with Alvin Duffy, the president of the Darling Bank.

Myra May Mosswell, communications secretary. Co-owner of the Darling Telephone Exchange and the Darling Diner. Lives with Violet Sims and their little girl,

13

Cupcake (Violet's niece), in the flat over the diner.

Club Members

Earlynne Biddle, a rose fancier. Married to Henry Biddle, the manager at the Coca-Cola bottling plant. Mr. Biddle is a supporter of Huey P. Long and the local chairman of the Share Our Wealth Club.

Bessie Bloodworth, owner of Magnolia Manor, a boardinghouse for genteel elderly ladies next door to the Dahlias' clubhouse on Camellia Street. Local historian, grows vegetables and herbs in the Manor's backyard.

Fannie Champaign, noted milliner and proprietor of Champaign's Darling Chapeaux. Recently married to Charlie Dickens, publisher and editor of the Darling *Dispatch.*

Mildred Kilgore, owner and manager of Kilgore Motors with her husband Roger. They live in a big house near the ninth green of the Cypress Country Club, where Mildred grows camellias.

Aunt Hetty Little, gladiola lover, senior member of the club, and town matriarch. A "regular Miss Marple" who knows all the Darling secrets.

Lucy Murphy, grower of vegetables and

14

fruit on a small market farm on the Jericho Road. Married to Ralph Murphy, who works on the railroad.

Raylene Riggs, Myra May Mosswell's mother and the newest Dahlia. Cooks at the Darling Diner and lives at the Marigold Motor Court.

Dorothy Rogers, Darling's librarian. Knows the Latin name of every plant and insists that everyone else does, too. Resident of Magnolia Manor.

Beulah Trivette, proprietor of Beulah's Beauty Bower, where all the Dahlias go to get beautiful. Artistically talented, Beulah loves cabbage roses and other exuberant flowers.

Alice Ann Walker, secretary to Mr. Duffy at the Darling Savings and Trust Bank. Alice Ann grows iris and daylilies. Her disabled husband, Arnold, tends the family vegetable garden.

CHAPTER ONE:
THE LUCKY FOUR CLOVERS

Friday, October 12, 1934

I'm looking over a four-leaf clover
I overlooked before.
One leaf is sunshine, the second is rain,
Third is the roses that grow in the lane.

No need explaining
The one remaining is somebody I adore.
I'm looking over a four-leaf clover
That I overlooked before.

> Lyrics by Mort Dixon
> Music by Harry M. Woods, 1927

It was raining cats and dogs on the evening of the show, but that didn't keep Darling from turning out in a big crowd — especially since the program was free. All the seats were taken in the basement meeting hall of the First Methodist Church, and Reverend Dooley, greeting folks at the door, was heard to mutter "Shoulda sold tickets." Donations had been encouraged, though, and almost everybody contributed a store-bought can or a quart jar of home-canned vegetables to the Darling Blessing Box, the contents of which would be distributed to folks who needed a little extra boost.

Everybody always looked forward to the show put on each October by the Lucky Four Clovers, Darling's acclaimed men's barbershop group. During the much-anticipated evening, the Clovers would regale their fellow citizens and supporters with old-fashioned melodies, patriotic Confederate tunes, several spirituals, a few Broadway hits — and of course their signa-ture song, "I'm Looking Over a Four-Leaf Clover," which they always sang at the beginning and end of the performance.

It would be a splendid evening, one that the whole community enjoyed, for the Clovers seemed, in an odd sort of way, to belong to the community and to speak for it and represent it, all at the same time. The Clovers sang from their hearts, and from the heart of Darling, too.

Clyde Clover had created the quartet back in 1917, the year Woodrow Wilson led the United States into the War to End All Wars and dispatched the boys of the Alabama

167th to France. They were happy to go, of course — all red-blooded young Americans thought it was their duty to make the world safe for democracy. It might not have been quite what they were expecting, but they did it anyway, and bravely.

All throughout the war, the Lucky Four Clovers kept Darling's patriotic spirits high. They sang "Over There" and "Pack Up Your Troubles in Your Old Kit Bag" and "It's a Long, Long Way to Tipperary." The one wartime song they didn't sing was "I'm a Yankee Doodle Dandy," because of course they weren't.

And when the Great War ended and the numb and battle-scarred survivors came home, the Clovers celebrated their return, and the music seemed to promise a new beginning. They still sang the old favorites, of course, but the Twenties were beginning to roar, and there was an avalanche of new music, bright and boisterous with the spirit of the age. They sang "Ain't We Got Fun," "Ma, He's Makin' Eyes at Me," "I'll See You in My Dreams," "Way Down Yonder in New Orleans," "Hard Hearted Hannah, the Vamp of Savannah," and (naturally) "Alabamy Bound." The decade's lively exuberance and boundless optimism was embodied in its music, and Darling (like everybody else in America) believed the party would go on forever.

It didn't. The fun came to an end on Black Monday, 1929, when the markets crashed. The Thirties didn't roar. They sighed and they sobbed, sometimes in minor keys. The favorites of those days — "Mood Indigo," "Willow Weep for Me," "Love Letters in the Sand," "Stormy Weather" — were melancholy, but for all their sadness, they were sweetly melodic.

And since almost every Darling family now had a radio (or a friendly neighbor who had a radio and was glad to offer an empty parlor chair), people spent their evenings listening. Everybody had a favorite show: the exotic, foreign-sounding *A&P Gypsies* (sponsored by A&P Food Stores); the down-home *Grand Ole Opry* on Nashville's WSM, with Dr. Humphrey Bates and His Possum Hunters and the Binkley Brothers' Dixie Clodhoppers; or the more sophisticated *Palmolive Hour* on Friday nights on NBC, where listeners could hear everything from opera to Broadway to jazz, sponsored by (of course) Palmolive Soap (*Keep that schoolgirl complexion!*). People listened at night, hummed and whistled and sang the tunes during the day, and played them (if they could) on their fiddles, guitars, ukuleles, autoharps, and the old Baldwin upright in the parlor.

Because it was such a musical era, the Lucky Four Clovers were Darling's favorite sons. The quartet was invited to perform for school events, church socials, community dances, weddings, and even funerals, where they sang "Just a Closer Walk with Thee" and "What a Friend We Have in Jesus," ending the service with "Rock of Ages." When the Clovers were invited to sing, the grieving family was assured of a grand turnout of mourners and could be confident that there wouldn't be a dry eye in the house.

Mr. Clover was dead by this time, and the membership of the quartet had changed, along with its repertoire. But the Clovers still performed their October show and always kept their audience completely enthralled. The 1934 fall show was special, for it was also a dress rehearsal — before a live audience — for the upcoming Dixie Regional Barbershop Quartet Competition, which was scheduled to take place in the Darling Academy gym in just a couple of weeks. It was a wonderful opportunity for the home-grown Clovers, and all of Darling was wishing them luck.

Ophelia Snow and Elizabeth Lacy, members and officers of the Darling Dahlias

Garden Club, had found seats together in the very first row. They were dressed in their Sunday best for the occasion, Ophelia in a pretty pink print silk with an ivory lace ruffle at the neck and Liz in a blue silk crepe outfit with long sleeves, a stylish shawl collar, and a pleated skirt that came to well below the knee — a pleasure to wear after those short, skinny flapper dresses of a few years back, which had never been much of a hit in Darling.

"What a swell turnout," Ophelia said to Elizabeth. She turned in her seat to peer at the crowd, which exuded the smell of wet wool, cigarette smoke, and Blue Waltz perfume. "I do believe everybody in town must be here, in spite of the rain. Looks like it's standing room only."

"Maybe Reverend Dooley can put some extra chairs up there by the stage," Lizzy said. Just as she said that, several young men came up the aisle carrying wooden folding chairs. With a clatter, they began setting them up on both sides of the platform at the front of the room.

Ophelia leaned a little closer. "I saw you and Mr. Moseley at the movie last weekend, Liz. *State Fair,* it was. Do you have something to tell me?"

Lizzy turned to look curiously at her

friend. "Well, I guess I can tell you I liked the movie. Will Rogers is a favorite of mine — he can be funny without half-trying. Janet Gaynor was great. I heard that some people were offended by the scene in the bedroom, but I didn't think it crossed the line. I mean, they were just *talking*."

Ophelia looked disappointed. "And that's it? You and Mr. Moseley aren't — ?" She waggled her eyebrows.

"No, we are *not*." Lizzy was emphatic. "Benton Moseley is my boss, and he's a friend. If there's a movie we both like, sometimes we go together. But that's all it is, Opie. And all it's ever been. Nothing more."

Lizzy was fibbing just a little bit, for when she first went to work in Mr. Moseley's law office, she'd had a huge crush on him — and quite naturally so. He was intelligent, good-looking, and very kind to a young woman just starting out on her secretarial career. Which of course she hadn't thought of as a "career," not at the time, anyway. Her job was just a temporary stepping stone on the path that led every Darling girl to marriage. And marriage to Mr. Moseley — why, that would have been any Darling girl's dream.

But that was years ago, and Lizzy had

made a firm effort to put that girlish silliness behind her. To her mother's great despair, she no longer saw her job as a parking place while she went looking for a husband. She and Mr. Moseley had worked together for so long and so well that they could read each other's minds, and when they went out together for a social evening, it was comfortable, companionable fun.

In the past few months, however, a rather unsettling difficulty had emerged in the office. The new CCC camp outside of town had been a welcome boost to Darling's economy, but it hadn't been much of a help for Mr. Moseley's law practice. Lizzy was beginning to fear that her job — which she needed, of course, to pay her bills — might not be as secure as she liked to believe. Last week, Mr. Moseley had even mentioned that he might have to cut her back to part-time.

"Maybe thirty hours, instead of forty," he had said casually. Too casually, Lizzy thought with a sinking feeling in the pit of her stomach. He was trying to act like ten fewer hours a week didn't matter, but of course it did — to her pocketbook.

"Nothing more, huh?" Ophelia repeated, sounding unconvinced. "Well, if you say so. But I still think that you and Mr. Moseley would make a really swell —"

She broke off "Oh, goodie! Here they come!" She sat up straight as four men emerged from a side door and stepped smartly onto the platform. "And don't they look *fine*?"

Oh, they did! Dressed in dark suits, starched white shirts, and their usual bright green bow ties, the Lucky Four Clovers looked confident, self-assured, and eager to please their audience. For the last couple of years, the quartet had enjoyed a stable membership. Portly Martin Ewing (owner of Cypress County's biggest cotton gin) sang lead and acted as the group's amusing master of ceremonies. Frank Harwood (a salesman at the Kilgore Dodge dealership, a bachelor, and very good-looking) crooned a rich baritone. Reginald Dunlap (owner of Dunlap's Five and Dime and the new husband of Liz Lacy's mother) sang a high, warbling tenor. And gray-haired Whitney Whitworth (the wealthy part-owner of the Darling Telephone Exchange) sang a full-throated bass but managed never to smile.

Everybody settled back happily into their seats as the quartet swung into "I'm Looking Over a Four-Leaf Clover." Then Mr. Ewing introduced himself and each of the other three men (although of course, everybody in the room already knew who they were). He followed that with a few cheerful words about how lucky they all were to live in the beautiful town of Darling, the luckiest little town on earth. And then the songs began.

The Lucky Four Clovers sang effortlessly, beautifully, with passion and precision, their voices blending harmoniously — and with no mistakes, not even one. They sang "Five Foot Two, Eyes of Blue, Has Anybody Seen My Girl?" and "Bye, Bye, Blackbird" and "I Found a Million-Dollar Baby (in a Five and Ten Cent Store)," and an old Stephen Foster ballad, "Jeanie with the Light Brown Hair." They sang several familiar hymns and a few Broadway tunes and the Confederate songs that everyone in Darling loved: "The Yellow Rose of Texas" and "The Battle Cry of Freedom" (the *Southern* version, of course) and "Dixie," with the audience joining in.

And at the end of the performance, after the Clovers had reprised their signature song and taken their bows, everybody in the room jumped to their feet, clapping and shouting and whistling. Two encores later, as Darlingians were putting up their umbrellas and sloshing back to their homes through the darkness and still-pouring rain, they were saying that the Lucky Four Clovers were the very best barbershop quartet in the entire South. Without a doubt — without a *doubt* — they would win the Dixie championship and put lucky little Darling on the musical map.

But while Darling folk are good and kind and industrious and have many outstanding talents, they are not very good at predicting the future. It isn't their fault, of course. It is fair to say that, as a species, humans are not very well equipped to look ahead. Nobody in the audience that night, for instance, could know that two of the Lucky Four Clovers were destined to have some very *bad* luck, very soon.

One would lose his voice.

And another would end up dead.

CHAPTER TWO:
THE DAHLIAS PLAN PIES

Sunday, October 21, 1934

"I swear, Bessie," Aunt Hetty Little said. "In all my born days, I have never seen a prettier pie pumpkin. Why, it makes my mouth water just to look at what's in that basket. I can picture the pies."

The bushel basket Aunt Hetty was looking at was filled with bright orange Winter Luxury pie pumpkins, grown by the Darling Dahlias in the large vegetable garden next to their clubhouse. The basket in the middle of their clubhouse's kitchen floor was heaped with the small pumpkins, known across the South as the best pie pumpkin anybody could ever hope to grow. And the Dahlias canning-kettle ladies, under the direction of master canner Bessie Bloodworth, were making sure that there would be plenty of pies this winter, all over Darling.

"They *do* look good, don't they?" Bessie said proudly. "You know, Aunt Hetty, those seeds came from my mother's garden. She got them from *her* mother's garden in the mountains north of Tuscaloosa. Gramma bought a packet of Winter Luxury from the Johnson and Stokes seed catalogue back when she set up housekeeping in 1895. Every year, she saved the best seed, and my mother kept up the habit. So have I. That's been —" She stopped, calculating. "Why, almost forty years now. Forty years!"

Ophelia Snow, whose husband Jed owned Snow's Farm Supply, shook her head admiringly. "Forty years' worth of pumpkin pies from one packet of seeds? Why, that is just plain amazing, Bessie!"

Mildred Kilgore turned from the kitchen counter, where she was slipping the skins off steamed pumpkin halves and cutting the flesh into one-inch cubes. "How do you save the seeds, Bessie? I don't think I know how to do that."

Bessie, plumpish and short, in her mid-fifties, might have been tempted to roll her eyes, but she didn't, because Mildred was a friend, even if she wasn't much of a gardener. "Why, there's nothing easier, Mildred." She nodded toward a colander that was filled with pulp that Liz Lacy had

29

scooped out of the pumpkins before she sliced them in half.

"You just stick that colander under the faucet and pick the biggest seeds out of that mess of fibers and stuff. Rinse them off clean and spread them out on a dish towel, separated as well as you can, so they don't get all stuck together. Should take them about a week to dry. Then drop them into an envelope and write on it what they are, with the date." She smiled reminiscently. "It's a really nice feeling, you know — planting the same seeds your momma and your gramma planted. Makes the pumpkins feel like members of the family, in a way."

"Not to mention that you don't have to lay out good money for seeds every year," Aunt Hetty said thoughtfully. "Although maybe if Huey P. Long gets to the White House, we'll have a little more money in our pockets."

Everybody knew that Aunt Hetty had to cut corners where money was concerned and was hoping that Senator Long would win the 1936 presidential election. He was making a lot of noise about his Share the Wealth program, traveling around the country promising that every family in America would get $2,000 a year. Not only that, but everyone over sixty would get a special $30-

a-month old-age benefit! Some people were skeptical ("Where's that money going to come from is what I want to know"), but others were in such dire straits that they were jumping at Huey Long's campaign promises like a rainbow trout jumping for a June bug. He was collecting quite a following.

"Franklin Roosevelt says he wants to give old folks a pension," Ophelia said, digging a pumpkin out of the basket.

"Well, then, why hasn't he done something about it?" Aunt Hetty asked testily. The oldest Dahlia but still spry and alert, she read the newspapers and prided herself on keeping up with the political news. She answered her own question. "He's afraid that if he does, people will say he's a socialist, so he's dragging his feet."

Bessie plunged her knife into a pumpkin and began sawing it in half. "Old Huey P. says people can call him anything they want," she said, "as long as they listen to what he's got to say."

For years, Bessie had been a big fan of Senator Long, the former governor of Louisiana, who was telling everybody within earshot that he wanted rich folks to share their wealth — which meant that the government would take money from rich people and give it to the poor. It was a popular message, and whenever he went on the radio, Bessie and the ladies who lived in her Magnolia Manor boarding house gathered around the RCA and listened. Most of them clapped.

Liz Lacy finished scooping the seeds out of a pumpkin Bessie had cut in half. Over her shoulder, she remarked mildly, "Mr. Moseley says that kind of talk makes Senator Long a bigger socialist than FDR. He thinks the president is waiting for the right moment to push his social security plan through Congress. We just have to be patient a little while longer."

"He'd better hurry," Ophelia said, "or he's going to disappoint a lot of people."

Agreeing, Lizzy turned back to her job, layering cleaned pumpkin halves into the big blue enamel pot. The pumpkins would steam on the back burner of the gas stove for fifteen minutes or so. When they were cool enough to handle, Mildred could slip the skins right off.

"If FDR does decide to push old-age pensions," Bessie retorted, "it'll be because Senator Long is nipping at his heels."

"That's what Henry says, too," Earlynne Biddle replied, hanging the dishtowel on the rack. Her husband Henry managed the

Coca-Cola bottling plant outside of town. "He says Roosevelt is good as far as he goes but he doesn't go far enough."

"If you ask me, he's gone way too far," Mildred said acidly. "That man has been in office for only eighteen months, and just look at all the programs he's come up with. The AAA and the CCC and the CWA and the FDIC and the FERA — crazy alphabet soup. Why, it's enough to make a person gag."

Mildred Kilgore and Roger, her husband, owned and managed Kilgore Motors, the local Dodge dealership, which hadn't exactly been doing a booming business during the Depression. It was hard to sell cars when people were worried about putting food on the table and shoes on the kids' feet. But the Kilgores had been staunch Hoover supporters and Mildred had never gotten over his trouncing. She criticized FDR every chance she got.

Bessie put down her knife. "Should I cut more pumpkins, or are we done for now?"

Mildred surveyed what was in her bowl. "Looks like I've got enough for two more quarts," she said. "That should fill up the pressure cooker."

"How many quarts will that make, total?" Ophelia asked.

"Sixteen," Mildred said. She grinned. "That's sixteen of Aunt Hetty's pumpkin pies. Best in Darling."

Earlynne began spooning the hot pumpkin cubes into sterilized quart Mason jars. "Best pies in the *world,*" she said.

The filled jars, capped with flat metal lids and shiny screw-on rings, would go into the club's new National pressure cooker, which the Dahlias had bought with the money they raised in their recent quilt raffle After ninety minutes at ten pounds' pressure, the jars would be cooled. Some of them would go straight to the Darling Blessing Box, others would join the canned fruits and vegetables on the shelves in the clubhouse pantry.

"Oh, yes, pies!" exclaimed Liz, the current president of the Dahlias. "That reminds me, girls. We need to make a plan for the community pie supper. It's a week from Friday, after the Dixie barbershop finals. The Dahlias have been asked to contribute a dozen pies." She picked up a notepad and pencil from the table. "While I have you right here, maybe you can tell me what kind of pies you want to make."

The Dahlias were the most active club in town and were always being asked to contribute to this and that. The club was founded back in 1925 by that dedicated gardener, Mrs. Dahlia Blackstone, who bequeathed them her house at 302 Camellia Street. Along with the dilapidated old house — now their clubhouse — had come an acre of sadly run-down gardens in the back, a half-acre of overgrown vegetable garden in the adjoining lot, and two beautiful cucumber trees. (They were really *Magnolia acuminata,* Miss Rogers reminded them. A librarian, she insisted that people use the proper names for things).

Some might have been daunted by the condition of the gift, but that was when the Dahlias showed what they were made of. They repaired the roof and replaced the plumbing and then turned to the unkempt gardens. The front yard had once been filled with azaleas, roses, and hydrangeas, and the backyard — over an acre — swept down toward a little wooded area and a clear spring surrounded by bog iris, ferns, and pitcher plants. Inspired by the zeal that all true gardeners feel when they confront a weedy, overgrown garden, the eager Dahlias rolled up their sleeves, got out their gardening tools, and marched out into the jungle.

They trimmed the clematis, mandevilla, and wisteria; cut back the exuberant Confederate jasmine and trumpet vine; and pruned the gardenias. They divided and replanted Mrs. Blackstone's favorite orange ditch lilies, as well as her crinum lilies, spider lilies, oxblood lilies, daffodils, and narcissus — far too many to count! They pulled weeds and dug out invaders and cleared the curving perennial borders to give the larkspur, phlox, Shasta daisies, iris, alliums, and asters more elbow room. They also pruned Mrs. Blackstone's many roses — the climbers, teas, ramblers, shrubs, and the rowdy, unruly Lady Banks, whose arching green branches had taken over an entire corner but whose gorgeous yellow blooms in early spring made it all worthwhile.

Then they hired Mr. Norris to bring Racer and plow the vegetable garden. Racer (his name was a Darling joke) was as slow as blackstrap molasses in January, but the old bay gelding knew exactly what to do when he was hitched to the business end of a plow, and he and Mr. Norris whipped the garden plot into planting shape in almost no time. The Dahlias got out their seeds and planted sweet corn, collards, chard, green beans, tomatoes, okra, mild bell peppers and fiery chili peppers, eggplant, squash, melons, cucumbers, sweet potatoes — and of course pumpkins, both the large and jolly jack-o'-lantern pumpkins and Bessie's Winter Luxury pie pumpkins.

36

In the natural way of things (and because they were very good gardeners), the garden had produced abundantly, yielding plenty of vegetables to sell at the Saturday farmers' market and give away to the Retirement Haven, the old folks' home over on Rayburn Road. And to put up in Mason jars, like the delicious little pie pumpkins they were canning today.

"Pies for the pie supper," Aunt Hetty said thoughtfully. "Well, let's see. My big old pecan tree struggled this year, what with all the rain and hot weather we had in August and September. But there'll likely be enough for a real nice pecan pie or two." She grinned mischievously. "With my secret ingredient, of course."

Everybody laughed, for they knew her secret ingredient. Aunt Hetty's cousin, Rondell Little, lived back in the hills and made the very best brandy — peach, apple, pear, cherry, whatever fruit he could get his hands on. Aunt Hetty used his brandy to flavor her pies. While Prohibition was in effect, Rondell's brandy was illegal, so everybody just whispered about Aunt Hetty's "secret ingredient." Now, almost a year after Repeal, it was still illegal, since Cousin Rondell didn't have Alabama's tax stamp. So everybody still whispered.

"I'll take a couple of these pumpkins and make a pumpkin pie," Bessie offered. She smiled. "I'll make it with pineapple — it'll be a special treat."

"There are quite a few green tomatoes still left on the vines," Liz said. "Green tomato pie is always a hit, and it's easy. I'll make that."

"Oh, and buttermilk pie," Ophelia added. "I'll make my mother's old-fashioned buttermilk pie."

"Put me down for a lemon icebox pie," Mildred said. "Mrs. Hancock saved me some lemons when her grocery order came in the other day. I'll make a cookie crumb crust."

Liz grinned. "Sounds like we have a plan, girls. Now, who'd like to call the other Dahlias and ask them what they'll be bringing?"

Aunt Hetty peered at Liz over her silver-rimmed glasses. "I would if I could, dear, but my party line is down."

"Again?" Mildred asked, raising her eyebrows. "Wasn't it down *last* week?"

"And the week before that," Aunt Hetty said with a scowl. "I'm afraid it's gettin' to be a regular thing. There are six of us on that line, and we miss our morning coffee-and-conversation." She looked pointedly at

Ophelia. "Claretta Manners is really stewing about it. She's writing a letter to the mayor. She says he ought to do something."

"I'm afraid Jed won't be any help," Ophelia said apologetically — as she should, since her husband was Darling's mayor. "Our line was out three days last week. He had some mayor's telephoning to do, and he was fit to be tied. He went over to the Exchange and talked to Myra May about it. She says that we're having all these problems because Darling has outgrown the old switchboard. To fix the problem, we need a new one."

Myra May Mosswell and her friend Violet Sims — both active members of the Dahlias — owned and managed the Darling Telephone Exchange, which was located in the back room of the Darling Diner, which they also owned.

"Well, if that's what it is, I hope they do it *soon,*" Aunt Hetty said emphatically. "I was one of the last to get on the telephone. But now that I've got used to having one, it's a tad bit hard to get along without it. I miss bein' in on the news as it happens."

Ophelia gave a regretful shake of her head. "Myra May says the new switchboards work better and faster, but they're pretty expensive. She and Violet have just about half of

39

what they need and are trying to get the other half from their partner. In the meantime, we just have to get along the best we can."

"Partner?" Bessie asked curiously. "I didn't know they had a partner. Who is it?"

Mildred lifted her chin. "Myra May just needs to get creative," she said in a teacherly tone. "If she put her mind to it, I'm sure she could come up with a solution."

There was a silence. Everybody knew that Mildred was thinking of events at Kilgore Motors, which had almost gone out of business over some mistakes her husband Roger had made — mistakes she would never let the poor man live down. But while Mildred carried a grudge longer than most, she was a creative manager who would try anything to boost sales. With that in mind, she had hired Frank Harwood as a salesman and posted a big sign in the window.

Buy a New Car and Get TEN Free
Driving Lessons!!

The fact that Mr. Harwood — the driving teacher — looked and sounded like Rudy Vallée didn't hurt a thing, of course. He even had a bit of the crooner's silver-tongued, intimate style. Darling's matrons were smitten, just as Mildred had hoped they would be. In fact, one of the more affluent women in town had persuaded her husband to purchase a new car, and another had bought one for herself.

"Well, my phone is working," Liz said. "At least it was this morning. And if it isn't, I'm sure Mr. Moseley won't mind if I use the office phone. How about if I make the calls?"

"If you don't mind, Liz," Aunt Hetty said.

"I'll take half of them," Bessie offered. "I'm sure I can find a time when my phone is working."

And that was how they settled it.

The Dahlias can always come up with a plan — especially when pies are involved.

CHAPTER THREE:
OPHELIA: GIRL REPORTER

Monday, October 22

Ophelia took off her pink sweater and hung it on the wall beside her desk at the Darling Dispatch. "It's warm for October," she remarked brightly. "Bet it hits eighty today."

Charlie Dickens, the editor of the *Dispatch,* glanced at the clock, which said half-past eight. "Running a little late, aren't you?" He went back to his two-finger attack on his Royal typewriter.

Ophelia sighed. It was hard to be a wife and mother and a working girl all at the same time — especially when the working-girl part of you held down not one but two jobs. "I would have called," she said apologetically, "but my phone was out."

Charlie stopped typing. "Again?" he asked, in the skeptical tone of a schoolteacher asking why the homework was late.

"Yes, again," she said. "Myra May says

Darling has outgrown the switchboard. We need a new one." Defensively, she added, "Actually, I'm late because Jed had to have a starched white shirt for a meeting."

She doubted that her excuse would hold any water with Charlie, though. The man had never ironed a starched white dress shirt in his life. He had no idea how much fussing it took. And since Ophelia had long since had to let her maid go, *she* was the one who did the fussing.

But her remark got his attention. He stopped pecking and reached for the open pack of Camels on his desk. "What meeting?"

Ophelia knew why he was asking. It was true that her husband was the mayor of Darling, but he was also the proprietor of Snow's Farm Supply and a blue-plaid-shirt-and-no-necktie kind of guy. Jed only wore a starched white shirt to church and somebody's funeral. Which meant that since this wasn't Sunday or a revival meeting day and nobody had died, something rather unusual must be going on.

"The Share the Wealth Society," she replied. "They're having a brown-bag lunch in the back room at Musgrove's Hardware. They're meeting every Monday now. Jed always goes."

Actually, Ophelia thought that *she* should be the one attending the meeting, since she was the one who shared most of the wealth in the Snow family. On Monday, Wednesday, and Thursday, she was a reporter, advertising manager, and Linotype operator for the newspaper, a job she'd had for several years. Last spring, she had been hired to work in the commandant's office at the nearby CCC camp on Tuesdays and Fridays, which meant a little more money coming into the family coffers.

Ophelia's two paychecks were as welcome as a cooling rain on a scorching July day, especially because the children (seventeen-year-old Sam and fifteen-year-old Sarah) always needed school clothes and supplies. The elder Snows, Jed's parents, needed help with the doctor and dentist bills. Ophelia couldn't begin to imagine how the six of them would get along without her money.

But however welcome it was, Ophelia's income was also a touchy subject at the Snow house. Since the Crash, farmers couldn't afford to buy much feed or equipment, so Snow's Farm Supply was barely able to pay its owner a salary, no matter how many hours a week he worked. Jed knew they needed Ophelia's money, but he didn't appreciate being reminded that his wife brought in more than he did. And even worse, one of her jobs took her out to the CCC camp, where she worked with dozens of strange men. With damn *Yankees,* and all of them in uniform, while Jed's heart belonged to Dixie. Altogether, it was a bitter pill for him to swallow.

But Ophelia knew that wasn't the only reason why Jed hadn't invited her to the meeting. The Share the Wealth Society was made up exclusively of *men.* Women weren't allowed.

"Huh." Charlie scraped a wood match with his thumbnail and lit his cigarette. "So your husband has decided to cast his lot with Huey P." His tone was sarcastic. "What makes him think there'll be any more wealth to share if Long makes it into the White House?"

"I don't know that he does, really," Ophelia said. She pulled out her chair and sat down at her desk, frowning. It sounded like Charlie had got up on the wrong side of the bed this morning, which was unusual these days. He had been a bear to work with before he and Fannie Champaign got married and settled into her apartment over the hat shop. But Fannie had worked miracles, and the grumpy old grizzly had turned into something closer to a well-mannered lamb.

Tentatively, she added, "What's so bad about Senator Long, anyway?"

Charlie blew out the match. He countered with, "Why does Jed have to wear a white shirt?"

"Because prosperous men wear white shirts and ties," Ophelia said, taking the cover off her typewriter. Jed had explained this, in detail. "Because Share the Wealth folks believe in dressing for success. If you dress like you're successful, you're more likely to be successful."

The men, anyway. She wondered what women wore when they dressed for success. *Ha,* she thought to herself, looking down at her pink and green cotton print dress, which she had sewn herself out of some yard goods she'd bought on sale at Mann's Mercantile for twelve cents a yard. *As if a woman would ever be able to dress for success.*

She turned to Charlie and asked again, "What's so bad about Senator Long?"

Charlie peered at her over his round, wire-rimmed spectacles. "You really don't know, do you." It wasn't a question.

"If I knew, I wouldn't be asking," she retorted.

But she supposed she did know. Huey P. Long — familiarly known as the Kingfish, after a character on the *Amos 'n' Andy* radio program — had been constantly in the news since the day he was elected as Louisiana's governor and started riling people up. Now, he was a senator and a Democrat, like President Franklin D. Roosevelt. He was also what people called a "populist." He and FDR were poles apart, politically speaking. As Jed put it, Long and the president were as different as chalk and cheese.

Since Roosevelt had settled in the White House the previous year and began pushing the New Deal, he had made a lot of changes to repair the damage done when the stock market plunged into oblivion. Some of the changes were welcome, like the repeal of Prohibition and the creation of the Civilian Conservation Corps, which was already creating work for thousands of unemployed young men. Others were controversial, like relief (which everybody hated, even the people who needed it) and plowing up the cotton so it wasn't a glut on the market.

Still, after four years of Herbert Hoover sitting on his thumbs, it was a relief to have a president who rolled up his sleeves and actually *did* something. As Will Rogers said on his Sunday night *Gulf Headliners* radio show, it didn't much matter what FDR did. "If he burned down the Capitol," Rogers had said, "we'd all cheer and say, 'At least he got a fire started.' "

But the Kingfish and his followers thought that the president ought to start a bigger fire, especially when it came to helping poor folks (who were about nine-tenths of the population). Senator Long was gearing up for a run at the White House in the 1936 election, and there were plenty of people in Darling who thought he had a very good chance.

Charlie Dickens, on the other hand, was an FDR supporter, so naturally, he didn't much like the senator. Which was why he called him "Huey P." in that sarcastic tone of voice.

Now, answering Ophelia's question, Charlie pursed his lips. "I guess you've never heard that Roosevelt called Huey Long one of the two most dangerous men in the country."

"No, I've never heard that," Ophelia said, surprised. "Why in the world would he say a thing like that?"

"Because Huey makes promises he can't keep," Charlie said. "Folks need hope, and that's what he gives them, in spades. He gets them all riled up, promising he'll give them everything they want. Jobs, money, better housing, better schools. Like this 'Every man's a king' slogan of his, and his plan to take money away from the rich to give to the poor. But even if he gets elected president, Long won't be able to deliver. People will be mad as hell and take to the streets. Roosevelt is afraid of a revolution."

Ophelia thought about this for a moment. Reluctantly, she supposed there was something to it — although when Huey P. was governor of Louisiana, he had delivered a lot of roads and schools. Of course, quite a few of his cronies had gotten rich in the process, but she supposed that was the way these things worked. People in government thought they had to take care of their friends, or they wouldn't have any.

She frowned. "Who's the other?"

Charlie pushed his glasses up on his nose. "The other what?"

"The other most dangerous man."

"Ah, him. General Douglas MacArthur."

"Oh," Ophelia said. Then, humbly, "I guess I don't understand."

"You don't remember when the Bonus Army was camping out in Washington, the summer of thirty-two? MacArthur ordered the cavalry and six tanks to charge on them. Those poor souls were *veterans,* just wanting the government to pay them the bonus they were due from the Great War."

"Oh," Ophelia said again, remembering.

"I guess somebody like that couldn't be a very good general, could he?"

"Right." Charlie went back to his rapid-fire, two-finger typing for a moment, then stopped, regarding her. "I don't suppose you'd like to go to that meeting. Share the Wealth, I mean."

"Of course I would," Ophelia said. "But I can't." She wrinkled her nose. "Jed says it's just men."

"Oh, yeah." Charlie chuckled sarcastically. "I forgot. Every *man* is a king. Huey P. doesn't say anything about women, does he? But you can go as a reporter, if you want to. Take notes, write up a story for next week's *Dispatch*."

"Gosh, that would be *swell*!" Ophelia said excitedly. "Thank you, Charlie." She had been stuck with Darling's women's news — the Mothers' Guild, the Quilting Society, the Dahlias — for way too long. She was eager to sink her teeth into some real reporting. Share the Wealth would be a great place to start.

Charlie held up a finger. "One caveat," he said. "I'm not going to run a story about how wonderful Huey P. is and what he's promising to do to help all us poor folks improve our lot in life. There's enough of that stuff out there. What I want is a story

50

about the men in the Share the Wealth Society — why they joined, what they're afraid of, what they want to see happen here in Darling that they're not seeing now. Individual stories about real people. Human-interest stories. Why-it-matters stories." He cocked an eyebrow. "You think you might be able to handle that assignment, Ophelia?"

"I can try," Ophelia said, a little doubtfully.

"Do it," Charlie said, and went back to his typing.

Ophelia stole a glance at her boss. His green celluloid eyeshade was pulled low and his cigarette dangled from one corner of his mouth the way it always did, the smoke curling in front of his face. As usual, his wire-rimmed glasses were perched on the end of his nose, his shirtsleeves were rolled to his elbows, and his gray vest hung open to reveal a loosely knotted tie.

But she thought his face was a little grayer, his shoulders a little more slumped, and he didn't seem to be attacking his typewriter with his usual ferocity. Ophelia wondered why. Now that the CCC camp was in full swing and spending several thousands of dollars a month in Cypress County, advertising and subscriptions were both back up, and the *Dispatch* was on a surer footing. Charlie ought to be in a better mood.

But maybe there was something wrong with the newspaper's equipment — always a possibility, since (as Charlie frequently said) it was older than dirt. She turned to look at the black Babcock cylinder press, a hulking four-pager that shook the floors and rattled the windows when it was chugging along at top speed on Thursday nights, when Charlie ran the home-print pages. It looked the same as always. And so did her Linotype machine, a prewar monster that she operated easily, even though women were not supposed to be strong enough to pull that heavy lever. The small Miles proofing press sat on the table beside the Linotype. Against the other wall stood the marble-topped tables where the pages were made up, the printers' cabinets with their drawers full of type fonts, and the stacks of paper, press-ready. And the smaller job press on which Charlie printed the flyers and invoices and business forms that filled in the income gaps as newspaper ad revenue waxed and waned.

But nothing looked amiss and she turned back, sneaking a sidelong glance at Charlie. Yes, he definitely didn't look as chipper as he had since he and Fannie were married. Maybe something was wrong at home, now that the honeymoon was over and the two of them had to learn to live together — a challenge in any marriage, as she herself had to admit.

But if that's what it was, she reminded herself sternly, it was none of her business. Jed was always warning her against sticking her nose where it didn't belong. "Do it once too often and somebody will smack you right in the kisser," he said, and she thought he was probably right.

So instead of asking Charlie if everything was all right at home, she took out her steno pad and flipped through the pages until she found the notes she had taken at the meeting of the Ladies Guild in the Baptist Church basement the week before. Then she rolled a long, column-width strip of paper into the old black Underwood she had bought for a dollar-fifty at Mr. Wheeler's yard sale and began to type. The machine was still a little stiff, even after her son Sam had cleaned it up and oiled it, but it wasn't long before her fingers were flying.

And this story was actually fun to write. The Ladies Guild had held its annual rummage sale on the Baptist Church lawn, where they had sold children's clothes, shoes, dishes, books, and tools, raising a grand total of $42.35 — almost a record, the organizers said. The entire amount would go toward buying groceries for the Darling Blessing Box.

Ophelia typed –30– at the end of the story and pulled it out of her typewriter. Charity, she thought happily, didn't have be doled out by the federal government in Washington, DC. There were plenty of ways to share the wealth right here at home. And *she* had a new assignment. She was going to that meeting after all — as a reporter!

CHAPTER FOUR:
CHARLIE DICKENS GETS A TIP

Charlie was working on the lead story for Friday's *Dispatch,* about Boomer Bronson falling off the roof of Claude Peevy's barn without killing himself, thankfully (although how thankful you were depended on what you thought about Boomer, Charlie reckoned). That Boomer was drunk as a skunk on Bodeen Pyle's white lightning probably figured heavily in his survival, although that wasn't the kind of detail that Charlie could include in the *Dispatch.*

Nor could he include the fact that this happened at midnight and that Claude was up there on the roof with Boomer, both of them naked as jaybirds. Or that when they were found by Mrs. Peevy, they were lying on their backs on a pile of hay, yodeling to the moon. Or what Mrs. Peevy might have said (or might have been imagined to say) when she came upon the scene.

Without these interesting details, Boomer's tumble wasn't much of a story — which was a sad thing, but nothing new. Once upon a time, Charlie had written feature stories for the *Cleveland Plain Dealer* and the *Baltimore Sun* — undercover stories, investigative stories, in-depth, tell-it-all stories that told readers what they didn't know. He had dug up the dirt on local politicians, blown the whistle on some notorious police corruption, and triggered a federal investigation that ended with a major-league crime boss going to jail. He had been read, applauded, rewarded, and even fired a time or two. He had been good. He had been *damn* good.

That was then. This was now. While Charlie had scored several big stories in the *Dispatch* — the killing of Rider LeDoux by the federal revenue agents at Mickey LeDoux's still on Dead Cow Creek, the embezzlement scheme at the CCC camp, and the sensational murder of the "Eleven O'Clock Lady" — there had not been one single shred of news worth reporting in the past few months. (Boomer's story, unfortunately, was more notable for the parts that couldn't be printed in the paper.)

And the only news on the horizon was the barbershop quartet competition being held in town next week. There certainly wasn't much excitement in that — just a bunch of guys singing close harmony on the stage at the Academy, with a big community pie supper afterward. Of course, if the Lucky Four Clovers were lucky enough to win, there might be a nice story in that. Local interest, anyway, with a focus on each of the four men. *If* they won. People said they were good, but Charlie wasn't enough of a music fan to know whether the hometown team stood even half a chance.

With an ironic twist of his mouth, Charlie pulled Boomer's story out of his typewriter and dropped it into the wooden tray on his desk, one of a stack of wooden letter trays labeled Page One, Two, Three, and Four. They were the same trays his father had used for the very same purpose back in the day when he edited and published the *Dispatch.* That was before the senior Charles Dickens succumbed to lung cancer and left the newspaper to his only son. Charlie, himself a newsman, had figured to sell it quick, pocket the change, and go back to his old job of crime reporter for the *Plain Dealer.*

But after the stock market took its fatal nosedive, the *Plain Dealer* (and every newspaper, everywhere) stopped hiring. Worse, nobody wanted to buy a newspaper with a shrinking subscription list, declining advertising revenue, and a faltering job printing business — in a two-bit Southern town where a halfway decent story came along once in a blue moon. His father's pride and joy was an albatross around Charlie's neck.

Well, the Boomer story, inconsequential as it was, filled out the rest of the page. In a couple of hours, Ophelia would take his stories and hers to the Linotype machine and begin setting up the four pages of what they called "home print": the local news; the church and club news; births, deaths, marriages, and travel (mostly weekend visits to family on the other side of the county). There was also Liz Lacy's Garden Gate column and whatever local ads Ophelia had been able to sell. That part of the job had to be finished in time to get the pages on the press late Thursday night.

On Friday, the home print pages would then be folded together with the four pages of ready print that Charlie bought from a syndicate called the Western Newspaper Union, as did the hundreds of other little newspapers around the country. The ready print pages contained the national and international news (mostly dismal, these days), the financial news (still disastrous), the women's column (twaddle), serialized fiction (trash), comics, and sports — although this year's World Series would make it to the national page, with good reason. The St. Louis Cardinals had just squeaked past the Detroit Tigers four games to three, with pitching brothers Dizzy and Daffy Dean each winning two games for the Gas House Gang. They were still dancing in St. Louis, where after the game, August Busch's new team of Clydesdales had paraded around the infield, pulling a shiny red beer wagon loaded with free bottles of Bud. This was the first wet Series since the "Thirsty-first" of July, 1919, when the National Wartime Prohibition Act had thrown three strikes at the beer industry.

In fact, the ready print ought to be loaded with news this week. Over in Germany, they were still talking about the extravagant Nuremburg rally the Nazis had staged for their man Hitler, whom they were now calling their Führer. Back home, investigators were still trying to figure out the cause of the fire that destroyed the *Morro Castle,* leaving 137 passengers and crew dead. The latest cost-of-living figures were out. The average cost of a new house (if you could afford one) was $5,970, but if you were renting, you could figure on spending an average of $240 a year out of your average annual wage of $1,600. And there had been three more kidnappings in the past seven days. A plague of kidnappers had settled on the land, it seemed, snatching anybody whose family might be willing to pay a ransom.

With any luck, the bundles of ready print would arrive from Mobile on the Thursday afternoon Greyhound bus, although that depended on whether the bus (which was no spring chicken) made the trip without breaking down. If all went according to Hoyle, the *Dispatch* would be in the mail carrier's flivver and on its way to subscribers on the RFD routes by early Saturday morning. Charlie himself would fill the newspaper racks around the square in time to catch the Friday night moviegoers and Saturday shoppers.

If there were any.

Shoppers, that is.

Business was picking up, thanks to the Darling Dollars scrip that Alvin Duffy, the new bank president, had persuaded people to accept, as well as the boost the merchants were getting from the CCC camp. But Charlie was convinced that the town would never again be anything like as prosperous as it had been before the Crash, which left the *Dispatch* in a big round hole.

He ground out his cigarette in the over-flowing glass ashtray that sat on his father's 1909 *Webster's New International Dictionary,* opened the bottom drawer, and pulled out a bottle of warm Hires root beer. He missed the powerful kick he used to get from Mickey LeDoux's tiger spit. But he had promised Fannie to stop drinking the hard stuff and he meant to keep that promise, even if it killed him. Which it very nearly did in the wee small hours of Friday morning, when he was finishing up the print run and — before he married Fannie — would have happily fallen into a jug of shine.

The days, though, he went home to fall into bed beside his wife and sleep the sleep of the righteously sober next to her warm, soft fragrant body — more than a fair trade for a daylong hangover.

Except that this week, he wouldn't be falling into bed beside Fannie, for the simple reason that she wasn't there, which was partly responsible for Charlie's gloom. Miss Champaign (to Charlie's chagrin, his wife continued to use her professional name) was the proprietor of Champaign's Darling Chapeaux, located on the west side of the courthouse square. She was also a professional milliner of some repute who had just completed thirty-some ladies' hats, her "fall line," as she called it. Charlie had helped her box them up and haul them to the L&N depot, to see them on their way to New York.

Fannie herself had left yesterday for her meeting there with Lilly Daché, a celebrated French milliner who provided custom-made hats for the Hollywood studios. Through Mme. Daché, one of Fannie's chapeaux had ended up in *Grand Hotel,* on the handsome head of leading lady Joan Crawford. Miss Crawford had been quoted in the *Hollywood Reporter* as saying that she "just adored" that "clever little hat." *Voilà!* Fannie was famous, and her hats were now in great demand.

Unfortunately, Fannie's celebrity came at a price, which was why she was in New York and Charlie was sleeping alone. His wife had rented an expensive suite in the Biltmore Hotel where she planned to display her fall line, so all the big hat buyers in the city could come and take a look. If they liked something they saw, they would pay Fannie for the design, and her hat would be copied and sold to swanky department stores like Macy's in New York and Wannamaker's in Philly. Now that Roosevelt was making it possible for more people to have a few dollars more in their pockets, ladies' hats were big business again.

And Fannie was not just a creative de-
signer of exquisite ladies' hats, she was a
businesswoman and a damned successful
one, at that. Charlie didn't know how much
she was making, exactly. He just knew it
had to be a *lot.*

But while Miss Fannie Champaign might
be a rising star in the millinery world, she
was still Mrs. Charlie Dickens. And while
Mr. Charlie Dickens certainly didn't object
to his wife's career (he had been all for
women getting the vote, hadn't he?), he *had*
expected that once they got married, she
would give up junketing all over God's
green earth and settle down to her Darling
hat shop, downstairs from their apartment
and cattycorner across the courthouse
square from his newspaper office.

As far as Charlie was concerned, this was
an ideal situation. Fannie had paid cash for
the building, so they didn't have to pay a
cent of rent. And she liked to cook and do
other housewifely things, which made her
husband's life exceedingly pleasant. After
several years of living alone in the two
upstairs rooms he rented from Mrs. Beedle
(five dollars a week, clean sheets but no
housekeeping, meals, or laundry), Charlie
was at last (you might say) in clover. Which
was one reason why batching it bothered

him so much, even if it was for just a couple of weeks.

But as Charlie's dad used to say, a mule could be sweet as apple pie at one end and kick you crazy at the other, and something much more disturbing than Fannie's absence had gotten under Charlie's skin. He dearly loved his wife, but she had an independent streak a mile wide and two miles deep. She had kept her account book herself before they were married, and she insisted on doing that now. She refused to allow him to look it over, a fact that gnawed at Charlie no end. Now that they were married and would be required to file a joint income tax return for 1934, he thought he ought to at least have some idea of how much his other half was making and how well she was managing her money. Her money? Well, that was up for discussion, he thought. Now that they were married, wasn't it *their* money?

So when he came back from putting Fannie on the Sunday morning train, Charlie made a momentous decision — one that was about to disorder his relatively well-ordered life. He sat down at the kitchen table with a cup of coffee and Fannie's account books and made a discovery that shook him all the way down to the soles of his wingtip shoes. In the previous year, his wife's hat business had brought in some $2,400.

Charlie stared at the number, scarcely believing his eyes. Twenty-four hundred dollars was a small fortune, fifty percent more than the average joe's salary and twice as much as last year's income from the newspaper! He gulped. He'd had no idea.

Of course, he reminded himself, Fannie had to pay for her materials, advertising, and shipping, all of which were detailed in her precise hand in the expense columns. But those charges amounted to not much more than $400. She obviously kept her overhead costs low. Then his attention was caught by something else: a regular expense of fifty dollars a month, with no explanation. Just two letters. JC.

Charlie was baffled. Fifty dollars a month? *Fifty dollars a month?* Why, that totaled up to $600 a year, a quarter of what her entire business brought in! Was JC a person or . . . or what? Was Fannie repaying a debt? Was she making payments on a piece of property? If it was real estate, where was it? If it was a person, *who* was he . . . or she? And even more importantly, why hadn't she told him? What was she hiding?

Why was she hiding it?

Didn't she *trust* him?

65

And then he thought of something else. There had always been a bit of a mystery about Fannie, for she had simply gotten off the Greyhound bus one day, carried her suitcase across the courthouse square, and started making hats. Darling had been deeply curious about her because she was an unmarried woman with no friends or family to welcome her to town — and no apparent reason to choose Darling over Mobile or Montgomery, or any other town for that matter. What's more, she made it abundantly clear that she was an *independent* woman who didn't need a man to support her or make her happy. And since Fannie was quite attractive, this fact alone was enough to make people take notice.

Now, Darling loves nothing in the world so much as it loves gossip, so plenty of rumors had been floating around since Fannie's arrival. *Out of the blue,* people said, or *Really, out of nowhere.* Various "informed sources" had told Charlie that Miss Champaign had been engaged once, that she had been married twice, that her fabulously wealthy husband had died, that her mobster husband had gone to prison for tax evasion and she had divorced him, and that she had inherited a potful of money from her father, who made an illicit fortune running guns from the Florida Keys to Cuba during the Spanish-American War. He had even heard that her mother was a rebellious heiress (possibly a Vanderbilt or maybe a Carnegie) who had given birth to Fannie out of wedlock and sent her to be raised by a couple in Atlanta.

But whether this was fact or fiction had mattered not a whit to Charlie. He had been so besotted with love and so eager to marry this beautiful lady that he had never once asked her who she really was and why she had come to Darling, and she had never volunteered the information. She was still a mystery — and up to now, it hadn't mattered. For all he cared, his wife could have killed somebody. Why, she might even be on the lam from the law. But regardless of who she was or what she had done, she was still Fannie. *His* Fannie.

But now, confronted by this unexplained, inexplicable six-hundred-dollar annual expense and given the empty pages in his wife's life history, Charlie found that he *did* care. He cared a very great deal, and his natural cynicism and reporter's instinct seized on the very worst possibility.

This payment . . . was it . . . could it be . . . *blackmail*?

What had Fannie done, that she was paying for it so dearly?

Baffled, Charlie had closed Fannie's account book with something like a sense of despair. And then he had gotten up from the table and done something he never imagined he would do. He wanted to find those canceled fifty-dollar checks, so he went into their bedroom and searched the closet, Fannie's dresser drawers — her stockings, her undies, her lacy chemises, her nightgowns, her shirtwaists — and the drawers in the nightstand next to her side of the bed.

But there were no checks to be found, canceled or otherwise. Which meant that she must be keeping them with all her other paperwork in the little office at the back of her hat shop. But Fannie had locked the shop up tight and must have taken the key with her, for it was nowhere to be found, either. The only window was the front display window, and he couldn't get in that way. He considered breaking the lock, but that would be costly, and (he had to admit) hard to explain.

Charlie was in a quandary. He had thought he knew the only important things there were to know about his wife: that she was sweet, loving, patient, and generous to a fault — witness her dealings with Rona

Jean Hancock (the Eleven O'Clock Lady) — a few months before. Now, all he knew for sure was that Fannie was hiding a secret, and at this point, it really didn't much matter what the secret was or whether it was good or bad. The fact was that it was a *secret.* And as his father used to say, there isn't a helluva lot of difference between a hornet and a yellow jacket when he is raising Cain under your shirt.

The Regulator clock on the wall of the newspaper office cleared its throat, whirred, and began to strike nine. At her desk, Ophelia stopped typing, pushed back her chair, and stood up.

"Are you ready for me to put the local stories on the Linotype?" she asked.

"They're all there," Charlie said, pointing to the trays. He picked up his Hires and took a swig. Of course, he could always just come straight out and ask Fannie where that $600 a year was going, and why. But she would ask him how he knew about it, and he would have to confess he had looked at her accounts, which would probably make her so angry that she would —

He couldn't begin to guess what she would do, but he knew that telling her would destroy the trust they had built up between them. Unfortunately, he didn't stop to ask himself whether his interest in (or perhaps more accurately, his obsession with) the way she spent her money signaled a lack of trust on *his* part. He just kept asking himself how he could discover who was getting Fannie's six hundred dollars a year. He was an investigative reporter, wasn't he? He had dug up hundreds of bigger secrets than this one, hadn't he? He ought to be able to figure this one out.

He was still trying to come up with ways to unravel this mystery when the telephone on his desk rang. He pulled it toward him and lifted the receiver from its cradle. "Dispatch office," he said curtly, into the mouthpiece. "Dickens here." He listened for a few seconds, then transferred the earpiece to his left hand and picked up a pencil.

"When did this happen?" he asked, and began jotting notes in the reporters' shorthand he'd used back when he was a real reporter and had real events to report. "Did you call the sheriff's office?" He jotted another line or two. "Do you know who —"

But the call had been abruptly cut off — whether because the caller had said all there was to say or because the switchboard had dropped the connection, Charlie had no way of knowing.

"Damn and blast," he muttered. Dropped connections happened too often these days. He should get Ophelia to dig into the problems at the Exchange. It would be an easy story for her, because she was friends with Myra May and Violet — they were all members of that garden club — and could get them to tell her what was going on.

But not now. He dropped the receiver in the cradle, grabbed his notebook and Rolleiflex camera (a relic of his *real* newspaper career, when he carried it everywhere) and pushed his chair back.

"Ophelia!" he shouted, reaching for his hat and his seersucker jacket. "Something's come up. Go ahead and get started on the local pages, but we may cut something. There's going to be another story."

And before she could ask him whether somebody's house was burning down or somebody had gone and got himself shot and killed, Charlie had shrugged into his jacket, jammed his fedora on his head, and was dashing out the door.

It was just a few minutes past nine.

CHAPTER FIVE:
LIZ HANDLES A CRISIS

Business had been pretty slow in Mr. Moseley's law office lately, which gave Liz Lacy plenty of time to work on the garden column she wrote for the *Dispatch.* This week, she planned to write a piece on "lucky" plants in recognition of Darling's Lucky Four Clovers. She had already gotten a good start on the column, because she was using material from a talk that Miss Rogers had recently given at a meeting of the Dahlias.

But today — Monday — had begun with a bang: a frantic eight-fifteen phone call from a panic-stricken lady whose voice Lizzy didn't immediately recognize. She had tried to get her to calm down and say who she was and why she was calling, but the woman just kept repeating, frantically, "I've been trying and *trying* to get through, but there must be something wrong with the darn phone system. I have to talk to Mr.

Moseley right now, please. Right this *min-ute*!"

And when Liz was finally able to make her understand that Mr. Moseley was out of town and wouldn't be back for a couple of days, the caller wailed, "But he promised I could call him any time, day or night!"

"If it's terribly urgent," Liz said reluctantly, "I can give you the number for Mr. Jackman's office in Montgomery. That's where he's working." Mr. Moseley wouldn't like the interruption, but Liz thought the woman sounded so frantic that she should try to help.

"Thank you," the woman said breathlessly. "I wouldn't ask, but I simply *have* to talk to him!"

Lizzy hung up, finished the last two bites of the cinnamon-sugar doughnut she'd picked up at the diner on her way to work, and then got out the yellow legal pad that contained Mr. Moseley's notes on his private meeting with a client the previous week. Their discussion concerned a certain painful domestic matter, some of it quite sensational, by Darling standards, anyway. It wasn't every day that the subject of divorce came up.

It was Lizzy's job to type the notes, which she did quite rapidly, paying only enough

73

attention to make sure she didn't make any mistakes. In the years she had worked for Mr. Moseley, she'd trained herself to mechanically reproduce his notes without recording the content in her brain. She did it by keeping her mind focused on another subject while her fingers transcribed Mr. Moseley's scrawls. Occupying her mind with something else made it easier for her to ignore the content of what she was typing, for of course she had to keep it confidential. Attorney-client privilege was one of Benton Moseley's most sacred principles. And since it was his, it had to be hers.

This morning, Lizzy didn't have to search for something to distract her as she typed. Over the weekend, she had been confronted with a troubling personal dilemma that she couldn't get out of her mind. She typed mechanically as she thought about it, remembering.

On Saturday morning, Lizzy had gone shopping at Hancock's Grocery, where she had been pleased to find a very nice pork roast for just sixteen cents a pound and enough fresh apples for an apple pie, perfect for the company dinner she planned to cook that evening for Captain Gordon Campbell, commander of the CCC camp outside of town. She had also scooped up some bargains: two cans of Van Camp pork and beans for six cents a can, a crisp head of lettuce for a nickel, three pounds of sweet potatoes for six cents, and a pound of bacon for a quarter — all good buys.

Old Zeke usually delivered groceries for Mrs. Hancock's customers, but he was laid up with a bad back, so that morning, Lizzy had to carry. Toting her two heavy shopping bags, she was walking past Grady Alexander's house when (by accident or design she never knew, but suspected the latter) Grady came out of his front door. He caught up with her quickly and took both bags out of her hands. It had been an awkward moment.

"Hullo, Liz," Grady said quietly. "It's good to see you. You're looking . . . grand."

"Thank you." Lizzy avoided his searching glance. "It's nice to see you, too, Grady." Fumbling for the right words, she said, "I've been meaning to drop you a note and tell you how sorry I am about your . . . your wife. It must be so hard for you."

They began to walk again, Grady falling into step beside her. "It is." His voice was low and rough. "I can't get used to it, Liz I keep thinking it's just a bad dream. I'm going to wake up and find out that the last few months have never happened."

Not knowing how to answer, Lizzy slid him a quick sideways look, trying to see his face. Grady had never worn his brown hair slicked down the way other men did, and the breeze tossed it loosely across his forehead. He hadn't shaved that morning, his dark eyes were troubled, and he had long ago ceased to flash the rakish, devil-may-care grin that had once lit his serious face.

She looked away quickly and shoved her hands in her jacket pockets. This was the man whom she had once expected to marry. After all, that was every Darling girl's dream, wasn't it? Like all the other girls she knew, Lizzy had grown up thinking she would find a husband, have his children, keep his house neat as a pin, and live happily ever after.

And why not Grady? He was tall and robust, good-looking, intelligent, and (she had thought) dependable. What's more — as Lizzy's mother repeatedly pointed out — he had a college degree and a steady job as the Cypress County agriculture agent. He would make a first-rate husband.

"You cannot object to him in any conceivable way," her mother had said, truly annoyed with her daughter. "You should catch him while you can, Elizabeth. You won't be young forever, you know. Why, you're almost an old maid already!" If truth be told, Lizzy very likely would have married Grady just to get away from her mother, a domineering woman who thought it was her job to manage her daughter's life.

But then the old man who lived across the street had died, and Lizzy had bought his house and renovated it, just the way she wanted it. It was too close to her mother, but except for that small flaw, it was a beautiful little house, so tiny that it almost looked like a dollhouse. It was just right for a single woman and her orange tabby cat — but too small for a daughter and her mother, and much too small for a married couple and their children.

Lizzy loved her house, but even more, she loved living there alone, because living alone gave her the solitude she needed to write. Growing up, she had written stories and poems, and she had long dreamed of writing a novel. But somewhere along the way, she had come to understand that taking care of a husband and children would mean that she'd have to give up her writing — temporarily, anyway, while the children were young, but maybe forever. When Grady proposed again, she had to say she just wasn't ready.

They had gone along in that way for a

several years — comfortable years, Lizzy had thought. And then *ka-boom!* Grady had dropped a bombshell. A year ago last spring, he had told her that he was marrying Archie Mann's pretty young niece, Sandra. That he *had* to marry her because she was expecting his baby.

At first, Lizzy felt as helpless and disoriented as if she'd been whirled off her feet and flung through the air by a tornado that came roaring at her out of the dark. *Pregnant?* She'd had no idea that Grady was even seeing someone else! How could this have happened, when the two of them had been so close for so long?

But when she could think more calmly, Lizzy reflected that maybe it wasn't so surprising, after all. She and Grady mostly saw things alike, but they had their differences, especially when it came to sex. He seemed to think that because they had been going out together for such a long time, he should be able to . . . that she should want to . . . that they should, well, go all the way.

Now, Lizzy was by no means a prude, and she certainly enjoyed parking with Grady in his old blue Ford on the hill above the country club golf course, where they could watch the moon rise and the stars fall on Alabama, to borrow the title of a popular

Guy Lombardo song. She enjoyed kissing Grady and she loved the feeling of his hands all over her — and she loved him, as well. She must, or she wouldn't let him touch her that way, would she?

But if Grady didn't have a built-in sense of limits, Lizzy did. Inside her somewhere there was a warning sensor that flickered when enough was about to become too much. She made him stop the minute she knew that if she didn't make him stop *now* she might stop wanting him to stop, which could be very dangerous. And it wasn't just because she was afraid she might get pregnant, although that was part of it, of course. She knew that if she and Grady had sex, he would jump to the natural conclusion that she was ready to marry him. And that would be wrong, for she wasn't. Not yet, anyway.

But Sandra (who was barely out of her teens) hadn't known how to make him stop, or maybe she hadn't wanted to. It didn't much matter whether Grady had insisted or Sandra had invited, however, for in the end it was all the same. Actions (especially that one) definitely have consequences. Sandra got pregnant and Grady, who was an honorable man, did the honorable thing. Right or wrong, like it or not, marriage was what Darling expected in a case like this, and the sooner the better. Grady married the girl.

Poor Lizzy might have felt betrayed and terribly angry, and it says something about her character that she didn't. Oh, at first she did, of course. For days, she was numb to everything but her own terrible pain. But it wasn't long before she realized that she was more sorry than angry. She was sorry for herself, but she was sorrier for Grady. And for Sandra, too.

For Grady, because he'd had to do what duty obliged him to do. He had married Sandra and he would take care of her and their baby. But Lizzy knew that somewhere deep down inside the dutiful husband and father there would be a doomed, dark center, like a fiery cinder grown cold and hard. Grady would become resigned and, yes, resentful. And she felt sorry for Sandra, because no matter how much she loved her husband, if Grady resented her, she would soon hate him and perhaps even his child. There would be no escape for either.

Still, Grady's marriage had come as an incredibly painful blow, and it took all of Lizzy's strength to pretend to her friends and her mother and Mr. Moseley that it didn't hurt. Darling thrived on gossip, and this little story of premarital lust and its consequences had tongues wagging all over

Cypress County. The Dahlias were the only friends Lizzy could trust not to bring up the subject, and the garden was the only place she could get away from the gossip. To help her escape, Mr. Moseley had found her a temporary job with Mr. Jackman, a lawyer and friend in Montgomery.

There, Lizzy had learned to live with her feelings and had put her spare time to use by writing a novel — a good one, too, even if it was her first. With the help of Mr. Jackman's wife and some remarkable good fortune, she had found a literary agent — Nadine Fleming — to represent her. Then (and even more remarkably, she thought) Miss Fleming had found a publisher for her book! Next week, she was scheduled to receive the galley pages of *Sabrina,* her historical novel about a wealthy, impetuous, and often imprudent young Alabama woman who lost her sweetheart at Gettysburg and was driven from her family plantation by marauding Yankee soldiers. "A rousing, romantic novel," Miss Fleming had said. "In an ordinary market, it should do quite well. Sadly," she had added, "this isn't an ordinary market. The Depression has crippled the publishing industry. But of course, we'll hope for the best."

Now, Lizzy was back in her old life and

on the job at Mr. Moseley's office. She had already started working on a second novel. It was proving to be more difficult than the first, but she felt that she was well on her way to becoming a writer — and a *published* writer, at that! She likely wouldn't make much money, but that didn't matter, really. Just seeing her book in print was reward enough.

But it was hard not to be painfully aware of Grady's new life as a married man, for he and Sandra had moved into the old Harrison place just down the block from Lizzy's house. She couldn't help noticing the attractive changes he was making in the old house (paint and a new roof had made a big difference), and the flower garden Sandra planted, and Grady Junior's freshly washed diapers hanging on the backyard clothesline and his little wooden baby swing in the oak tree in the front yard. She supposed this was good, in a way, and even healing, for it required her to come to terms with the fact that Grady's life was moving on, just as hers was. She was more or less back on an even keel when something else happened — something so inexpressibly dreadful that she could still scarcely bear to think of it.

Late in the previous winter, the Darling

grapevine had reported that Grady's young wife was pregnant again. This news was met with a universally cheerful anticipation, for Sandra and Grady were legally married now and all Darling celebrates every Darling baby with enthusiastic delight. And since there had been no baby showers for Baby Number One (couples who had to get married didn't get a shower), Darling made up for it with Baby Number Two, which by the law of averages ought to be a girl. Sandra's sisters gave a shower, her aunt-by-marriage Twyla Sue Mann gave a shower, and the ladies at Sandra's church generously forgave her for her earlier moral lapse and gave a shower, too. Of course, times were tough and most of the gifts were hand-me-downs (with a little added lace and some embroidered bunnies), but it was the thought that mattered. Sandra must have been delighted.

As it turned out, though, Sandra wasn't carrying a baby. Tragically, what was growing inside her was an especially virulent cancer. First the Darling doctor, then the doctor in Monroeville, and then two more doctors in Mobile had said there was nothing they could do for her, and apparently, they were right. In the middle of September, all Darling (including Lizzy) attended the funeral and went with Grady to bury his young wife in a pleasant corner of Darling Cemetery, out on Schoolhouse Road. Everybody said she looked very pretty, laid out in her wedding dress with her hair beautifully done and Grady Junior's little wooden horse in her hand. All agreed that Cecil Prudhorn (who engraved all the Darling headstones) had done an outstanding job with her monument — pink marble with a little angel carved on one corner. They left flowers on her grave and went home.

That had been a month ago. Now, on this Saturday morning, seeing the man she'd once loved for the first time since he became a widower, Lizzy was having a hard time finding the words to comfort him, for the truth was that it wasn't a bad dream. The past few months *had* happened, and there was nothing he could do to escape them. What could she say that would help?

Finally, she settled for something she knew to be inadequate. "I know this must be terribly, terribly hard, Grady. Sandra was so young and pretty, and everybody is saying that she was a wonderful mother." This was true, for the Darling grapevine, quick to accuse but also quick to forgive, had found much to admire in the way Grady Junior's young mother had doted on her little boy. She added, "You must miss her.

And little Grady — he must be bereft."

Grady nodded. "He's staying with Sandra's mother right now, over in Monroeville." He cleared his throat. "He's a pretty big handful for her, but I can't . . . well, I'm working, you know, and I can't take care of him." He brightened. "I'm going to pick him up later this morning, though. I'll have him for the rest of the weekend. It's good for me. He's such a sweet little guy, and it gives his grandma a break."

By this time, they had reached Lizzy's house and she took the shopping bags out of his hands. "Thanks for carrying my groceries, Grady. I appreciate it." She hesitated, still fumbling for words. "I hope you and your little boy have a nice weekend." She turned to go.

"Wait, Liz." Grady thrust his hands into his pockets. "Hey, listen, I was wondering. Would you . . ." He took a breath. "Would you like to have supper with Junior and me tonight? Nothing special, of course. The kid likes hotdogs and canned beans, so that's what we're having. We might even cook them over a fire in the backyard, with marshmallows on a stick." He grinned. "For him, that's a big adventure."

Lizzy was nonplussed. How *could* he? Why, his wife had only been gone a few weeks! She herself had never been a person who paid much attention to what people might think, but this would be . . . well, unseemly. And anyway, she couldn't, even if she wanted to. She raised her eyes to his. "I'm sorry, Grady. I have other plans."

Because she spent her evenings and weekends writing, Lizzy didn't have much time for socializing. But she and Mr. Moseley went to the movies occasionally, the new editor of the newspaper in Monroeville had taken her out to dinner twice, and last week, she had gone horseback riding with Captain Campbell. That had been fun, and she had reciprocated with an offer to cook dinner for him that night, which is why she had bought the pork roast and was planning an apple pie. Afterward, they were going to the Palace Theater to see Katherine Hepburn and Douglas Fairbanks Jr., in the new movie *Morning Glory.*

But that wasn't the whole story, and she hurried to add the rest. "Even if I didn't," she said, "I don't think it would be a very good idea."

His lips thinned in the way she knew so well. "I don't see why not," he said stubbornly.

"I think you do." She took a deep breath and said what had to be said. "It's too soon,

Grady." And then, since that still wasn't the *real* reason, she said, "And anyway, we can't turn back the clock. What's done is done. We're not the way we were when we were . . . together. We're different people now."

He put his hand on her arm, his voice harsh, entreating. "It doesn't have to be that way, Liz. I've never stopped loving you, in spite of . . . in spite of Sandra and little Grady and all the rest of it. We *can* start over again. It will be better this time, because we know what's important. We —"

"No," she said, pulling away from his hand and turning rapidly so he wouldn't see her tears. "We can't."

He gave her a searching look, and his voice grew even harder. "You're not getting off so easily, Liz. This is *important.* I won't allow it."

She had not known what to say to that, so she had simply turned and walked away.

And even though she and Captain Campbell had spent a very nice Saturday evening together and made plans for another date, Lizzy couldn't forget the pain in Grady's voice or the undisguised pleading in his eyes. *How truly terrible it must be for him,* she thought, *to lose his wife and be left with the care of his motherless little boy.* By Sunday

87

morning, her compassion had threatened to overrule her common sense, and it was all she could do *not* to reach for the telephone and invite Grady and little Grady to come over for Sunday lunch. She could make sandwiches out of the leftover pork roast and they could eat outside at the picnic table, where anybody who walked past could see them and know that there wasn't any . . . well, hanky-panky.

She had steeled herself against the impulse. But the thought of Grady had tugged at her heart all through Sunday.

Now, on Monday morning, she was still thinking about Grady as she finished typing. She took Mr. Moseley's notes out of the typewriter, carried them into his office, and dropped them into the green "In Progress" folder in his desk drawer. She adjusted the venetian blind at his window, brushed a fly off the windowsill, and then pulled open his closet door so she could see herself in the full-length mirror.

Today, she was wearing one of her favorite work outfits: a slim-fitting gray wool and silk noil tweed skirt with kick pleats and a white silk crepe blouse with a pretty cowl neckline and the puff sleeves that were so popular — together, a bargain for only

$3.49 plus postage from the Sears and Roebuck catalogue. (When you had a Monday-through-Friday job and were trying to write a book on the weekends, you didn't have time to drive to Mobile or Montgomery to go shopping.) She fluffed her loose brown hair, licked her little finger, and smoothed an eyebrow. She leaned forward, examining the wrinkles between her eyes — age wrinkles, surely — and frowned, thinking once again of Grady. What *was* she going to do?

Then, with a sigh, she went back to her desk in the reception room. The Moseley law office, a longtime fixture in Darling, was located on the second floor of the Dispatch building. If she worked late on a Thursday night, when Charlie Dickens was printing the Friday paper, the old Babcock press ran like a locomotive, rattling the windows and shaking the floors. But all was quiet now, and she took a deep breath and looked around.

Besides her desk, the reception room had three chairs and a leather sofa for people who were waiting to see Mr. Moseley, as well as several floor-to-ceiling bookshelves. A stand in the corner held a dictionary that had once belonged to Jefferson Davis, open (at Mr. Moseley's instruction) to the word "integrity." The floor was covered with a pair of worn Oriental rugs, and the wood-paneled walls were hung with diplomas and maps and the gilt-framed oil portraits of the three senior Mr. Moseleys. (Mr. Benton Moseley — who had inherited the law firm from his father, who had gotten it from his father and uncle — had a renegade streak and refused to sit for his portrait.)

Yes, it was all very old-fashioned and staid and decorous. But it seemed to Lizzy to represent what people were seeking when they climbed the stairs: if not justice, then something close to it, something established, reliable, constant, and trustworthy. Something that would help them define the difference between what was right and what was wrong and understand what consequences would follow from what they had done or failed to do. Even those who had broken the law had to respect what they found here.

And if she needed another way to think about justice, she could look out the front windows and see the Cypress County courthouse on the other side of the street. It was an imposing red brick building with a white-painted dome and a clock that told the right time and a bell that rang so loud and clear that everybody in town could hear it and be comforted by it.

Yes, Lizzy thought, justice was like that. It was solid, something you could count on to be the same way every day, for everybody — unlike life, which was completely unpredictable and unfair and full of unnerving surprises. Like Mr. Moseley remarking, too casually, that he might have to reduce her hours. Like Grady marrying Sandra out of the blue and Sandra unexpectedly dying and leaving behind a bewildered husband and a bereft little boy. That was life for you, and it had nothing to do with justice or people getting what they deserved.

And now Grady seemed eager for them to be together again, and Lizzy felt the way she did when she and Myra May were girls and got on the Ferris wheel at the county fair, and a cable snapped and the big wheel started going around, faster and faster and faster, with all the riders screaming in terror and excitement. It had taken the entire Darling volunteer fire department to stop them, and poor Al Barkley broke his arm when he tried to grab their gondola as they went whizzing past. Everybody said it was a wonder they hadn't gone spinning out into space.

That was the way she felt now. There was no point denying that she had been in love with Grady once, or that she'd had to learn (hard lesson!) not to love him, but without hating him or hating Sandra. And she hated the thought of hurting him now. But she could see where this was going, and what she saw both terrified and excited her at the very same time, just like that spinning Ferris wheel.

She was still thinking about this when the telephone on her desk jangled. She picked it up and said "Law office. Good morning. How may I help you?"

"It's long distance from Montgomery, Liz," an operator said, and Lizzy recognized Violet Sims' voice. It must be her turn on the switchboard. "Please hold while I connect you." There were several clicks, then several more, then, "Go ahead, please," and Mr. Mosely was on the line.

"Liz?" he said impatiently. "Liz, is that you? Are you there?"

"I'm here," Lizzy said. "What can I do for you?"

He sounded exasperated. "I've been trying to get through for the last ten minutes, but something must be the matter with Darling's phones. Anyway, I got a call here from Regina Whitworth. She sounded pretty frantic. Have you finished typing those notes?"

"I just got them done," Lizzy said. "They're in the green folder, in your desk drawer."

"Good. Now, here's what I want you to do." Mr. Moseley was being authoritative. "Close up the office and go over to the Whitworths' house. When you get there, talk to Mrs. Whitworth and find out as much as you can about what's going on — but don't upset her any more than she is already. Just get the facts, then telephone me at Jackman's office. Do it quick. Depending on what you find out, I may need to come back sooner than I planned."

"What's happened?" Lizzy asked. "What's going on?"

"Danged if I know," Mr. Moseley replied impatiently. "It's a crisis of some sort. So just *go,* will you?" As an afterthought, he added, "If you run into the sheriff, see what you can find out from him. But don't let him in on whatever you learn from Mrs. Whitworth. Remember client privilege." He paused and added sternly, "Got that, Liz? *Client privilege.*"

"Got it," Lizzy said. "I'm on my way."

She put down the phone, feeling her skin prickle. Obviously, some sort of crisis had happened. She put her notebook and pencil in her pocketbook and settled her dark blue, narrow-brimmed sailor hat on her head. Mr. Moseley was expecting her to investigate, and she wouldn't let him down.

What's more, she would do her job so well that he would have to concede that she was indispensable. He would give up the idea of cutting her back to part-time.

Chapter Six:
Myra May Is Stymied

At the Darling Diner, next door on the east to the Dispatch building, Myra May Moss-well was cleaning up after the last breakfast customer had finished his coffee and gone out the door.

Wearing a blue bibbed apron over her red blouse and khaki slacks, she collected the empty mugs from the tables, dumped the coffee grounds out of the big urn, and began sweeping the floor behind the counter. From the kitchen, she could hear the comfortable chatter of Raylene and her helpers as they started lunch preparations. From the back room, she could hear the murmuring voices of Violet and Lenore Looper as they managed calls on the switchboard of the Darling Telephone Exchange — as well as little Cupcake's sweet giggles as she played telephone with her dolls under Violet's chair.

Myra May smiled to herself. Customerwise, it had been a good morning. Now that the CCC camp was in full swing out by Briar Swamp, more money was coming into town. Myra May always measured the size of the crowd not just by the cash that ended up in the register (including the brightly colored Darling Dollars, the emergency scrip still in circulation after the bank had nearly failed the year before), but by how much chow her customers put away. This morning, they had disposed of a large urn of coffee, six quarts of orange juice, three dozen eggs, two-and-a-half pounds of thick-sliced bacon, a quarter of a good-sized smoked ham, four pounds of thin-sliced red potatoes, a four-quart pot of grits, three dozen biscuits, and five quarts of Raylene's redeye gravy. The men (the diner's breakfast crowd was exclusively male) liked to eat.

The men also liked to listen to the morning farm and market reports while they were downing all that chow, so the Philco on the shelf behind the counter was tuned to Mobile's radio station WALA. (Supposedly, the letters stood for "We Are Loyal Alabamians.") Myra May cared more about what she had to pay for pork chops at Hancock's Grocery than what pork bellies were selling for at the East St. Louis stockyards, so she reached up and turned the dial to WGN, broadcasting from the Drake Hotel in Chicago. The nine o'clock *Music for Your Morning* show had just begun, and the announcer was playing a recording of Bing Crosby crooning "Dancing in the Dark." She turned up the volume and began to sing along. Smiling happily and swinging her broom in time with the music, she sang all the way to the last two lines of the chorus: "We can face the music together, dancing in the dark."

If somebody asked you who you thought was the prettiest woman in Darling, Myra May Mosswell would not top your list. She had a strong face with a square forehead, a square jaw, and deep-set eyes that seemed to bore straight through a person. If you had just met her, you might think she was checking to see if your hair was combed and your socks matched, but that wasn't it at all. She was checking to see if you had half a brain — and she stopped checking as soon as she figured out that you didn't. If there was one word to describe Myra May, "direct" would do it. If you wanted a few more words, you could try "does not suffer fools gladly."

Myra May's best friend and partner, on the other hand, easily came to everyone's mind as the loveliest woman in Darling.

Violet Sims was petite and picture-pretty, with bouncy brown curls, a warm smile, and a soft heart. She and Myra May shared the diner, the Exchange, the flat upstairs, and little Cupcake. People who knew them explained their friendship as an illustration of the old saying, "Opposites attract," and since they were two very different people, perhaps that was true.

But whatever held the two of them together made for a very strong bond. As far as business was concerned, Myra May's no-nonsense, let's-get-this-damn-job-done-*now* manner was complemented by Violet's sweet-natured charm and friendliness, which put everyone immediately at ease and made them want to pitch in and help. On the personal side, Violet's accommodating and sympathetic personality balanced Myra May's prickly impatience and smoothed out life's little bumps.

Several years before, Myra May and Violet had purchased the diner and the Darling Telephone Exchange from old Mrs. Hooper, who had been forced to sell when her feet and ankles swelled so badly that she couldn't stand behind the counter. With the purchase had come a good-sized vegetable garden out back, a ramshackle garage for Bertha (Myra May's old green Chevy touring car), and a very nice upstairs flat with lots of windows and a pleasant view of the Cypress County courthouse on the other side of Franklin Street.

The flat was occupied by Myra May, Violet, and Violet's adorable three-year-old niece, whom they had informally adopted after her mother's death. Cupcake had strawberry curls, dimples in both cheeks, and the bluest of blue eyes. She was the apple of her mamas' eyes and the darling of Darling's fond heart. (Darling swore that she was every bit as cute as Shirley Temple, whose latest movie, *Bright Eyes,* was a huge hit everywhere.) The diner's kitchen was under the expert management of Raylene Riggs, Myra May's mother, who lived south of town at the Marigold Motor Court. The Exchange was ably managed by Violet, with the help of a well-trained team of switchboard operators — the Hello Central girls, as some Darling wag had once called them.

But nothing is ever perfect, and as it happened, there was an unfortunate fly in this otherwise delightful ointment. Myra May and Violet owned only *half* of the Exchange. The other half inconveniently belonged to Mr. Whitney Whitworth, who was not an accommodating partner. When they first bought Mrs. Hooper's half of the Exchange,

Myra May and Violet had offered to buy his half, too, but they couldn't afford what he was asking. Now they could, but his price had gone up — way up, and out of their reach. Before, Mr. Whitney Whitworth had been an occasional pain in the patootie. Now, he was a serious thorn in their side.

The problem was that while their partner was glad to pocket half the profits, he did nothing to help with the management of the Exchange. Worse, over the past two years he had objected to every single one of the improvements Myra May and Violet proposed to make — and there were plenty of those, since they were still using the original switchboard, which was over twenty years old. The Hello Central girls did the best they could, but calls had to wait, or were abruptly disconnected, or (worse) switched to the wrong numbers. What's more, the party lines caused lots of problems, and people were demanding private lines — which they couldn't have because the old board didn't have enough capacity. Making the switchboard work, Violet said despairingly, was like trying to poke a cat out from under the porch with a rope. You just couldn't do the job with the only tool you had.

The problem, unfortunately, was *progress.*

When the Exchange first started out back in 1913, most Darlingians got along just fine without a telephone. There were fewer calls, so one operator working part-time could easily handle the switchboard. But more and more people wanted telephones, and more and more telephone wire was strung on more and more poles around town. Violet now had to keep one or two and sometimes even three girls on duty. The poor things were packed shoulder to shoulder in front of the old switchboard like sardines in a can. On a warm, humid day, in that small back room, they were hot enough to sizzle.

Myra May kept abreast of the advances in telephone technology and felt that if they brought their equipment up to date, they could provide a much more reliable service. In fact, she was convinced that things were getting to the point where modernizing wasn't just an option. It *had* to be done, or one morning Darling would wake up and all the telephones in town would be dead as doorknobs. She had investigated and found a new exchange system with automatic features that would solve these problems. It would also allow Violet to reduce the number of Hello Central girls and — most attractively — it had a "secret service" feature that would keep the operators from listening in, which was always a problem in a small town.

Sold by the Kellogg Switchboard Company in Chicago, the new equipment cost $1,000 down, with the rest on a monthly payment plan. A thousand dollars was a lot of money, of course, especially in these difficult days. But Myra May could come up with five hundred from what was left of her father's small estate. If Mr. Whitworth would ante up the other half of the cost, they could get the job done quickly, and make the monthly payments out of the savings.

He wouldn't.

"No, thank you," he had said pleasantly. "I see no need to improve our little enterprise, Miss Mosswell. It seems to be functioning quite adequately."

"But you don't hear the complaints," Myra May had protested. "It is *not* functioning quite adequately. In fact, we're just damn lucky if it functions at all. What's more, if we replace the switchboard, we can reduce the number of operators. In the long run, we'll save enough money to pay for the thing twice over."

"No." Mr. Whitworth smiled a small smile. "Perhaps I should remind you —

once again, Miss Mosswell — that I am a *limited* partner."

And that was the rub. Mrs. Hooper had signed a paper saying that the money she originally got from Mr. Whitworth to start the Exchange was all she was ever going to get, while Mr. Whitworth would receive his share of the profits, forever. He might be invited to invest more, but it was his privilege to say no. Which he did.

And it wasn't because he didn't have the money, Myra May thought resentfully. Mr. Whitworth's wife Regina had inherited a cotton plantation on the Alabama River from her grandmother, Helene Marie Vautier. The Whitworths lived in a nice brick home on Peachtree, a street of nice brick homes. Mr. Whitworth was a past member of the Darling Town Council, and he sang with the Lucky Four Clovers. He belonged to the Darling Rotary Club, the Benevolent and Protective Order of Elks, and the Share the Wealth Society. He drove the 1923 Pierce-Arrow that his wife had inherited from her grandmother, a fine old car that everyone in town had come to recognize. He was known to be a thrifty man who managed the family money carefully — a sterling citizen, as far as Darling was concerned.

But none of this was of any comfort to Myra May. She felt totally stymied by Mr. Whitworth's refusal to carry his fair share of their joint business responsibilities — regardless of his "limited" partnership. And in this unfortunate situation, she and Violet were not alone, for Mr. Whitworth was a "limited" partner in at least one other Darling business. She had heard that he treated his other partner in the same way, pocketing his share of the profits (if there were any) and refusing to put a dime into maintaining or expanding the business.

Which is where matters stood on that October Monday. Things were, however, about to change, for just as Myra May finished sweeping and put her broom away, the front door opened and Sheriff Buddy Norris came in. And from the grave look on his face, Myra May concluded that he hadn't come in for a nice hot breakfast and some friendly conversation.

Something was going on in Darling, and the sheriff didn't like it.

CHAPTER SEVEN:
THE DAHLIAS BLOOM AT
THE BEAUTY BOWER

A few blocks away from the diner, at the Beauty Bower on Dauphin Street, Beulah Trivette had just taken a stack of fluffy pink terry towels out of the laundry basket and put them into the cupboard. She was humming happily because it was Monday, and because Beulah considered herself to be the luckiest woman in Darling.

With good reason, too, for Beulah Trivette had everything her heart desired: her husband Hank, who might not be the handsomest guy in town but was certainly the *sweetest.* And her smart son, Hank Junior, who had won Darling's grade school spelling bee last week with the word "malfeasance," which Beulah had never once in her life even *heard,* and there was Hank Junior standing up in front of everybody and spelling it pretty as you please. And her lovely blond daughter Spoonie, and good friends, and the Beauty Bower, her very own hair salon.

The Beauty Bower was located in what had been a screened-in porch at the back of the Trivette house. Hank had enclosed the porch for her, installed two shampoo sinks, two hair-cutting stations, and big wall mirrors. He had also wired the place for electricity for hair dryers and the new electric permanent wave machine that Beulah mail-ordered from a firm in Minneapolis.

Beulah had wallpapered Hank's new walls with floppy pink cabbage roses and painted the ceiling and wainscoting a matching pink. She painted the plywood floor pink, too, but discovered the problem with that when the first rainy day arrived and she had to get out the mop. So she spattered the pink with yellow, blue, and purple and put a purple rug in front of the door. Then she put a sign out front and she and Bettina Higgens, her beauty associate, tied on their pink ruffled salon aprons and picked up their combs and scissors. They had a vital mission: they were dedicated to making all Darling women beautiful, one head of hair at a time.

Beulah looked forward to Mondays because most of her Monday customers were Dahlias. They would share their weekend news and brighten one another's day with little bits of this and that. They agreed with Beulah that even a little beauty — a smile, a helping hand, bright marigolds along a walk, pink roses blooming beside an old house — goes a long way toward making people happy in this gritty, grimy old world. And if not happy, then perhaps a little easier to live with, which is important when bad things happen to good people and everybody finds themselves scrambling to get by.

Among the Dahlias who had standing appointments on Mondays was Verna Tidwell. Verna always came at eight, because she had to be on the job at the courthouse at nine and she liked to get her hair out of the way early. Bessie Bloodworth and Aunt Hetty Little both came in at eight-thirty, which was not a problem, because Bessie liked to have Bettina do her. After that, Earlynne Biddle came at nine, and Mildred Kilgore at ten. By that time, Beulah would have caught up with most of the weekend news and was ready to face the week wellinformed.

The bell over the door dinged and Beulah looked up, expecting Bettina, who could always be counted on getting to work before the first appointment. But it was Verna, dressed fit to kill in her best gray gabardine suit, a red blouse, red pumps, and the jaunty red felt newsboy hat that Fannie Champaign had made for her. Verna had two jobs — she was the county treasurer *and* the county probate clerk — so she always tried to look nice. But this was unusual.

"My gracious," Beulah said admiringly. "Don't we look swell this morning! Special occasion?"

Verna took off her cap and jacket and hung it on the rack by the door. "I'm driving over to Monroeville to have lunch with some ladies. They have a Girl Scout troop over there, you know." Shaking her head to Beulah's offer of a cup of fresh-brewed coffee and an oatmeal cookie, she sat down in the shampoo chair and put her head back in the sink.

"No, I didn't know," Beulah said, taking the cap off the shampoo bottle. "You're interested in Girl Scouts?" She ran the water, making sure it was hot, the way Verna liked it. "I've always wished that Spoonie could be a Girl Scout." She fluffed up Verna's brown hair, testing it with her fingers. "You're a little dry, sweetie. When we've got you shampooed, I'll use some of my special hair conditioner." Verna wore her brown hair in a sleek bob with square-cut bangs, like that flapper movie queen, Louise

Brooks. The style was a little out of date. These days, hair was all fluffy curls, à la Katherine Hepburn and Norma Shearer. But the bob was a perfect fit for Verna's no-nonsense, get-straight-to-the-point style, so Beulah suggested she keep it.

"Whatever you say, Beulah. Where hair is concerned, you're the boss." Verna closed her eyes as Beulah went to work. "Well, maybe she can," she said after a moment. "Spoonie, I mean. Be a Scout. I'm thinking about starting a troop here in Darling."

"Oh, really?" Beulah began to massage the shampoo through Verna's hair. "That is an absolutely *swell* idea, Verna! And with your organizing ability, you're just the person to do it, too."

"Well, I don't know," Verna said slowly. "There are some old fogies in this town that don't like the idea, you know." Her voice became mocking. "Girls getting out there, hiking, having adventures, coming up with new ideas — why, that's what boys are supposed to do. It's downright immoral, that's what it is. Dangerous, too."

Beulah chuckled and shook her head. "Well, yes, I suppose some folks *do* think it's immoral when a girl gets a new idea. My mother truly thought it was a scandal that I would go off to Montgomery on the

Greyhound, all by myself, and get my beauty certificate and start up my own business. And there are plenty who still don't think women should have the vote." Which was true, although women had been voting for president since 1920. They were blamed — unfairly — for Harding, Coolidge, Hoover, and now Roosevelt.

She turned on the faucet again and began to rinse Verna's hair. "But if you start a troop here in Darling, Verna, I will personally see to it that Spoonie is right there for every meeting. And her friends, too."

"Thank you, Beulah," Verna said gratefully. "That will be a big help. But I've got a lot to learn before I get started on this project. So don't say anything to Spoonie about it just yet."

"Oh, I won't," Beulah said. "But whenever you want some help, you be sure and let me know. If there's a thing in this world I believe in, it's *girls.*"

She took down a bottle of her freshly made special-recipe hair conditioner (one egg yolk whisked in a cup of warm water with a teaspoon of cottonseed oil) and poured a generous amount over Verna's hair. She was working it in when the telephone rang, three quick shorts — the Bower's telephone signal. And since Bettina still hadn't come in, Beulah had to hurriedly dry her hands and go to the phone.

The call was from Alice Ann Walker, another Dahlia. Alice Ann always took an eleven o'clock lunch hour on Mondays. Today, she had to reschedule, because Mr. Duffy, her boss at the Darling bank, was gone for the day and she couldn't get away. In a moment, Beulah had her fingers back in Verna's hair.

"Three shorts," Verna said. "You're back on the party line?"

" 'Fraid so." Beulah sighed. "Myra May says she had to put us back on the party line until they get a new switchboard at the Exchange." She made a clucking sound. "It's a serious problem for poor old Mrs. Hubbard across the street. She's losing her hearing and she confuses her ring — two shorts and a long — with ours. She's always running to answer our calls."

"Ha," Verna muttered. "Maybe she just likes to listen in. I have the same problem on my party line. Eudora Crawford keeps her telephone beside her chair and picks up every time it rings, no matter who it's for. I have to tell her to hang up and then listen to make sure she does." She puffed out an irritated breath. "I've been trying to get a private line, but Myra May tells me the same thing. Darling *obviously* needs a new switchboard."

Verna was getting so worked up that Beulah thought it was time to change the subject. While she was rinsing out the conditioner, she said, "We had an exciting weekend at our house. My Hank got lucky." She chuckled at her own little joke. "He got picked to sing lead with the Lucky Four Clovers."

"He did?" Verna's eyes popped open. "What happened to Mr. Ewing? He was singing lead when the quartet put on their show Friday night."

"He was. But he's been suffering with pimples in his throat, and they've gotten so painful he almost can't eat. Mrs. Ewing says he's living on eggnog, which won't hurt him a bit, of course. It's just fresh eggs and cream and sugar." Beulah reached for a fresh pink towel. "Anyway, Doc Roberts told him if he wanted to get better, he had to stop singing for a while."

"How *unlucky*!" Verna exclaimed. "He's been with the Clovers forever."

"He's really downcast, poor man," Beulah said sympathetically. She wrapped the towel around Verna's head. "And of course it's put the Clovers in a terrible fix, with the Dixie Regional coming up."

"That's right," Verna said. "Liz called me about bringing a pie for the pie supper afterward. I told her I would, but I haven't decided what kind to make." She sat up. "So Hank is taking Mr. Ewing's place for the competition?"

"Yes, and now there's no living with him." Beulah chuckled. "He feels so lucky to be a Clover that his head has swelled up four sizes too large for his hat." She took a pink hair-cutting cape off the shelf. "I told Liz I'd bring an apple pie. That Red Rebel tree in the backyard is positively loaded and the squirrels and possums are already raiding it. I need to get out there and start picking."

Verna pushed herself out of the shampoo chair and headed over to Beulah's hair-cutting station. "Well, you tell Hank congratulations from me. I know he'll do a good job." She sat down in front of the mirror. "What songs are they doing in the competition?"

"Their trademark, of course," Beulah said. She hummed a few bars of "I'm Looking Over a Four-Leaf Clover" as she shook out the cape and tied it around Verna's neck. "And I think they've decided on 'Yes, Sir, That's My Baby.' " She glanced up at the clock. "Gosh all get out, it's eight-twenty. I wonder what's keeping Bettina."

But just as she began to comb out Verna's wet hair, the door flew open and Bettina rushed in.

"Sorry to be late," she said breathlessly, whipping off her brown sweater and hanging it next to Verna's gray jacket. "Something unexpected came up this morning."

"That's all right, sweetie," Beulah said in a comforting tone. "Bessie isn't here yet." She nodded to the shelf where the electric coffeepot sat, with cups and a plate of fresh oatmeal cookies. "If you didn't get your coffee, the pot's on. Help yourself. Have a cookie, too."

"Thanks. I've already had breakfast, but another cup of coffee would be swell." Bettina straightened the collar of her pink-and-brown plaid cotton dress, then went to the coffeepot and began pouring a cup. "I am *so* sorry, Beulah. My phone isn't working or I would have called to say I'd be late."

"*Your* phone too?" Verna asked.

"It's our party line," Bettina said, sounding disgusted. "It's out about half the time." She added sugar to her coffee and stirred. "Anyway, I was just ready to walk out the door when Buddy stopped by to say he's working on a case and we'd better not figure on supper tonight. I told him that was a crying shame, because I got up extra early and baked his favorite shoofly pie for dessert. Seein' as how he hadn't had breakfast yet, he sat down and had a piece right quick." She smiled a private little smile that implied that there was more to the story than she was telling.

Beulah always tried to look past the surface and see the real beauty in people, deep down. But even she had to say that Bettina, a tall, angular young woman with mousy brown hair and a face full of freckles, was not the prettiest flower in the garden. In fact, Beulah had worried that while Bettina had the soul of an artist when it came to hair and nails, she might be destined to dry up on the vine. It wasn't hard to end up an old maid these days, for matrimonial pickings were pretty slim. If a young man wanted a halfway decent job, he had to take the train to Memphis or Chicago, so most of Darling's eligible bachelors had left town.

But to everybody's surprise, Bettina had caught the attention of one of the county's most marriageable men. He was Buddy Norris, who had recently been elected to fill the term vacated by the untimely death of Sheriff Roy Burns.

Beulah picked up her comb and scissors and began to even up Verna's ends. "Well, at least Buddy got a piece of shoofly pie before he went to work," she said, combing and snipping. "That brings back memories. My grandma used to make shoofly pie every Sunday morning. We had it for breakfast before we went to church. It was our special Sunday treat."

Verna turned her head so quickly that she almost got Beulah's scissor point in her eye. "How come Buddy had to cancel for supper, Bettina?"

"Careful, hon," Beulah said, using both hands to gently turn Verna's head back straight again. "Maybe it's not something Bettina can talk about."

"Actually, I don't know." Bettina went to a cupboard and got out a clean pink and white checked apron. "All he said was that it looked like he might have a pretty big case to work on, and he never likes to take time out from an investigation for personal reasons." She gave them a bright smile. "He may be just plain old Buddy Norris, but he's *very* professional."

There went Verna's head, swiveling again, and Beulah pulled it back. But this time Verna resisted. "Hold on a minute, Beulah," she said, turning her shoulders so she could look at Bettina. "I want to know. Bettina, what's this about a 'pretty big case'? What's going on?"

Beulah rolled her eyes. That was so like Verna. She always had to know every single little detail and was never satisfied with an explanation. After "what?" her next questions would be "who?" and "when?" and then "why?" and "how much will it cost?" Which of course was an asset, given her job as county treasurer. You wanted somebody at the courthouse who cared about keeping the records straight.

Bettina frowned. "Somebody disappeared is all he said." She tied her apron behind her back. "He didn't tell me the details. He just wolfed down his pie and left."

"Disappeared?" That got Beulah's attention and she turned, too. "You mean, like in 'ran away'?"

"Or got kidnapped?" Verna asked with interest.

"Kidnapped? Oh, surely not, Verna." Beulah was horrified at the thought. "Not here in *Darling.*"

"I don't know why not," Verna said. "It doesn't just happen in books, you know. They finally caught the man who kidnapped the Lindbergh baby — Bruno Hauptmann. That's real life for you. A lot more dangerous than fiction."

Bettina shuddered. "I keep thinking about

117

that sweet little Lindbergh baby," she murmured. "And his poor mama and daddy. It's sad as sad can be, that's what it is."

"And it's not just that baby," Verna went on, warming to her subject. "People are getting kidnapped everywhere. Didn't you read that story in the *Dispatch* a couple of weeks ago? More than two thousand people in this country were abducted and held for ransom in just the last two years. *Two thousand!* Why, it's a crime wave! And it's happening in little towns and big cities, everywhere. Nobody's safe."

Bettina's eyes were big. "You're right, Verna," she breathed. "All a crook has to do is grab you and tie you up and hide you in the coal shed or an abandoned cellar." She shuddered. "And then send your relatives a note saying how many thousands of dollars they have to fork over, or he'll kill you."

"Thousands of dollars?" Still combing and snipping, Beulah gave an ironic chuckle. "That's why a crook would never bother to kidnap anybody in Darling, Bettina. People in this town have barely enough money to pay the rent and buy a week's groceries. You could turn all of us upside down and shake us and you wouldn't get more than a pocketful of loose change."

"Not everybody in this town is dead

broke," Verna retorted. She gave a knowing sniff. "Who do you suppose keeps businesses like Kilgore Motors alive? *Some* people have enough money to buy new cars."

Beulah turned to Bettina, feeling that they had done enough speculating and really ought to get down to brass tacks. "Did Buddy actually *say* somebody was kidnapped?"

Bettina smoothed the wrinkles out of her apron. "Not specifically, no," she said. "What he said was that somebody disappeared. Which could mean almost anything, I guess. Somebody didn't get home after the movies last night, or got drunk and is sleeping it off in a barn somewhere, or —"

"And he didn't say who it was?" Verna asked, turning her head again. "Or when or how much —"

"Verna, sweetie." Patiently, Beulah turned Verna's head straight and began to snip. "If you will just let me finish cutting you, you can go right over to the sheriff's office and ask Buddy yourself. If he won't tell you, walk down the block and ask Charlie Dickens. He's in the news business. If somebody's been kidnapped, he'll know who it is."

But Verna didn't have to wait until Beulah had finished cutting her, for at that moment, Bessie Bloodworth opened the door and came in. Short, heavy-set, and fifty-something, Bessie had thick, dark eyebrows and loose salt-and-pepper curls that always looked mussed, as if she'd been combing them with her fingers. She was wearing a dark blue straw boater with a red ribbon and a navy cotton dress with a red rickrack border on a white sailor collar — which Beulah knew for a fact Bessie had bought from the Sears and Roebuck summer sale catalogue for 99 cents, because she remembered seeing it there.

Bessie didn't bother with her usual cheerful "hello" or "how is everybody this morning?" or even "I hope that coffee is hot." She just jumped right in with "Have you heard the news?"

From the tone of Bessie's voice, Beulah knew right away that it wasn't *good* news. Bessie (who owned and managed the Magnolia Manor, a boarding house for genteel elderly ladies) was Darling's resident historian. She knew everything there was to know about every single one of the local families, but she rarely bothered her head with current events. When Bessie announced gleefully that she had *"news!"* it was usually about something that had taken place twenty-five or fifty years before, and she had just dug it out of a letter or a newspaper clipping and couldn't wait to tell you about it so you could be as thrilled and excited as she was.

All three of them turned to look at her. "What news?" Bettina asked nervously.

Beulah paused in mid-snip. "Has one of your ladies died?" This was a continuing concern, since the Magnolia Manor residents were of advanced years and in varying stages of decrepitude.

"I guess you haven't heard, then." Bessie took off her hat and headed for the coffeepot.

"No, *we* haven't heard, Bessie," Verna said tartly. "But *you* obviously have. What's going on?"

Bessie picked up the pot and a cup and began to pour. Still holding onto her news but aware that her audience was getting annoyed, she gave them a hint. "It's Whitney Whitworth."

"What about Mr. Whitworth, Bessie?" Beulah asked.

"Mr. Whitworth?" Bettina frowned. "Who is he?"

"Mr. Whitworth is the reason your party line is out of order, Bettina," Verna said crisply. "And why Beulah and I have no private lines."

"What?" Beulah and Bettina chorused at once, and Beulah added, "Just what are you saying, Verna?"

"It's a fact," Verna replied flatly. "Ask Myra May — she'll tell you. She has all these plans for modernizing our telephone system. But Whitney Whitworth owns fifty percent of the Exchange, and he just flat refuses to chip in his share. Which is a mystery to me, since the Whitworths have plenty of money. Although," she added thoughtfully, "I understand that the money came from Mrs. Whitworth's side of the family, which I suppose might make some difference."

"Maybe not," Bessie said in an ironic tone. "Never having married, I'm no expert on husbands. But from what I hear, most of them think it's their responsibility to manage *all* the money in the family, regardless of where it comes from."

Bettina spoke up. "Well, whoever is holdin' onto that money," she said plaintively, "I wish they'd turn loose of some of it. Can't somebody have a *talk* with Mr. Whitworth? He needs to know he's a stumbling block in the path of Darling's progress. I am ready to get my phone fixed any day now." She picked up a towel. "Come on, Miz Bessie, and we'll get started on your shampoo."

But Beulah still didn't have an answer to her question. Scissors poised, she glanced at Bessie. "What *about* Mr. Whitworth, Bessie?" she repeated. "Has something happened to him?"

"I reckon you might say so," Bessie replied in a meaningful tone. She sat down in the shampoo chair. "Roseanne heard from DessaRae this morning that he didn't come home last night. The man has *disappeared.* Mrs. Whitworth is beside herself, of course. She's called the sheriff."

"Oh, my goodness," Beulah said. "Well, DessaRae should know."

Everybody else nodded. This was one of those situations where, if you understood who worked for whom in Darling, you would understand everything. Roseanne had cooked for Bessie at the Manor for going on ten years now. DessaRae, a Creole from Louisiana who had married Roseanne's second cousin (now passed on), worked for the Whitworths. Normally, DessaRae and Roseanne wouldn't talk on the telephone during working hours. But as Bessie went on to explain it, the fact that Mr. Whitworth hadn't come home made this call an acceptable exception. DessaRae had called to ask if Roseanne had any dried lemon balm, so she could brew up some calming tea for poor Mrs. Whitworth, who was quite beside herself with worry.

Roseanne had told DessaRae that she didn't have any lemon balm, but she knew that ImaJeen did. ImaJeen cooked for Mrs. Forenberry over on Cherry Street. DessaRae should call over there and ask. ImaJeen had made up a little packet and sent it over by her husband Doobie, who had been pulling weeds out of Mrs. Forenberry's petunias when he was sent on the errand.

So by the time DessaRae was able to brew Mrs. Whitworth some lemon balm tea, Roseanne, ImaJeen, and Doobie would have known that Mr. Whitworth hadn't come home the night before. An hour later, that number would have easily tripled or even quadrupled. It was well understood that if you wanted to find out what was *really* going on in town, you had to ask the help. The colored folks always know what's what — although they also know how to keep a secret and who to tell it to, which most likely won't be their employers.

"Well, what did I say?" Verna demanded, then added smartly, "It's a kidnapping, that's what it is. And the Whitworths have *plenty* of money, even if most of it came from Mrs. Whitworth's side of the family. I wonder how much ransom the kidnappers are asking for him."

"Five or ten thousand at least, I would think," Bessie said. "How much did they ask for that lady that got kidnapped in Indianapolis?"

"They got ten thousand for her," Beulah said. "I read it in the paper."

"So *that's* why Buddy can't come to supper tonight," Bettina said, taking the cap off the shampoo bottle. "He's investigating a kidnapping! Well, I must say I'm surprised that such a thing could happen in little old Darling, but it's good to know what's going on."

She turned on the faucet in the sink and adjusted the temperature. "You just put your head back, Miz Bessie, honey. You can tell us the rest of the story while you're gettin' beautiful."

CHAPTER EIGHT:
BUDDY NORRIS INVESTIGATES

"Mr. Whitworth has *disappeared*?" Myra May asked blankly. "What's that supposed to mean, Buddy?"

Buddy Norris sat down on his usual stool — the third one from the end nearest the door — and folded his arms on the counter. Watching Myra May's face, he replied, "What I just said, Myra May. Whitney Whitworth didn't come home last night." Casually, he added, "Don't suppose you know anything about it."

If she did, she wasn't letting on. "Dunno how come you're asking me," she said, turning away to rearrange a pair of salt and pepper shakers. "Have you talked to his wife? She'd be the one to tell you where he is."

Buddy was disappointed. He had hoped that Myra May — who, after all, was Mr. Whitworth's business partner — might have some information.

"Yes, I've talked to Mrs. Whitworth," he replied. Regina Whitworth was a quiet lady — surprisingly young and rather attractive — who was rarely seen around town. In fact, Buddy could remember running into her only a couple of times before she had called him to her house just before seven that morning. He added, "Do you reckon you could rustle me up a cup of coffee?"

As Myra May went to the coffee urn, Buddy caught a glimpse of himself in the mirror behind the counter and brushed his brown hair back off his forehead. Roy Burns' nickel-plated sheriff's star was pinned to the pocket of his khaki work shirt, which was about as close as he ever got to a uniform. People said that his cleft chin and wide forehead made him the spit and image of Charles Lindbergh, the famous airplane pilot who flew all the way to Paris, and whose baby boy had been murdered by a kidnapper a couple of years before.

Personally, Buddy thought he might look more like Lucky Lindy if he didn't have that scar across his cheek, which he'd got when Big Daddy Boudreaux got drunk and pulled a knife on him over at the Red Dog, a juke joint on the colored side of the L&N tracks. Big Daddy had slept it off in one of the town's two jail cells upstairs over Snow's

Farm Supply, and Buddy let him go with a talking-to the next morning. He didn't believe in holding a grudge against a man who was too drunk to know what he was doing — unless he did it a second time. Then it was time to take the matter seriously.

Myra May slid a mug of coffee across the counter. "Have you had breakfast yet? Raylene might be able to round you up something."

"I had me a piece of shoofly pie," Buddy said. He half-smiled as he remembered the thank-you kiss he had bestowed on the girl who had baked the pie. "But if Raylene is still in the kitchen, I figger I might could get around some ham and —"

"This is for the sheriff," Raylene Riggs said, coming out of the kitchen with a plate of buttered toast and ham and eggs, soft and sunny-side up, gently basted with hot bacon grease, just the way Buddy liked them. Myra May put the plate in front of Buddy and added silverware and a mug full of hot coffee.

"There you are, Sheriff," she said. "Now, what's this about Mr. Whitworth?"

Buddy appreciated the use of his new title. He'd grown up in this town and his old man still lived a few blocks down on Robert E.

Lee. Lots of people called him Buddy, like they did when he was a little kid — and like he was still wet behind the ears. He was glad that Myra May and Raylene weren't in that bunch.

"I was hoping you could maybe shed some light on that," Buddy said. "Either you or Violet."

Myra May raised her voice. "Hey, Violet. Somebody wants to talk to you." To Buddy, she said, a little more sharply, "What makes you think *we* know anything?"

"Just lookin' for some help is all." Buddy raked his fork across one egg and sopped up the yellow yolk with a piece of buttered toast. Myra May's tone, he thought, was a little more challenging than usual. "For starters," he added mildly, "I thought you or Violet might've heard something on the Exchange or over the breakfast counter." He smiled, being friendly. "You girls remind me of spiders in the middle of a web, you know? Something happens in Darling, you gen'rally hear about it before anybody else."

It was true. Sheriff Burns used to say that the women who worked behind the counter at the diner were the best informed in town. And back when he was still just a deputy, Buddy had learned that when something happened, he could save a lot of time by

129

sitting down with a cup of coffee and a piece of lemon meringue pie and asking Myra May and Violet what they knew about it. Nine times out of ten, they had picked up something he hadn't heard, just by listening to the conversations at the tables and the counter, or by being curious about a call that went through the Exchange. Or in Raylene's case, just by *knowing,* however that worked, which Buddy didn't pretend to understand.

"Spiders, huh?" Myra May gave him a slight smile that acknowledged the truth of what he had said, then shook her head. "But not this time, at least not so far as I'm aware." She turned to Raylene. "You know anything about the whereabouts of Mr. Whitworth, Mama?"

"Can't say that I do," Raylene said, in her rich, husky voice. She looked troubled. "But I have to admit that I've never been able to tune into that man. He's different — not like most other folks, you know."

"Oh?" Buddy sopped up the last of the egg yolk. "Different like how?"

Everybody knew that Myra May's mother had "the gift," as Buddy's grandmother had called it. For instance, Raylene could tell you what somebody wanted to eat before he ordered. She said it was like tuning a radio to a distant station. When people wanted something, they sent off a signal, loud if they wanted the thing a lot, soft if they were only so-so about it. When the signal was loud and her internal radio was working right, Raylene picked it up. When the signal was weak or she wasn't tuned in, she got a lot of static.

"Different like how?" Buddy repeated curiously.

Raylene frowned. "He hides himself. On purpose." Her frown deepened. "He's like . . . Oh, I don't know. A tin can, maybe."

"A tin can?" Buddy was interested. "How's that?"

"Well, you know." Raylene waved her hand vaguely. "All you've got to go by is the label somebody pasted on it, which may or may not be right. You can't see what's really inside."

Myra May chuckled. "What Mama is saying is that when Mr. Whitworth comes in here, which he doesn't very often, she never knows whether it'll be meat loaf or fried chicken. That bothers her."

Buddy reckoned that if you were in the psychic business, a tin-can kind of person might be frustrating. But that wasn't helping him much, since all *he* had to go by was the label. What he needed was somebody who could tell him where Mr. Whitworth might be this morning and why he hadn't come home the night before.

"Oh, hi, Buddy. What's going on?"

He turned as Violet Sims came out of the Exchange, which was in the spare room tacked on at the back of the diner. She was wearing a pretty blue and yellow cotton print dress, a yellow ribbon in her brown hair, and a yellow sweater with the sleeves pushed up to her elbows. As usual, her outfit was a sweet, girlish contrast to Myra May's red shirt and khaki slacks. Tilting her head, she smiled at him and he returned the smile appreciatively. Violet held a special place in his heart, but he knew better than to let Myra May see how he felt. She was the jealous type.

"What's going on is what the sheriff wants to know, Violet," Myra May said. "Seems that Mr. Whitworth has disappeared."

"Disappeared?" Violet's eyes widened and her hand went to her mouth. "You don't suppose somebody might've *kidnapped* him, do you?"

"What makes you say that?" Buddy asked.

"Well, everybody's getting kidnapped these days, aren't they?" Violet said. "I heard on the radio about a girl down in Mobile who got kidnapped just last week. She was

132

ransomed for I don't know how much. A lot."

"Three thousand dollars," Raylene said.

Buddy whistled.

"Whitney is one of the few people in this town who's rich enough to make it worthwhile to kidnap him," Myra May said drily. "They wouldn't get more than two bits if they kidnapped *me*."

"Oh, come now, Myra May," Violet objected. "You know we'd scrape up every penny we could find."

"I know you would, dear," Myra May replied sweetly. "And if you shook out Cupcake's piggy bank, you might get as much as a whole dollar. If you're lucky."

Buddy forked up the last bite of ham and chewed. It was blanketed with Raylene's good redeye gravy, which he would put up against anybody's in the world. "I was wondering whether you might've picked up anything on the Exchange about Mr. Whitworth," he said. "You know, somebody callin' his house or mentioning his name or . . ." He let his voice trail off suggestively.

Violet pursed her lips. "Nobody called his house," she said, and her glance slid to Myra May. "Anyway, we have our rules, you know."

Actually, it was Myra May's rule. She was

on record as saying that if she got wind of so much as one single shred of gossip that might have *possibly* come from the switchboard, she would fire the loose-lipped operator on the spot, no excuses accepted.

But he also knew that listening in was pretty much unavoidable, since it was too much to ask any human being — let alone a nineteen-year-old girl — to sit in front of the switchboard for eight hours a day with her headphones on without overhearing something. And since Myra May and Violet owned the switchboard (well, half of it, anyway), they figured that listening was a little bonus they got with their investment. So they broke their rule whenever they found it convenient.

Buddy put down his fork, feeling that it was a little difficult to conduct an official interrogation while you were enjoying ham and redeye gravy.

"I know you're not supposed to listen in," he said, "but you do. Sorry, ladies, but this is a police matter. Mr. Whitworth didn't come home last night. He still wasn't there when Mrs. Whitworth got up this morning, and she's pretty frantic. I am investigating this as a missing person case. I'd really appreciate you givin' me a hand here."

Myra May narrowed her eyes. "If you

know anything, Violet, you might as well tell him." She slid a glance at Buddy. "We've got nothing to hide."

Buddy wondered why Myra May thought she had to say that, but Violet was speaking. "Well, Lenore Looper was on the night shift. But I happened to be on the switchboard yesterday afternoon when Mr. Dunlap called Mr. Whitworth."

"And?" Buddy prompted.

"Well, of course I —"

Buddy sighed. "And?" he repeated.

"And they agreed to get together at Mr. Dunlap's house yesterday evening. It was about the Clovers, as I remember. Something about Mr. Ewing having to drop out of the Clovers because he has pimples on his throat."

"That's unlucky," Myra May remarked.

Buddy thought that this was probably unrelated. "Anything else?"

Violet frowned. "Well, there was a call this morning —"

"Buddy Buddy Buddy!" cried Cupcake, running out of the Exchange and careening toward him, laughing, arms flung wide. "Jackie Jill fell up a *hill*!"

"Did he really now? That's pretty amazin'." Buddy reached down, scooped up the little girl, and nuzzled her neck. She was wearing pink corduroy bib overalls and smelled like talcum powder and roses. She wriggled with delight when he blew the curls on the back of her neck.

"And Humptiddy Dumptiddy cracked his head!" She bounced on Buddy's knee, clapping her hands.

"That's enough, Cupcake," Violet said firmly, taking her out of Buddy's arms. "The sheriff is here on business."

Cupcake wrinkled her nose. "One two buckle my shoelaces," she retorted with dignity. "Three four —"

"I wonder if there's a good little girl who would like a glass of orange juice," Raylene remarked in a thoughtful tone. "I'm sure if there is, we can find —"

"Me, me, me!" Cupcake cried. Buddy set her on the floor and she ran around the end of the counter. She and Raylene disappeared into the kitchen.

Feeling the need to bring the conversation back to the central issue, Buddy took his notebook and a pencil out of his shirt pocket, and looked at Violet. "You were saying something about a phone call this morning. Somebody called the Whitworth house?"

"Not so far as I know." Violet leaned against the counter. "It was Mrs. Whitworth, calling Mr. Moseley's office. I stayed on the line until Liz Lacy answered, because I wasn't sure she'd got to work yet. Liz had just left here with one of Raylene's cinnamon-sugar doughnuts. They're her favorite." She turned to Myra May. "Myra May, you might tell Raylene they're all gone so she can —"

Buddy cleared his throat.

"Sorry," Violet muttered. "Anyway, I stayed on the line, but just long enough to hear Liz answer and Mrs. Whitworth say she had to speak to Mr. Moseley. That's when I got off."

"You didn't hear anything else?"

Violet hesitated. "Only that Mr. Moseley was doing a deposition in Montgomery and wouldn't be back for a couple of days."

Depozition, Buddy wrote. *Montgomry.* He wondered why Mrs. Whitworth was calling a lawyer. "Anything else?"

"Well, it seemed like Mrs. Whitworth was pretty upset. She must have really wanted to talk to Mr. Moseley because she called him, long distance. But of course, I got off the line as soon as they were connected."

Upset. Long distance. Buddy had the feeling there was more. "And then?"

Violet sighed. "And then Mr. Moseley called his office — long distance again —

137

and talked to Liz. But I didn't hear anything they said. And that's *all,*" she added, with a note of finality. "Honest."

"All that callin' back and forth happened this morning?" Buddy asked.

Violet nodded. "Sometime after eight, because Lenore had just gone home. She worked the board last night, so if you want to know anything about that, you'll have to ask her."

"Thanks," Buddy said, "I will." He looked at Myra May. "I'm wondering when was the last time *you* talked to him. To Mr. Whitworth, I mean."

"Me?" Myra May raised an eyebrow. "You're asking because . . ."

"Because you're his business partner," Buddy replied. "Because I'll be talking to his other business partner. And some more folks, too," he added, because to tell the truth, he wasn't exactly sure who he would be talking to. He had never investigated a missing person before, and Mrs. Whitworth had been too upset to give him any good leads. She was genuinely frightened, he had thought. All she could do was cry and wring her hands, so pale and hysterical that he'd thought she was maybe going to faint on him, and he sure as hell didn't know what to do about that. He had left in kind of a hurry.

"Well?" he prompted, after a minute.

Violet looked at Myra May. Myra May looked at Violet, shifted and frowned. "Yesterday. I talked to him yesterday."

Buddy made a note. "Morning, afternoon, evening?"

A pause. "Afternoon," Myra May said guardedly.

"Here?"

"Upstairs. So we wouldn't be disturbed."

"I was there, too," Violet added helpfully.

Buddy scribbled some more. "What did you talk about?"

Myra May sighed heavily. "What we always talk about with that man. How important it is to expand the switchboard. How many people will benefit. How much money we'll save."

Buddy raised his eyebrows. It sounded like a normal kind of business discussion to him. "And he said . . ." he prompted.

"No," Myra May said darkly. "He said no. Again."

"She means," Violet explained, "that this is an ongoing discussion. We *have* to expand the Exchange. Myra May has picked out the equipment that will do the job and we've got enough money to cover our share of the cost. But Mr. Whitworth keeps saying no. He says he's what's called a 'limited partner.' Which means he only put the money into the business at the beginning. He doesn't have to put in anything else."

"Which is just *nuts.*" Myra May scowled darkly. "We know he must have the money, but every time we ask, he just flat refuses. We've tried to buy him out of his damned fifty percent, but he's asking so much we can't afford it. So we're stuck."

"Must be frustrating," Buddy said. He could see their point of view.

"We're not the only ones who have this problem," Violet added. "Reginald Dunlap at the Five and Dime — Mr. Whitworth is partners with him, too. And there may be others."

Frowning, Buddy scribbled faster. *Reginal Dunlop.* He wasn't much of a speller, especially when it came to names. "Others? Like who?"

"You don't know that for a fact, Violet," Myra May said cautiously. "That's just Mr. Dunlap's notion."

"But it's something Buddy should know," Violet protested. To him, she added, "Mr. Dunlap says Mr. Whitworth owns a share of Bodeen Pyle's whiskey still."

Buddy wasn't sure he believed it, but he

wrote the name down anyway. *Bodene Pile.* "Thank you," he said. "Anybody else? How about friends? Do you know who his friends are?"

Violet and Myra May exchanged looks. Myra May shrugged. "Maybe the Clovers?" Violet hazarded.

"Okay." Buddy wrote that down. "How about places Mr. Whitworth might go? People he might want to see — if he left Darling, I mean."

Myra May looked at him. "*Has* he left Darling? Did he take his car?"

His car. Feeling the flush climb his cheeks, Buddy folded his notebook and stood. "What do I owe you for breakfast?"

"It's on the house," Myra May said. "You're doing your duty. We want to help."

"Thank you," Buddy replied humbly. Why in tarnation hadn't he thought to ask Mrs. Whitworth whether her husband's car was gone, too? It was because she was crying, that's why. Roy Burns would never have made that mistake. He *had* to learn how to handle weeping females, or he'd never be able to do his job.

"Humptiddy Dumptiddy," Cupcake announced loudly and with great seriousness in the kitchen. "Jackie Jill pushed him down the hill and he broke his head."

141

At the rear of the diner, a young woman stepped out of the door of the Exchange. "Is Sheriff Norris here?" she asked.

Buddy turned, surprised. "Present," he said, realizing that she must be the other switchboard operator on duty this morning.

"You've got a phone call," the girl replied. "He says he's your deputy."

"You can take it at the switchboard, Buddy," Violet said. "Come on, I'll show you." Buddy grinned. Far as he was concerned, Violet could call him Buddy any day of the week.

The Exchange was a narrow room with the telephone switchboard on one side and a cot for the nighttime operator on the other. Buddy had never seen a switchboard before and was surprised at its complexity. The thing was a four-by-six-foot vertical panel, with rows of lighted sockets and a horizontal board with plugs and jacks. The operator — wearing what looked like earmuffs over her head and a funnel-shaped mouthpiece around her neck — sat in front of this contraption and plugged the right jack into the right socket. It all looked very advanced and mysterious to Buddy, but he could see one thing at a glance. It really was quite easy for the operator to hear every word that anybody said — or to put it a different way, it was hard *not* to hear.

Violet handed him a headset and inserted a plug into a blinking socket on the switchboard. "You're connected. You can talk."

"Yo, Wayne," Buddy said, into the funnel. "What's up?"

The man on the other end was Wayne Springer, Cypress County's new deputy. The sheriff's office was only a two-man shop, and when Buddy won the special election to fill Roy Burns' empty boots, somebody had to fill his. Wayne came with five years of experience as a deputy over in Jefferson County, where his training had included target practice with a .38 Special, which was one of the reasons Buddy had hired him. (Buddy could shoot a squirrel out of his dad's peach tree with his .22 rifle, but he still wasn't comfortable with the notion that he might actually have to shoot somebody with the revolver he sometimes carried on his hip — which was why he didn't carry it more often.)

The other reason Buddy had hired Wayne was that he was from way over by Birmingham. Jobs were hard to get, and there had been a dozen would-be deputies, but Wayne was the only one with no local kinfolk. Buddy reasoned that if you and your deputy were in a tight spot, you didn't want him

143

wondering whether the man they had cornered up in the barn loft was his mother's favorite cousin's son. The deputy might hold his fire — or conversely (and just as likely), he might shoot when he didn't need to. In Buddy's opinion, a stranger was more likely to be objective when it came to apprehending people.

Buddy listened to the tale Wayne was telling him on the phone. "Well, that's a bad hill when it's muddy," he said. "Several accidents there in the past. Where are you now?"

He listened some more, then said, "Spook Hill is out on the Jericho Road. You want to go past the airfield a good mile, maybe mile and a half. I'm going over to the Five and Dime and see Mr. Dunlap about this Whitworth thing. You reckon you can handle that accident without me?"

He listened to Wayne's reply, feeling grateful that his deputy had enough experience to be confident in dealing with just about anything. "Nothing from Mrs. Whitworth?" he asked. "No ransom calls yet?" He nodded. "Right. Okay, see you later."

He handed Violet the telephone gear. "Thanks," he said. "Sorry for the interruption."

Violet pulled the plug. "Myra May can be

a little abrupt," she said softly. "But she wants to help — she really does. I know she'll worry about Mr. Whitworth until she hears he's okay, so let us know as soon as you've located him. He *is* our partner, after all. She wants another chance at convincing him to help us modernize." She paused, frowning. "No ransom calls?"

"Nope." Buddy had the feeling there wouldn't be.

"What do you suppose has happened to him?"

"Hard to say," Buddy replied thoughtfully. "Sometimes folks just get a little tired of the life they're living and they chuck it and take off for parts unknown." He grinned. "Or a guy gets a little drunk and knows his missus is waiting up for him — and doesn't want her to see him in that condition. So he goes someplace to sleep it off."

Violet looked doubtful. "That doesn't sound much like Mr. Whitworth. I don't know him that well, but he's never struck me as the type to get so drunk he can't make it home."

"Well, don't you worry your pretty head about it," Buddy said expansively, resisting the urge to give Violet a quick kiss on the cheek. "We'll get it straightened out."

But Buddy wasn't as confident as he liked

to pretend. He hadn't thought to ask about the car — a dumb mistake, the kind an amateur would make. And he couldn't quite put his finger on it, but there had been something about his conversation with the tearful Mrs. Whitworth early that morning that had made him uncomfortable. He wasn't sure she was telling him the truth, at least, not all the truth. But he didn't give a lot of credence to Violet's idea of a kidnapping. For one thing, there hadn't been a ransom demand — at least, not yet. Wouldn't kidnappers holding a man as well-off as Mr. Whitworth start calling first thing?

And there was Raylene's puzzling remark about the tin can. Since he'd been sheriff, Buddy had run into more tin cans than he would have thought possible, here in little Darling — people who were labeled one thing on the outside and were entirely something else when you managed to pry the lid off. He was often surprised at the number of secret lives that were lived in such a little town.

"He hides himself," Raylene had said. "On purpose."

If Whitney Whitworth wanted to hide himself — that is, actually *hide* himself — where was he likely to go?

CHAPTER NINE:
LIZZY MAKES A DISCOVERY

Lizzy loved to walk, especially on a pretty October morning, when the air was so crisp that just breathing it made you feel fizzy and the sugar maple leaves blazed like somebody had put a match to them. Of course, Darling was small enough that you could walk anywhere you wanted to go in a half hour or less, and if you had to go any farther, a bicycle was as good as a car.

In this case, she had to walk only six or seven blocks. She cut across the courthouse lawn and went past the Old Alabama Hotel, which served the most elegant meals in town, with Mrs. LeVaughn playing soft dinner music on the grand piano in the lobby. Past Pete's Pool Parlor, with its outdoor barbecue barrel belching fragrant smoke and somebody breaking a rack of balls with a CRACK! loud enough to be heard on the street. Past Brady's Barbershop (Haircuts 2 Bits), its signboard plastered with Huey P.

Long's grinning picture and the words "Every Man's a King!" in big black letters. Somebody had drawn a crown on the senator's head and penciled in "Vote for Huey."

And then, as Lizzy passed Kilgore Motors' showroom window, she saw that the jazzy pumpkin-colored 1934 Dodge convertible coupe that had been there the week before was gone, replaced by a sedate black Dodge sedan. The coupe must have been sold, she realized with a pang. She didn't actually *need* a car, and she certainly couldn't afford one, not with her job in jeopardy. But that didn't keep her from admiring the swell-looking convertible and wondering who had bought it — and who was getting the free driving lessons from Frank Harwood. Must be somebody who lived out of town, she decided, since she hadn't seen anyone driving it.

Lizzy had almost reached Mimosa Street when she saw Grady Alexander's old blue Ford coming up Robert E. Lee toward her. If there'd been a store she could duck into, she would have, but there wasn't. He slowed and she thought he intended to pull over to the curb and stop. To prevent him, she pointed to her wristwatch and shook her head, pantomiming apology. He gave a regretful shrug, waved, and mouthed "I'll call you" before he drove on.

Lizzy felt as if she had dodged a bullet somehow, although she couldn't have said exactly what that meant. She just knew that she didn't know what she was going to do about Grady, and the uncertainty was at once unsettling and intriguing. She took a relieved breath and went on.

Usually, Lizzy took her time when she walked, especially this time of year. She enjoyed the golden marigolds and purple fall asters and orange chrysanthemums that bloomed in the small front yards and the fire-engine red geraniums that decorated the porches. Life had been tough in Darling and while things were looking up, people hadn't forgotten their hard-learned lessons of self-reliance and frugality. She turned the corner onto Mimosa Street, where almost everybody had a garden — fresh collards and snap peas in the spring, sweet corn and green beans and tomatoes in the summer, sweet potatoes in the fall. Most folks also kept a dozen hens and a rooster in a back-yard coop, so they could have eggs for breakfast and chicken and dumplings for Sunday dinner.

But while the morning air was enticing and the neighborhood was pleasant, Lizzy moved along briskly. For one thing, there

149

was nobody in the office to answer the telephone, so she ought to get back to her desk as quickly as she could. For another, she was prickling with curiosity about what was going on. She kept thinking of those notes she had typed that morning — for they were notes of Mr. Moseley's discussion with Mrs. Whitworth.

Scrupulously, Lizzy had directed her attention elsewhere while she typed. Still, she couldn't miss the general drift, which would certainly raise a Darling eyebrow or two. According to the notes, Mrs. Whitworth suspected her husband of misusing the money she had inherited from her grandmother just before she got married. (The timing was important. In Alabama, any money a woman inherited before she got married belonged legally to *her* and not to her husband.) Mrs. Whitworth wanted Mr. Moseley to look into the situation, find out what had happened, and advise her about what she could do, if anything.

When he had asked, "Are you thinking about divorce?" she had answered emphatically. "I don't have to consider it. I've already made up my mind. I'm going to divorce Whitney." For Darling, this was a sensationally scandalous declaration. If people knew, their party lines would be

150

buzzing with excitement — assuming their party lines were operating, that is.

The Whitworth home was on Peachtree. It was a substantial brick house with white pillars across the front and green-painted shutters at the windows, set back from the street by a well-tended yard studded with live oaks. A graveled drive led to a two-car garage at the back. The house wasn't as palatial as some of the plantation homes Lizzy had visited, but for Darling, it was impressive.

Lizzy climbed the front steps to the green-painted front door and rang the doorbell. A moment later, its chime was answered by a thin-faced, angular woman of indeterminate age, with skin the color of dark chocolate and graying hair in tight curls all over her head. She wore a black maid's uniform with a frilly white collar and a white apron.

When she saw Lizzy, her face broke in a wide smile and her dark eyes flashed with pleasure. "Miz 'Liz'bet', good mawnin'!"

"Why, hello, DessaRae. It's good to see you. How are you this morning?" Lizzy was surprised and then she wasn't. She remembered hearing that after old Miss Hamer died a few months before, her maid, DessaRae, had been hired by Mrs. Whitworth for day work, cooking and cleaning.

Growing up, Lizzy had been under the benevolent charge of Sally-Lou Hawkins, a colored girl who had been more of a friend and companion than a nanny, and who (once her young charge was grown up) had stayed on as a maid to Lizzy's mother. Sally-Lou had become a member of the Lacy family, and DessaRae — Sally-Lou's auntie by marriage — had visited so often that she was like family once removed.

Lizzy still had fond memories of going into the kitchen after she finished her homework and finding Sally-Lou and Des-saRae laughing together over slices of red velvet cake and cups of tea. Often, she would walk with Sally-Lou over to Maysville to visit DessaRae, finding her dressed in one of her colorful Creole outfits, stirring up a pot of spicy sausage and okra gumbo big enough to share with all her neighbors. She would never forget the tiny kitchen that smelled of woodsmoke and hot lard and had a slanted floor that was perfect for marble-racing with Sally-Lou's kid brother, Fremon, a year older than Lizzy.

"I's fine," DessaRae replied to Lizzy's question. She threw a quick glance over her shoulder and leaned forward, lowering her voice. She spoke with a strong Cajun accent that sometimes made her difficult to understand. "But Miz Whitworth ain't jes' real good, I's sorry to say. You might oughta come back when she's feelin' better."

Lizzy shook her head. "I'm sorry, but I need to see her, DessaRae. I work for her attorney, Mr. Moseley. He asked me to talk to her right away. It seems like there's something serious going on. Do you know what it is?"

It was very likely that she did. The colored help always knew everything about the white folks they worked for, things that nobody else (and sometimes not even family) knew. It wasn't that they listened on purpose; most people just forgot they were there and said things they might not have said if they'd remembered. Most of the colored help wouldn't think of telling family secrets to other white folk; that would have been disloyal. But Lizzy had often wondered how much Sally-Lou and DessaRae and their maid friends and relatives shared with one another. She knew they knew a *lot,* and most of it was probably pretty embarrassing, or worse.

So she wasn't surprised when DessaRae hesitated, frowning. "Yes'm, I reckon I do know a little something. But you better ask Miz Whitworth." Hesitantly, she added, "You know the sheriff's been here a'reddy?"

"The sheriff?" Lizzy said in surprise. "No, I didn't know."

"Well, come on in, then." DessaRae opened the door and stood back. "Miz Whitworth, she be in the breakfas' room. Straight down the hall to the back of the house."

Lizzy had met Regina Whitworth when she came to the office to talk to Mr. Moseley. She remembered her as shy and somewhat uncertain, in her mid-thirties, some fifteen years younger than her husband. She was slender and pretty, although she seemed not to be aware of that. Her creamy skin, large, luminous brown eyes, and graceful hands were her most attractive features. Her dark brown hair was long, and she wore it in a loose bun at the nape of her neck.

This morning, though, her hair was down on her shoulders. She was wearing a prim-looking navy silk crepe dress with a high collar and lace cuffs on the long sleeves. She sat at a small dining table in front of a window. The table was set for two, with an unused plate, cup and saucer, and empty juice glass on a linen mat, opposite. She held a teacup in her two hands.

"Miz Whitworth," DessaRae said gently, "you got some comp'ny. Mr. Moseley sent Miz Lacy over here to see you."

Regina Whitworth spoke in a muted voice. "DessaRae, I told you I didn't want to —" She turned. "Mr. Moseley?"

"I'm his secretary," Lizzy said uncomfortably. "He telephoned from Montgomery and asked me to talk to you. He'd like me to let him know how he can help."

Deftly, DessaRae gathered up the unused dishes and silver, leaving the linen mat. "You just sit yo'sef down there, Miz 'Liz'bet, and I bring you some coffee. Or would you like tea?"

"Coffee will be fine," Lizzy said, taking the empty chair as DessaRae left the room.

The sunshine fell through the wide window and spilled across the table. Beside the window, an ornate birdcage hanging from a wrought-iron stand held a bright yellow canary, pleasantly chirping. Outside, the grass was neatly mowed and trimmed along a wide border of flowers. A brick patio outside the window was centered with a birdbath and several rosebushes, and an unruly sweet autumn clematis grew against the garage, a little distance away.

Quickly, DessaRae was back with a cup and a pot and poured hot, fragrant coffee for Lizzy. "You want a doughnut, too, Miz 'Liz'bet'?" she asked solicitously. "Or maybe some eggs? Got some nice brown eggs. Be

155

glad to scramble you some."

"No, thank you, DessaRae," Lizzy said. "I've already had breakfast." DessaRae left, this time closing the door.

Lizzy looked at Mrs. Whitworth across the table. She was pale and composed — with an effort, Lizzy thought. Her eyes were red and it was clear she had been crying. Her dark hair swung against her cheek, half hiding her face.

"Mr. Moseley asked me to tell you that he can drive down from Montgomery," Lizzy said, "if it's necessary. Can you tell me what happened?"

"Well, no, I can't, not really," Mrs. Whitworth said. She set her teacup in the saucer and reached for a cigarette. "Mr. Whitworth went out last night and didn't come home. When I got up this morning and realized he wasn't here, I called the sheriff. He came over and asked me some questions. After he left I called Mr. Moseley's office." She paused. "It was you I talked to on the phone?"

"Yes," Lizzy said.

Mrs. Whitworth nodded. "And then I called Mr. Moseley in Montgomery, at the number you gave me. I told him Whitney was gone. I don't . . . I don't know why I called him. I guess I was grasping at straws."

She struck a match but her hand was trembling so that lighting her cigarette was difficult. "Or maybe I just wanted somebody on my side."

On her side? Lizzy thought this was odd, but then, this whole thing must be difficult, especially under the circumstances — her plan to divorce her husband, the missing money. "You said Mr. Whitworth went out. What time was that? And did you know where he was going?" She took her notebook and pencil out of her pocketbook. "I need to make notes," she added, "so I don't forget anything important when I talk to Mr. Moseley. You won't mind, I hope."

"Not if it's for Mr. Moseley," Mrs. Whitworth said. She pulled nervously on her cigarette, slanting a glance at Lizzy. "I suppose you know why I hired him."

"I think so," Lizzy said tentatively, not sure how much she should reveal about what she knew. In the cage, the canary spilled out a cadenza of brief liquid song. Liz skipped the issue of Mrs. Whitworth's accusations of theft. "You're considering . . . divorce."

Mrs. Whitworth sighed. "Yes," she said. "And to answer your question, I have no idea where my husband went after he left. He was here for dinner, and then he . . . he went out, about eight, without telling me where he was going. I was in my bedroom, reading, but I heard the car." She turned her head to one side and blew out a stream of blue smoke. "I had a . . . a headache. I read for a while, then went to bed. That must have been around ten o'clock."

Lizzy frowned. There was something in Mrs. Whitworth's voice that made her question what the woman was saying. But she wrote it down, anyway. *Headache, reading, bed at ten.* What other questions should she ask? What would Mr. Moseley want to know?

After a moment, she said, "Did he often . . . has he ever been gone all night?"

Mrs. Whitworth pressed her lips together. "To tell the truth, Miss Lacy, I couldn't tell you. I sleep better by myself. We've had separate bedrooms for years."

She tossed her head and as her hair swung back, Lizzy caught a momentary glimpse of what it concealed: a large bruise on her jaw, and a patch of badly abraded skin. Lizzy felt instantly sympathetic. It looked very much as if she'd been hit — quite hard. Had Mr. Whitworth done that? And she was wearing a dress with long sleeves, on a warm October morning. Lizzy suspected that her arms were bruised, too. They must have had

158

an argument, and Mrs. Whitworth was too ashamed to say so.

"And sometimes I sleep late," Mrs. Whitworth added, half-defensively. "I wouldn't know if my husband had been out all night or not."

"Then how did you know *this* time?" Lizzy asked, her eyes on the telltale bruise.

Nervously, Mrs. Whitworth smoothed her hair forward. "I went past his room and the door was slightly open. I glanced in."

Lizzy was sure now that she was right. In her notebook, she wrote *bruise.* And then, because that didn't tell the whole story, added *scrape.* The abrasion was as ugly as the bruise. *Husband hit her,* she wrote, and underlined it.

"When I looked in," Mrs. Whitworth went on, "I saw that his bed hadn't been slept in." She nodded toward the window. "I went out to the garage and saw that his car was gone. So I knew that he hadn't come home. That's when I called the sheriff."

Lizzy followed her glance. Wide enough for two cars and sheltered on this side by the vigorous clematis, the garage was only a little distance from the house. The main garage door was shut, but the side door was open and she could see a car inside — a car the color of pumpkin. She realized with a

159

start that the Whitworths must have bought the car she had admired at Kilgore Motors. But that wasn't relevant at the moment.

"What kind of car does your husband drive?" she asked, but then she remembered. "Oh, it's a Pierce-Arrow, isn't it?"

"Yes." Mrs. Whitworth's voice dropped so low that Lizzy could scarcely hear her. "That was my grandmother's car. It's really my car — I mean, it was part of my inheritance when I married Whitney. But I didn't drive, then, so my husband drives it. He's rather . . . fond of it." She pressed her lips together as if to keep them from trembling, and turned away.

"And you haven't heard from him since last night?" Lizzy asked tentatively. "No phone calls or anything?"

"No telephone calls," Mrs. Whitworth said. "Nothing." She laughed nervously. "No ransom demands, either."

"Ransom demands?" Lizzy asked.

"That's what kidnappers usually do, isn't it?" Mrs. Whitworth said. "They ask for money. That's what I read in the newspaper. I've been waiting."

Lizzy blinked. "So you think your husband might have been *kidnapped*?" She felt a little foolish. That idea hadn't even occurred to her, but she could see the logic of it. Mr.

Moseley had probably thought of it, too.

Mrs. Whitworth shook her head. "I don't know *what* to think," she said, her voice rising in a thin, tremulous wail. "Really, Miss Lacy, I'm at a *loss*!"

There was one thing, though, that weighed against kidnapping. "You said that his car is gone," Lizzy pointed out gently, wanting to comfort her. "Doesn't that suggest that he drove off by himself?"

Mrs. Whitworth took a deep breath. "Not necessarily. They might have made him drive them away." Her eyes widened and her voice dropped to a dramatic whisper. "At gunpoint." As if in response, the canary offered a few tentative bars of song, then lapsed into silence.

Lizzy persisted. "But you didn't see any signs of a struggle? Anything out of the ordinary around the house — or in the garage?"

"No," Mrs. Whitworth said, "but that doesn't mean . . ." Fighting back tears, she bit her lip. "I don't know what to say, Miss Lacy. Whitney has never done anything quite like this before. It's just so . . . so *strange*."

Lizzy had one more question. She waited until the other woman seemed calmer, then said, "When you talked to Mr. Moseley, you

161

said that you thought your husband had taken money that belonged to you — that was part of your inheritance, I mean. Did you discuss this with him?"

If she had, Lizzy thought, that might explain what had provoked the argument that resulted in the bruise — and why the man had disappeared. If he feared that his wife was going to charge him with theft, he would have reason to leave town. By this time, he could even be in New Orleans. Or Atlanta.

"No," Mrs. Whitworth said, looking away. "I haven't brought it up with him yet. Mr. Moseley was going to look into the accounts and see how much is gone. After that, we were going to discuss what should be done."

That sounded like the right approach. There was no point in setting off an alarm until it was clear how much damage had been done. Lizzy nodded and closed her notebook. "Is there anything you'd like Mr. Moseley to do this morning? I know he wants to be helpful."

"I can't think of anything." Mrs. Whitworth bit her lip. "I guess maybe I overreacted when I called him in Montgomery. The sheriff had just left, you see. He asked me all kinds of questions, and I just got . . . well, scared."

"Scared? Scared about what?" Lizzy asked in surprise. Buddy Norris, the sheriff, wasn't the kind of person who would frighten a wife whose husband had disappeared.

"Just . . . just scared," Mrs. Whitworth said evasively. "I can't really explain it. The past couple of weeks have been really difficult, you see, and —"

The phone rang, and Mrs. Whitworth jumped. The kitchen door opened and DessaRae said, "Want I should answer that, ma'am?" From the swiftness of her response, Lizzy thought the maid must have had her ear to the door — which was just like DessaRae. She always had to know what was going on.

But Mrs. Whitworth had already gotten up, and Lizzy knew what she was thinking. *Kidnappers, maybe with a ransom demand.*

"No, never mind, DessaRae. I'll get it," she said. She went to the telephone, which stood on a little table in the corner of the room. Lizzy held her breath.

"Hello?" Mrs. Whitworth said in a muted voice. She turned away and lowered her voice even more. "I'm sorry. I can't talk right now. I have a visitor."

Lizzy let out her breath. It wasn't kidnappers.

"Thank you," Mrs. Whitworth said. "That's sweet, but I'm not badly bruised. Don't worry." She glanced over her shoulder at Lizzy. "Yes. I'll phone you when I can." She put the phone down and turned with a smile — a strained smile that cost a tremendous effort, Lizzy thought.

"A friend," she said, coming back to the table. "Just wanting to know if I'm . . . all right."

Lizzy wondered how the friend had known about the bruising, but she couldn't think of a tactful way to ask. She put her notebook into her purse. "Well, then. I'll stop bothering you and let you get some rest. You have our office telephone number. Please feel free to call me if there's anything you need." She paused and added, with real concern. "I wonder, though — do you think it might be good to have Dr. Roberts look at that bruise on your face? It looks rather serious."

Hastily, Mrs. Whitworth brushed her hair forward. "It's nothing," she said. "I just . . . fell. On the back step. Clumsy me." She gave a nervous little laugh. "Don't worry Mr. Moseley about it, please."

Fell on the back step? Lizzy didn't believe that for a moment. "Well, whatever you think. But to me, it looks serious." She pushed back her chair and stood, and the canary burst into cheerful song. "Please let us know the minute you hear any news about your husband."

"I will," Mrs. Whitworth said. "Thank Mr. Moseley for me, please. And thank you for your concern."

The kitchen door opened again and DessaRae came out with a small paper sack in her hand. "I'll walk you to the do'," she said. "These here cookies are for Sally-Lou. You can take 'em to her tonight when you go 'cross the street to your momma's house."

"I can do that," Lizzy said, but she thought that this seemed rather peculiar. Now that her mother was married to Mr. Dunlap (a blessed event that had taken place that summer) Sally-Lou was back on the job again, but not as a live-in maid. She left for the day before Lizzy got home from the office — and DessaRae certainly knew that.

DessaRae went out with Lizzy, closed the door behind her, and handed her the sack. " 'Scuse me," she said in a low voice. "Had something to tell you. Didn't want to say it where Miz Whitworth could hear."

Sensing something important, Lizzy put the sack into her pocketbook. "What's going on here, DessaRae?"

"I don' know," DessaRae said, shaking her head. "An' I don' know where Mr. Whitworth has got off to. But I do know it's got somethin' to do with —"

The door opened behind them. "DessaRae!" Mrs. Whitworth's tone was sharp. "Don't detain Miss Lacy. Get back in here right now and do your work."

DessaRae ducked her head. "Yes'm," she said softly. To Lizzy, she said, "Now you give that there sack to Sally-Lou," and went into the house.

Which left Lizzy wondering what in the world DessaRae had been talking about.

Chapter Ten:
Charlie Chases a Story

When Charlie Dickens grabbed his camera and rushed out of the Dispatch office, he headed straight for the shed behind Fannie's hat shop, where he kept his car parked. Although his old green Pontiac had certainly seen better days, it got him where he wanted to go — usually. But when he reached the shed, he saw that the left rear tire was flat as a pancake. Irritated (flat tires only happened when you were in a hurry), he pulled off his seersucker jacket, jacked up the car, wrestled the spare tire out of its rack, and made the change. He would drop the tire at Jake Pritchard's Standard station and pick it up on the way back.

The October air was crisp, the morning sun was warm, and the trees were just beginning to exchange their summery greens for the gaudy colors of autumn. Charlie sometimes heard people say that you had to drive to the northern part of the state or up to the Smokies to see colorful autumn trees, but that just wasn't true. In another week or two, the hills and river bottoms would be flamboyant with the burnished gold and copper of the Southern sugar maples, the throbbing red and plum-purple of the sweet gums, the emphatic chartreuse of the fringe trees, the rich bronze of the bald cypress. Even considering what he might find at the end of the road, it was a fine day to be chasing a story.

After he dropped off the tire at Jake's, Charlie swung down the Jericho Road, past the Cypress Country Club, the county fairgrounds, and Darling's airfield. The airfield had been built in the 1920s, when barnstormers flew in three or four times a summer and people had the money to buy an airplane ride. The most recent airshow, though, had been the summer before last, and since nobody in town owned or flew an airplane, the runway was overgrown with Johnson grass. The damned stuff was named for Colonel William Johnson, who owned a plantation over on the Alabama River. He had planted it for cattle forage a couple of decades before the Civil War and now it was everywhere, as bad as kudzu and nobody could figure out how to get rid of it. Charlie knew about this because he'd written a story about it. That's how he knew most things. He wrote about them.

Six or seven miles past the airfield, just before you got to Ralph Murphy's place, the road narrowed and dipped down a very steep hill. In fact, it had been Lucy Murphy, Ralph's wife, who had made the telephone call that had jerked Charlie away from his typewriter. Ralph worked on the railroad, and early that morning, Lucy had driven him to the L&N depot in town to catch the first locomotive out. She was on her way back home when she saw the car, wheels up, off the road and down the embankment at the foot of Spook Hill. She couldn't see who the driver was because he was pinned under the car, but she could tell he'd been dead for a while.

She had driven home as fast as she could and telephoned the sheriff's office. She owed Charlie a big favor, so as soon as she got off the phone with the sheriff, she had phoned the newspaper. It was her tip that had sent him off in hot pursuit.

Spook Hill was a notoriously steep grade that seemed to go downhill forever. In the rare January or February when there was enough snow or ice, the hill made for some pretty exciting coasting for Darling kids. It was just as exciting when it was muddy, too, because Alabama's red clay roads were slick when it rained — slick as bear grease, the old folks liked to say. What made the hill even more exhilarating was the drop-off down the embankment to the left, sixty feet or more to Spook Creek at the bottom. Snowy, muddy, or bone dry, if you were driving down that hill you'd be glad your brakes were working. And scared silly if they weren't.

It had rained the day before and the road's red mud was slick and gooey. Charlie wasn't too sure about the brakes on his old Pontiac, so he stopped at the top of the hill. Ahead, at the bottom, he could see a black Ford Model T pulled over to the uphill side of the road and two men standing beside it with their hands in their pockets, one of them smoking a large cigar. They wore dark blue uniforms, cop hats, and side arms. The Alabama state shield was painted on the car door, the words *Jericho State Prison Farm* under it. Somebody else had spotted the wreck.

Surveying the situation, Charlie thought it wouldn't be so good if somebody else came barreling down the hill while people were standing around at the bottom, trying to figure out what to do. So he climbed back into his car, started it, and parked it diagonally, blocking the road. He pulled the handbrake and got out, carrying his Rolleiflex. Staying close to the uphill side of the road, he worked his way down to the bottom. There, he recognized the heavy-set man with the grizzled hair and brushy mustache as Warden Burford, from the prison farm.

He put out his hand. "Charlie Dickens, Darling *Dispatch,*" he said. "I understand there's been an accident."

The warden was red-faced, with a substantial belly that hung down over his belt. "Down there," he said gruffly, jerking a thumb in the direction of the drop-off. "Engine's cold. Looks like it's been there all night." He nodded toward the other man. "Jimmie Bragg, my assistant. He saw the car on his way to work this morning and notified me."

Charlie shook hands with Bragg, a short, wiry man with dark hair and a scar across his chin. "Sheriff's on his way?" he asked.

"S'posed to be," the warden replied. "The deputy said he'd get out here soon as he could." He shook his head. "Last time somebody got in trouble on this hill, it was a supervisor from Montgomery, come to see if we was feedin' the boys right. Only he didn't manage to turn his car over. He hit that tree." He indicated a large sweet gum on the wooded uphill side of the road. Its trunk bore the scars of more than one vehicle encounter. "Goldurned lucky, too. Smashed the motor back in his lap and stove in his ribs real bad, but he crawled out alive."

Charlie looked down at the road. Tire tracks — ruts in the soft mud — led to the edge and then veered sharply off. He stepped to the embankment and looked over. The car was on its roof, wheels in the air, about twenty feet down the steep drop-off, lodged against a boulder. The front end was pointing uphill, toward the road, so Charlie figured it must have vaulted end over end when it went over the edge. From this angle, it was hard to identify the make of the vehicle, but he could see one sleeved arm flung out onto the dirt, unmoving. Holding his camera at his waist and looking down into the viewfinder to center the image, Charlie took a photo, then turned the crank to advance the film and took another.

They heard the sound of a motor and the warden turned to look up the hill. "Reckon that's the deputy now," he said.

Charlie glanced up to see Buddy Norris's new deputy, Wayne Springer, parking his dinged-up black 1927 Chevy next to the

Pontiac at the top of the hill. He walked down slowly, pausing as he went to study the tire tracks. When he got to the bottom, he introduced himself, then followed the tracks to the edge and peered over, surveying the scene for several moments.

Springer was tall and rail thin, with a narrow, sun-darkened face, high cheekbones, and a beaked nose. Charlie wondered if there might have been a Cherokee or two somewhere on the man's family tree. He wore a blue denim shirt with a deputy's badge pinned to the pocket, faded blue jeans, and a battered black cowboy hat with a hawk's feather stuck in it. Yep, part Cherokee, Charlie decided.

"Helluva bad hill," Springer said gruffly, hitching up his jeans. "If you don't know it's here, you can come over the top way too fast. Reckon that's what happened?"

"Could be." The warden took his cigar out of his mouth, regarded it gloomily, then tossed it into the bushes. "We lose somebody down here at the bottom every couple of years. Folks who drive out this way gen'rally know to keep it slow. Guess this feller didn't." He pointed down the embankment. "We checked. Driver's dead. Stone cold dead," he added, as if to reassure himself that there was nothing that might have been done for the man. "Likely been out here all night."

"Had to be." Jimmie Bragg spoke around his cud of chewing tobacco. "I was at Pete's place shootin' pool yestiddy evenin'. I quit about eight." He spat. "That car wasn't here when I drove back to the farm."

Springer stepped back to the edge and peered over again. "You sure about that?" he said over his shoulder to Jimmie. "How do you know? You wouldn't have seen it from the road."

"See them tracks?" Jimmie pointed to the ruts in the mud. "They're deep enough for me to have seen 'em. If 'n they'd been here, I would've stopped and got out to look. It was still light when I come along." He pointed to the other side of the road. "Them's my tracks, there. I know to stay on the uphill side when the road is muddy."

Springer knelt down to have a look at the ruts. He studied them for a moment, then stood. "Anybody know whose car this is? Know the driver?"

Warden Burford said, "No idea." He looked at Bragg. "You recognize it, Jimmie?"

Jimmie cocked his head. "Yeah. Seen it a time or two in town. A Pierce-Arrow — old but kept nice. Not a car you forget easy, once you seen it."

Pierce-Arrow? Charlie thought, and then, *I know that car.* There was only one Pierce-Arrow in Darling. It belonged to Whitney Whitworth. He shivered. So unless somebody had stolen the car, that arm flung out there in the dirt must belong to Mr. Whitworth.

"Wonder why that fancy car was all the way out here," the warden remarked casually. "There's no place else to go on this road but the prison farm, and that fella surely wasn't comin' to see *us.*"

Charlie considered. It wasn't quite true that there was no place to go on this road but the prison farm. Past the prison farm, the Jericho Road dwindled to a narrow, rutted track, ending in a marshy morass at the northern edge of Briar Swamp. For the past few months, the boys over at the CCC camp had been doing their level best to drain the swamp, but that was never going to happen, at least not in as big a way as they thought. There were a couple of thousand acres of quagmire out there, nothing but bald cypress up to their knees in water and tupelo gum and hummocks of buttonbush and black willow and pawpaw. Folks would tell you that there was nothing in that swamp but silent flooded lands and mosquitos damned near big enough to carry you away, if the alligators didn't chew off your feet first.

But folks told you that for a reason. There *was* something out there in that quagmire, although Charlie had never been quite sure where. And it didn't bother him that he didn't know, either, for this was one of those cases where the less a man knew, the better off he was. Bodeen Pyle's moonshine camp was out there in the swamp, and the road they were on was the only way in and back out again. And Bodeen Pyle would be a damned dangerous man if somebody tried to get in the way of what he did for a living.

Which of course the warden wouldn't mention within earshot of the deputy, and for one very simple — and very good — reason. The prison farm — or so it was rumored — was one of Pyle's best customers. The steady supply of shine that was made available to inmates and their guards was responsible for the fact that Jericho ran smoothly and had very few escape attempts. The warden would want to protect Pyle's operation, especially since Deputy Springer was new to Darling and still pretty much a cipher. Charlie had heard that old Sheriff Burns knew about Jericho's arrangement with Pyle, but he also knew when to let well enough alone. He had been fond of saying that as long as the local moonshiners kept to themselves and stayed out of trouble, he would stay out of their way. The warden had never met Springer, though, and had no idea how he would view the little arrangement. He probably couldn't be too sure of Buddy Norris, either. He was being cautious.

Charlie cleared his throat. "I know that car," he said. "It belongs to Whitney Whitworth."

The deputy tipped his cowboy hat on the back of his head and looked over at Charlie. "So it does," he said drily, and Charlie realized that he had known this all along. "Tell you what, Dickens. If you've got more film in the camera, how about you walk up that hill a piece and take some pictures looking downhill? Get three, four good shots of those ruts, too." To Burford, he said, "Looks like we got some work to do here, warden. Gotta turn that car over on its wheels."

"We're not waiting for the sheriff?" the warden asked, clearly not sure where he stood with this deputy.

Springer shook his head. "He knows we're here — said he'd be out when he could. He told me to go ahead and do what had to be done. And what's gotta be done is turn that thing over and see if that's Whitworth dead under there, or somebody else."

Jimmie Bragg spoke up. "How 'bout I git a few of the fellers from the farm and a tractor to do the job?"

Springer said he thought this was a good idea, and the warden nodded. Twenty minutes later, a half-dozen men wearing black-and-white striped prisoners' uniforms arrived in a wagon pulled by a forty-horsepower Massey-Harris tractor with cleated steel wheels and driven by a big, bald prisoner named Mango, also in a striped uniform. It took them all of twenty minutes to right the wrecked car, retrieve the dead driver, and lay him out beside the road. His face nearly obliterated, he was not a pretty sight. His own mother probably wouldn't know him, Charlie thought with a shudder.

Then they attached a chain to the wreck's rear bumper and dragged it up the embankment as Charlie took photos. The Pierce-Arrow, a large seven-passenger sedan, had indeed been a splendid car, once. It was painted pale beige, with a contrasting dark roof and a great deal of chrome on the radiator and lights. Now, the roof was pancaked flat across the tops of the seats, the front-end grill was caved in, and there was a dent in the rear.

The driver must have died instantly, Charlie thought, crushed under that heavy vehicle. He imagined what it would be like to come over the top of that hill in the dark and plunge down the other side, maybe only half-aware that this was a dangerous business, and then go flying off the road and do a somersault in the air. If it was your time to go, it might not be a bad way to leave this earth.

Charlie took several photographs of the car and of the deceased Mr. Whitworth, bizarrely frozen by rigor mortis into a sitting position. The latter were so graphic that he knew he couldn't run them in the newspaper. Sensational stories might be the blood and bones of big-city newspapers, but his father had always said that if the *Dispatch* had a motto, it would be "All the news that's fit to be read (by Darling Sunday School teachers)."

Still, as Charlie continued to snap the shutter, he was thinking that he might try selling the grislier shots to the Associated Press. Just last May, the AP had run photos of the bodies of Bonnie Parker and Clyde Barrow, ambushed and shot to death on a rural road in Bienville Parish, Louisiana, by a six-man posse of Texas and Louisiana officers. A boisterous crowd flocked to the

179

ambush spot. Several women cut off bloody locks of Bonnie's hair and pieces of her dress to sell as souvenirs, and a man tried to hack off Clyde's trigger finger. Photos of the killing had been plastered all over the newspapers. The public appetite for such things was insatiable. Newspapers were delighted to deliver.

Even without the photos, though, the story Charlie was already writing in his mind was going to command attention. Whitney Whitworth was very well known, not just in Darling but in the surrounding area. So the first question that would pop into everyone's mind was likely to be "What the heck was Whitney Whitworth doing on Spook Hill all by himself, on a Sunday night?" Charlie wanted to know the answer to that question, whether he would be able to print it or not.

Springer had been examining Whitworth's body, giving him a long and careful going-over. With the dead man's billfold in his hand, he straightened and came over to Charlie. In a low voice, he said, "Get a couple of good close-ups of the rear end of that car, will you? When they're developed, I want copies. One of every shot you've taken."

"Oh, yeah?" Charlie smiled to show that

he was asking a casual question. "Any reason why, in particular?"

The deputy didn't smile back. "When I think of a particular reason, I'll tell you," he said shortly. He turned away and climbed up the hill, pausing now and again to bend over and study the car tracks in the mud like some old Indian tracker. When he got to his car, he started it, pulled around Charlie's Pontiac, and drove slowly down to where they were all standing. He got out, carrying a black rubber raincoat that he handed to Burford.

"Warden, I don't have a sheet for the body, but this raincoat will do. I'd appreciate it if a couple of your men could wrap Mr. Whitworth in it and put him into the rumble seat of my car. I'll take him into town to Nolan's funeral parlor."

"What about the Pierce-Arrow?" the warden asked. "We can tow it to the farm? We've got some other junked cars there."

"Nope." The deputy nodded at the man who was driving the tractor. "I'd prefer it if Mango here hooked it up to his tractor and pulled it into town, to the sheriff's office."

"I'll go with Mango," Jimmie Bragg volunteered. He grinned at the tractor driver. "Make sure he don't try to escape."

"Okay by me," the warden said. He pulled

181

another cigar out of his shirt pocket, giving Jimmie a stern look. "But you stay on that tractor with him, Bragg. And you and Mango come on straight back to the prison farm — no stopping at Pete's Pool Parlor. You hear?"

"Yassuh, boss," Jimmie said, and gave an exaggerated salute.

The warden regarded him suspiciously. "Tell you what," he said. "I'll drive along behind, just to make sure there's no funny business. Somebody's got to pick up the mail, anyhow. Might as well do that while I'm in town."

"Okay, then," the deputy said. "Here's what we'll do. I'll lead the way. Jimmie, you and Mango come next. Warden Burford, you bring up the rear." He turned to Charlie. "We're going to be pretty slow, Dickens. Why don't you go on back to town and get started on those photos?"

Charlie resisted the sarcastic temptation to salute and say "Yassuh, boss." But as he drove back to the Dispatch office and got to work developing the photographs, he couldn't help wondering. What had the deputy spotted out there on that hill that he hadn't? What could be of such interest in his photos that Springer wanted copies — and wanted them fast?

182

Other people, too, had questions that morning, as they observed a cavalcade of several vehicles crawling slowly along Darling's main street. Curious about what was going on, they went to their windows or stepped out onto their front porches or stopped on the sidewalk to watch and wonder.

First came the sheriff's deputy in his old black Ford roadster, a passenger wearing a raincoat sitting rigidly in the rumble seat, head bent forward, one arm flung stiffly to the side. Darlingians who gave this curious spectacle a casual glance might have concluded that Deputy Springer (who, everyone agreed, was proving to be a diligent lawman, with just the right sort of experience to back up the inexperienced young sheriff) was hauling a drunk to jail. Obviously, the fellow had consumed a little too much of Bodeen Pyle's powerful tiger spit and would spend the rest of the day sleeping it off in one of the two cells in the second-floor jail over Snow's Farm Supply, next door to the sheriff's office.

But those who took the trouble to step down off their porches and walk out to the curb for a better look could see that the man in the deputy's rumble seat was no drunk at all, but a very bloody, very dead *corpse.*

Whose corpse, they couldn't be sure, for the head was bowed and the face was hidden.

However, these curious Darlingians didn't have to wait long for an answer to their shocked and breathless question: *Who in the world . . . ?* A half-block behind the deputy sheriff came a slow, heavy, steel-wheeled tractor, clanking ponderously along the street like one of Colonel George S. Patton's army tanks. It was followed by a black Ford with the Alabama state shield and the words *Jericho State Prison Farm* painted on both sides, driven by a portly, important-looking officer smoking a cigar the size of a corncob. The tractor was driven by a large Negro with a shiny bald head, wearing striped prison garb, a skinny uniformed man perched behind him. The tractor was towing a wrecked ivory-colored Pierce-Arrow, splattered with red clay mud, the roof smashed flat.

And the instant Darlingians saw that car, they knew whose corpse it was.

CHAPTER ELEVEN:
LIZZY GETS A LETTER

Before she went back to Mr. Moseley's law office, Lizzy took a minute to walk around the corner to the post office. Thaddeus Flagg, the postmaster, was a stooped little man who wore a green eyeshade, a red knitted cap, a purple sweater, and black fingerless gloves, even in the heat of summer, when everybody else was sweltering. He claimed to be deaf, but everybody knew he could hear what he wanted to hear, especially when it was gossip. They also suspected that he read their postcards and the return addresses on their mail — and wouldn't put it past him to steam open a promising envelope over that little teakettle he kept on a hotplate in the back room.

"Whose mail?" Mr. Flagg demanded testily, as if he had never seen Lizzy before in his life — which was of course ridiculous, for she went to the post office every day to pick up the office mail.

"Mr. Moseley's, please," Lizzy said meekly and waited while he stomped off in the direction of the wooden cubbyholes arrayed across the back wall of the post office. Darling was behind the times, for nearby Monroeville had real post-office boxes with brass-plated doors and little glass windows and combination locks, so you didn't have to ask the postmaster for your mail. Lizzy's mailman (a pleasant fellow named Tootie Blue) carried the mail in a big leather shoulder bag and delivered hers right to her door. But businesses and professional people who got a *lot* of mail, like Mr. Moseley, rented a cubby.

Mr. Flagg was gone for several minutes, and when he came back, his hands were full. "Too much mail again today," he growled, as if the postal service imposed some sort of limit. "Tootie's out sick, so yours is here, too." He thumped the mail on the counter.

"I'm sorry," Lizzy said contritely. She saw her name on the top envelope, from Nadine Fleming, of Fleming and Finlay Literary Agency, in New York City, and her heart jumped. It wasn't something *bad,* was it? More revisions to her book — again? A delay in the publishing schedule? Or maybe the editor had decided he didn't like what she had done and wouldn't be publishing it

186

after all! Miss Fleming had told her not to count her chickens until they had hatched — that is, until the book was actually published.

Mr. Flagg peered down at the envelope in Lizzy's hand. "Literary agency." He grunted. "A rejection notice, I reckon." He shook his head gloomily. "You young girls. Never content with what you got, allus shootin' for the moon. Oughtta get yerself a husband and settle down to a real job."

"I *have* a real job," Lizzy protested, but Mr. Flagg pretended not to hear.

"That feller you used to go around with — the county farm agent. He's single again now." He squinted at her over the tops of wire-rimmed glasses. "And so is yer boss. Y'see? You got *two* choices, which is more than most young girls your age got. You don't take one of 'em, you're gonna end up an old maid. Mark my words. A wrinkled, skinny old maid."

Lizzy knew it was pointless to argue with Mr. Flagg. She bundled up the mail, thrust it into her handbag, and said goodbye. "And thank you," she added, politely.

"Don't mention it," Mr. Flagg said with a dark emphasis. "You just mind what I say, girl. An old maid."

■ ■ ■ ■

Lizzy hurried back to Mr. Moseley's law office, took off her hat, and plugged in the electric percolator. She put the bundle of mail on her desk, sat down, and reached for the phone.

It took the girl on the switchboard three tries to put the call through to Montgomery and Mr. Moseley, but finally Lizzy had him on the other end of the line and was reporting on her visit with Mrs. Whitworth. She had taken out her notebook and now went through her notes, pausing when she got to the words *bruise, scrape,* and *husband.* She told Mr. Moseley what she thought, then added, "I suggested that she see Dr. Roberts, but she refused. She is *very* upset, although she tries to hide it. She thinks her husband might have been kidnapped."

"I doubt that," Mr. Moseley said. "No ransom demand, I suppose. No notes, no phone calls."

"No. She got a phone call while I was there, but it was from a friend, evidently asking about the bruise on her cheek." She thought of the car she had glimpsed through the window. "By the way, I'm pretty sure that the Whitworths bought the convertible coupe that was in the show window at Kilgore's last week. I saw it in their garage — at least, I think I did. I didn't get a close look."

"Oh, too bad," Mr. Moseley said regretfully. "I had my eye on that car. The only thing that deterred me were the suicide doors. That design is dangerous."

"Suicide door?" Lizzy asked. "What's that?"

"It's a door that's hinged at the rear, rather than the front. If it's not latched, the airflow can swing the door open, and the driver can fall out. It happened over in Georgia not long ago — the driver was killed when he went around a corner. I understand there may be a lawsuit." He paused. "But back to the question at hand. I don't think there's anything to worry about. Whitworth probably picked up a bottle of moonshine, took it out somewhere, and is sleeping it off He'll show up back home looking hang-dog and guilty."

"I suppose so," Lizzy said, although she wasn't so sure. "You're not coming back to Darling, then?"

She didn't expect him to. When he was in Montgomery, Benton Moseley spent his evenings (and nights, too, probably) with a wealthy socialite named Daphne, a charming, twice-divorced lady who belonged to the elegant, ultra-fashionable country-club set. So while Mr. Flagg and her friend Ophelia (and sometimes others) might suggest that Lizzy and her boss would make a compatible couple, she understood that this was entirely out of the question. Not that she was disappointed, of course.

"Doesn't sound like there's anything I need to do there," he replied. "I'll finish up my depositions here and be back on Wednesday or Thursday. Keep in touch with Mrs. Whitworth, will you? Check on her this afternoon. And call me when Whitworth shows up." He paused. "Anything interesting in the mail?"

"I haven't had a chance to go through it yet," Lizzy replied, glancing at the letter on top of the bundle. She said goodbye and hung up.

The coffee had finished perking, so she poured herself a cup and sat down with Miss Fleming's letter. Lizzy still couldn't believe her good luck in finding a literary agent. Of course, the woman had never been terribly encouraging, for the Depression had had a dreadful effect on the publishing business.

"Even established writers with a long track record are having a hard time," Miss Fleming had told her when they talked on the phone. "People are finding whatever jobs they can. Ghostwriting, movie scripts, advice to the lovelorn. It's terribly, terribly difficult. You're doing excellent work, Miss Lacy, and in a different economic climate, I'm sure you'd be published immediately. These days, I'm afraid not. I'll do my best of course, but please don't expect *anything*."

But to Miss Fleming's surprise and Lizzy's astonishment, her novel *had* found a home — and an illustrious home, at that — at Scribner's. Amazingly, her new editor was Maxwell Perkins, who had published F. Scott Fitzgerald and Ernest Hemingway and Thomas Wolfe! Mr. Perkins had been remarkably generous with his time, making all sorts of editorial suggestions to tighten Lizzy's plot and strengthen her characters. She had made all the changes he suggested and sent the manuscript back. Miss Fleming had told her to expect galleys — but now, a letter? Had Scribner's decided not to publish *Sabrina*?

Anxiously, she skimmed the typewritten page and then sat back in her chair, whooshing out a relieved breath. Miss Fleming wrote that Mr. Perkins was quite pleased with her revisions and would be writing to tell her so himself. In the meantime, he had a suggestion for the title.

"He would like to call it *Inherit the Flames*," Miss Fleming wrote. "I think it is most appropriate, for it catches a bit of what you represent so well in the novel: the fiery cataclysm of the Civil War and the passions that swept those years. If you agree, I'll let him know."

Inherit the Flames, Lizzy thought, and then said it aloud. "Inherit the Flames." She had liked *Sabrina*, but she liked the sound of this much better. She would write to Miss Fleming and tell her so. She opened the bottom drawer of her desk, took out her handbag, and opened it to put the letter away.

When she did, she saw the paper sack that DessaRae had given her — for Sally-Lou, the maid had said — when she left the Whitworth house. Curious now, she opened the sack and peeked in. Inside were two of DessaRae's pecan cookies, which she remembered eating when she was a girl.

But there was something else in the sack, too. A folded bit of torn paper. On one side was what looked like part of a grocery list: *mayonnaise, sugar, coffee, lard.* On the other side were three sentences, written in a faint pencil in DessaRae's tight, careful script.

Tell Sally-Lou you need to talk to Fremon

right away.

Tell him I told you to ask him what he saw last night.

And don't take no for an answer.

·✦·

Fremon? Lizzy stared at the note, puzzled. Sally-Lou's kid brother Fremon Hawkins worked at Jake Pritchard's Standard station out on the Monroeville Highway. Lizzy knew him well. At least, she *had* known him, years ago, when she was a girl and Sally-Lou (just fourteen and still a girl herself when she came to work for Liz's mother) was her nursemaid and friend. Lizzy had often gone with Sally-Lou to her mother's house on the other side of the L&N tracks. She and Fremon would play with his pet turtle, Myrtle, or climb the catalpa tree with their slingshots and practice knocking cans off the back fence. Or they would take cane fishing poles with red-and-yellow cork bobbers and a lard bucket full of fishing worms and the three of them — Sally-Lou, Fremon, and Lizzy — would walk down the tracks to where Spook Creek flowed deep and dark under the railroad bridge. They spent many lazy summer days in the shade of the cottonwoods and sweetgums along the banks, fishing for bluegills, bass, and catfish.

But that was a long time ago, when the freedoms of a small-town childhood — and the inattention of her mother — made such friendships possible. Lizzy had seen Fremon around town, of course, and had heard that he was married and had children. But they hadn't talked in years. Why was DessaRae telling her to speak to him now? And what *had* he seen? Was it something to do with Mr. Whitworth?

Lizzy glanced at the old Seth Thomas clock on the opposite wall. It was almost quarter to eleven. Now that her mother was married and helping to manage her new husband's Five and Dime, Sally-Lou was working for her again. She did the washing on Mondays, out back in the wash house, where she heated the water in a copper boiler on the old wood-fired stove, to keep the heat out of the house. The telephone was inside, of course, in the hallway. She might not hear it, but it was worth a try.

Lizzy was about to hang up, but the phone was answered on the fifth ring. "Dunlap residence," Sally-Lou said breathlessly. "Mr. an' Miz Dunlap ain't here jes' now. Would you like to leave a message?"

Mr. and Mrs. Dunlap. Lizzy smiled. Her mother's recent marriage had been as surprising as Grady's, but in a much more gratifying way. Mrs. Lacy (now Mrs. Dunlap) believed that it was her job to tell her daughter how to live her life. This had been bad enough when she was a girl, but as Lizzy grew older, her mother's interference had become almost intolerable. When she announced that she was getting married, Lizzy had been overjoyed. From now on, her mother was Mr. Dunlap's problem!

"Hello, Sally-Lou," Lizzy said. "It's Liz. Actually, I wanted to talk to *you.* Is now a good time? You're not too busy?"

"Oh, good mawnin', Miz Lizzy," Sally-Lou said cheerfully. "Sorry — I was hangin' sheets on the line and it took me a while to git to the phone. What can I do for you?"

Lizzy was relieved that her mother had a private line. She couldn't think of a way to slip easily into the subject, so she took a deep breath and dived in. "I just got back from the Whitworth house. Mr. Moseley asked me to go over there this morning, because Mr. Whitworth has . . . well, he seems to have disappeared."

"Disappeared?" Sally-Lou repeated, sounding surprised. "That man Aunt Dessy work fo'?"

"Yes, that's the one. His wife is worried about him." Lizzy pressed on. "When I was leaving, your aunt gave me a note."

195

A silence. Then, "What fo' Aunt Dessy done write you a *note*?"

Lizzy understood why Sally-Lou's tone was suddenly guarded. In the years since Sally-Lou had taken care of her, they had both learned that friendship wasn't always a safe bridge between the colored folks in Maysville and the white people in Darling. They still felt as warmly toward one another as they did when they had gone fishing under the railroad trestle. At least, Lizzy did, and she thought Sally-Lou did, too. But they were grown up now. As adults, they had to recognize that they lived on separate planets and that it was difficult to bring the two into the same orbit. It could even be dangerous — not so much for Lizzy, but for Sally-Lou. And even more, for Fremon.

Lizzy swallowed uncomfortably and answered Sally-Lou's question. "DessaRae wrote the note because she wasn't sure we'd have a chance to talk where Mrs. Whitworth wouldn't hear. She gave it to me when I was leaving, in a sack with two pecan cookies. She told me to give the cookies to you tonight, when I go over to my mother's."

"Well, that don't make no sense a-tall," Sally-Lou said testily. "I leave here at fo', and Aunt Dessy knows you don' never come over here till after supper." Her voice sharpened. "That woman is a pistol. What she got up her sleeve this time?"

DessaRae, Sally-Lou's aunt by marriage, had a reputation for doing outrageous things. Like the time she took the train to New Orleans to be in the Mardi Gras parade and came back with her face painted and wearing a fabulous feathered headdress. On the job, she wore the standard maid's uniform, but at home in her tiny Maysville house, she wore madras plaid skirts and ruffled blouses and wrapped her head in yellow and red tignons. She kept a parrot she called Pierre LeToot, who could whistle like an old steamboat and had a vocabulary of nearly two hundred words, half of them obscene. DessaRae was also said to practice voodoo, although Lizzy doubted the truth of that rumor.

"I'll read you her note." Lizzy put it on the desk and smoothed it out. "It says, 'Tell Sally-Lou you got to talk to Fremon right away. Tell him he has to tell you what he saw last night. And don't take no for an answer.' "

"Talk to Fremon?" Sally-Lou said, sounding genuinely puzzled. "Why? What that boy see? How does Aunt Dessy know? And how come it matters to *you*?"

They were all pertinent questions, but

Lizzy had no answers. She cleared her throat. "I think it must have something to do with what's happened to Mr. Whitworth. Mr. Moseley has asked me to find out whatever I can about it." She paused. "Does Fremon still work at Pritchard's Standard station?"

"Yes," Sally-Lou said slowly. "But you don' want to talk to him there, wi' all them men around."

Lizzy agreed. It wasn't "all them men" that were the problem, however. It was just one man: Jake Pritchard's cousin Jumbo, a big, burly man with a menacing look who occasionally hung around the station. The Klan had been much more active in Cypress County during the 1920s than it was now — the Depression had taken a bite out of its membership. But Jumbo Pritchard still led the robed and hooded group when it marched in the Confederate Day parade. He would make things tough for a colored man seen talking to a white woman. In fact, any encounters outside of the everyday working relationship could prove to be a problem for Fremon, and Lizzy didn't want to cause him any trouble.

"Does your brother still live in Maysville?" Lizzy asked. "Maybe I could go to his house. Or talk to him on the phone." She might have suggested that he come over and mow her lawn or paint her front porch swing, but she didn't want to put him in that position. It was dishonest. And demeaning. Fremon had been a proud boy. She hoped the man hadn't changed.

"He do. But his wife won' 'preciate you comin' to their house," Sally-Lou said firmly. "An' his neighbors might see you an' be wonderin' why a white lady be doin' what she's doin'. Plus he don't have no telephone."

Lizzy felt embarrassed. Of course, Fremon didn't have a phone. Most folks in Maysville didn't.

Sally-Lou was silent for a moment. Finally, she said, "I reckon I could ask him if he'd come over to your house wi' me after supper tonight — later, after it's dark. I could sit on the back porch whiles you an' him talk."

"Oh, would you?" Lizzy asked in a grateful rush. "Thank you very much."

"Cain't promise," Sally-Lou said. "But I can try." She hesitated. "Not sure I should tell him why, though. You reckon?"

"I agree." Lizzy hated to do it that way, but she was afraid he might not come if he knew why he was being asked. Especially if he had seen . . . *Seen what?* She couldn't

199

know the answer to that, though, until she had talked to Fremon.

"I won't, then." Sally-Lou chuckled wryly. "That boy will prob'ly say more if he took by surprise an' don't got the time to plan it out ahead."

Lizzy agreed with that, too, but she didn't like to say so. "What time do you want to come?"

"Let's say seven-thirty. You at Mr. Moseley's office today?"

"Yes. I'll be here until five."

"I'll phone Fremon over at the Standard and see what he says. If 'n you don't hear from me, let's count on seven-thirty. We'll come to the back door."

"Thank you," Lizzy said again. "I really appreciate this, Sally-Lou."

"Don' thank me yit," Sally-Lou warned, and hung up.

Lizzy sat back in her chair, thinking. She was caught up on her work for Mr. Moseley, and she had gone just about as far as she could — for the moment — with the Whitworth affair. Fremon might be able to add something tonight, or he might not, in which case the whole thing would simply have to wait until Mr. Whitworth turned up.

In the meantime, she could work on "The

Garden Gate," the weekly column she wrote for the *Dispatch*. She had already started it, so she reached into the drawer, took out the pages she had done, and set to work.

CHAPTER TWELVE:
THE GARDEN GATE
BY ELIZABETH LACY

Looking For Luck? Find it in Your Garden!

At a recent meeting of the Darling Dahlias Garden Club, Miss Rogers (Darling's librarian and noted plant historian) gave a talk on plants that can bring their owners good fortune. She was speaking in honor of Darling's own Lucky Four Clovers — our town's hands-down favorite to win the Dixie Regional Barbershop Quartet Competition. She has given me permission to use her notes for this column. Thank you, Miss Rogers, and good luck, you Lucky Four Clovers. Your hometown friends are rooting for you!

The Four-Leaf Clover (*Trifolium repens*). Miss Rogers reported that she found one of these lucky clovers recently growing beside the path to the library. Following the advice of an old saying, she picked the clover and put it in her shoe, so she could have good luck until the next new moon.

Another legend has it that when you find a four-leaf clover, you'll see a fairy. (Unfortunately, that hasn't worked out so well for Miss Rogers, maybe because Darling's fairies have moved somewhere else.) In Ireland, a four-leaf clover can protect you from evil spirits. In ancient Rome, it could protect you from poisonous snakes. On the Ivory Coast of Africa, a four-leaf clover is a symbol of power: find one and you can be chief of the tribe.

The four-leaf clover seems to be a universal symbol of good fortune, perhaps because it is rare everywhere but occurs just often enough to keep us looking. People who count such things tell us that one out of every ten thousand clovers has four leaves. The Latin name of this plant, *Trifolium repens,* describes its usual three leaves and its habit of creeping across the ground. Miss Rogers suggests that if you find a four-leaf clover, you might call it *Quadrifolium repens.* She even proposed that the Lucky Four Clovers consider changing the name of their quartet to *Quadrifolium repens,* but this suggestion was met with great disapproval.

Jade plant (*Crassula ovata*). This lucky plant's common names tell us why people treasure it: money tree, money plant, lucky plant, dollar plant, and prosperity plant. Usually grown as a houseplant, the glossy round leaves of the jade plant resemble valuable jade coins. In Asia, where it is especially prized, jade plant is often given as a gift to a new business, to a new bride and groom, or to an infant. It is also given as a New Year's gift, to bring wealth and good fortune throughout the year. Carry several of the shiny green "coins" in your pocket and see if they bring you some silver.

Lucky bamboo (*Dracaena sanderiana*) looks like bamboo, with its woody, segmented stalk and bright green leaves, but it's not invasive. A houseplant often grown in water, its genus name (*Dracaena*) comes from a Greek word that means "female dragon," so-called because of its paradoxical association with independent strength and compliance. (The flexible stems of lucky bamboo are often bent into intricate shapes.) In China, this plant goes by the name *fu gwey: fu,* for luck and fortune; *gwey,* for power and honor. The number of stalks of *fu gwey* suggest different kinds of luck: three for happiness and long life; five for wealth; seven for good health. Groups of stems (three times three stems; three times five; three times seven) are thought to bring happiness, wealth, and health several times over. Another lucky thing about this plant: it requires almost no care at all. If you're growing it in water, though, be sure to replace the water every few days to reduce algae growth.

Morning glories (*Ipomoea*) in your garden are said to bring you peace and happiness — and guaranteed to bring a smile when you see them. If you put morning glory seeds under your pillow, your sleep will be restful and free of bad dreams. The Aztecs believed that the plant was a way of connecting with the Sun God; carrying the seeds would bring great good fortune. In voodoo tradition, the root of one plant in this genus, jalap (*Ipomoea jalapa*), is reputed to bring good luck in anything relating to money, but especially in gambling — and flirting. Carry the woody tuber in your pocket or attach it to a chain or ribbon and wear it as an amulet.

Buckeye (*Aesculus glabra*) nuts — dried, oiled, polished — are also carried in the pocket or worn as an amulet. The buckeye tree is a relative of the chestnut and the nut is the same rich, mellow brown, but don't try to eat it. (It will make you sick.) Like the jalap root, the buckeye was thought to attract good fortune in the form of money — and the ladies. (Miss Rogers said that she wouldn't go into that part of it in her talk, but if you're interested, drop in at the library and she can show you where to look that up.)

Sunflower (*Helianthus annuus*). If you have planted sunflowers around your house or in your backyard, you are doubly lucky. Those large, sunny yellow flowers are guaranteed to brighten your day and bring you good fortune. At the same time, the tall, sturdy plants will serve as a shield to protect your home from bad luck. Other traditions: Pick a sunflower at sunset, wear it in your buttonhole the next day, and you'll have good luck all day long. Sleep with a sunflower under your pillow; before sunset the next day, you will learn a truth you are seeking.

Persimmons, peaches, oranges, and pomegranates. Sometimes called the "four fruits of good fortune," each of these symbolizes a different aspect of good luck. Persimmons represent friendship, happiness, and a smooth path through life. (In Korea, a persimmon can also scare away a tiger — although Miss Rogers does not recommend that you try this.) The peach symbolizes contentment in marriage and longevity. The orange stands for prosperity and financial success. The pomegranate (which has a great many seeds) represents good fortune through many children. Keep a bowl of these four fruits in your home and eat one every day, and you will certainly have good fortune.

Miss Rogers ended her talk by saying that it is all well and good to trust in luck, and it certainly won't hurt to have a four-leaf clover in your shoe, a sunflower in your buttonhole, morning glories on your fence, and a persimmon, a peach, an orange, and a pomegranate in a bowl on your table. But she has more confidence in the words of Thomas Jefferson, who said, "I'm a great believer in luck, and I find the harder I work the more I have of it."

The Dahlias thanked Miss Rogers for another informative talk and then adjourned for cookies and punch, provided by Refreshment Committee members Ophelia Snow and Earlynne Biddle. Earlynne says that several people asked her for her persimmon cookie recipe. If you're one of them, here it is.

EARLYNNE BIDDLE'S PERSIMMON COOKIES

1 cup persimmon pulp* (about 2 to 3 ripe persimmons)
1 teaspoon baking soda

1 cup sugar

1/2 cup butter, at room temperature

1 egg, beaten

2 cups flour

1 teaspoon cinnamon

1/2 teaspoon ground cloves

1/2 teaspoon ground nutmeg

1/2 teaspoon powdered ginger

1/2 teaspoon salt

1 cup chopped pecans, walnuts, or what have you

1 cup raisins

Preheat the oven to 375 °F. In a large mixing bowl, beat the persimmon pulp, soda, sugar, and butter until creamy. Gently stir the beaten egg into the persimmon mixture, along with flour, spices, salt, nuts, and raisins. Using a teaspoon, drop dough on a greased baking sheet and bake for 12 to 15 minutes. Makes about 3 dozen.

*Earlynne says persimmons are very sharp-tasting unless they are dead ripe and soft, but please don't leave them on the ground to get that way, or the raccoons and possums will have a feast and you'll come up empty-handed. Bring the persimmons in, wash them, and let them ripen in a paper bag (not in your icebox) until they're squishy. Peel them, take out the seeds and chop, then put them in a big bowl and whack them with your potato masher. After that you can put them through a potato ricer or a food mill and you'll end up with perfect persimmon pulp. Or, if you've got a mesh laundry bag (Earlynne got hers from the Sears and Roebuck catalog), put your peeled, seeded persimmons in the bag and squeeze. However you do it, clean up afterward. Persimmon pulp dries sticky. Earlynne says it is the very worst glue you've seen in all your life.

CHAPTER THIRTEEN:
BESSIE GOES TO THE
FIVE AND DIME

About the time that Liz began working on her garden column, Bessie Bloodworth (freshly shampooed, cut, curled, and combed out) had just left the Beauty Bower and was on her way to do some shopping.

The previous year, Bessie had served on the Bridge Club's Calendar Committee with Mrs. Whitworth, and she was tempted to make a quick detour over to Peachtree Street and tell that poor woman how distressed she had been to learn that her husband had been kidnapped. It would certainly be the courteous thing to do, but Bessie reluctantly decided against it. Mrs. Whitworth was probably pacing the floor and biting her fingernails, waiting for the kidnappers to call about the ransom. Bessie certainly hoped that her telephone was working.

Anyway, the courthouse clock said it was after eleven. The residents at the Manor —

the Magnolia Manor, the genteel boarding house for elderly ladies that Bessie owned and managed — had given her their Monday list of things to pick up. She had better get started or she wouldn't get home in time for lunch.

Bessie was headed for the Five and Dime, on the south side of the courthouse square. On her list: three yards of narrow cream-colored lace to trim the pink cotton nightie Leticia Wiggens was making; a card of small brass safety pins for Miss Rogers; a Charm-Kurl Permanent Wave Kit for Maxine Bechtel; and a bar of Lifebuoy soap for Mrs. Sedalius, who had shown Bessie a magazine ad so she would be sure to get the right brand: "I value my daintiness too much to ever take a chance with BO, so naturally I use Lifebuoy!"

None of Bessie's ladies were what you might call well-off (in fact, Maxine was two months behind on her board bill), and they all cut corners where they could. Most folks had to do that these days, especially older ladies who had no children to take care of them. Everybody at the Manor was on pins and needles to see what President Roosevelt was going to do about getting them an old-age pension. Leticia even went so far as to declare that if FDR was on the ballot in

1936, she wouldn't vote for him *unless* he got a pension bill through Congress. Most agreed that aid for the elderly was sorely needed, but some accused Mr. Roosevelt of getting his idea — social security, it was called — from Frances Perkins, his secretary of labor, and said that it was one of the soft-headed notions you got when you made the mistake of installing a woman on the president's cabinet. Bessie herself was a staunch supporter of Louisiana's senator Huey Long, who understood what folks needed and promised to get it for them. In the meantime, the residents at the Manor had to watch every penny they spent.

Darling was too small and out of the way for a Woolworth's (the nearest was down in Mobile). But Darling folk were just as happy with their Five and Dime, which was owned by Reginald Dunlap. Dunlap's sold just about anything under the sun as long as it had a five- or ten-cent price tag. The rock-bottom prices were designed to make shoppers feel rich, because they could buy lots of different things (even if they didn't always need them). What's more, everything was *on* the counter within easy reach, instead of being on shelves *behind* the counter, the way it was at Mann's Mercantile. At Dunlap's, you could pick something up and finger it and sniff it while you decided whether or not you could get along without it. If you didn't, there wasn't any clerk to frown and make you feel guilty for giving him the trouble of putting it back on the shelf.

Five-and-dimes had gotten off to a rocky start. Frank Woolworth's first store (in Utica, New York, back in 1878) was a failure. Nothing daunted, he put up the same red-and-gold sign, Woolworth's Great Five Cent Store, at another location — another failure. Landlord problems closed the third store, and the fourth (in York, Pennsylvania) went broke in three months. But shoppers flocked to the fifth store, in Scranton, which boasted mahogany counters with glass dividers and glass-fronted showcases, bright lighting, and polished wooden floors. By 1912, when the company went public, there were 596 stores and the sale of stock brought over $30 million. In the Threadbare Thirties, department stores everywhere went out of business, but not the dime store. It was designed to weather tough times.

Darling's Five and Dime was one of a handful of stores conveniently located on the courthouse square, the hub of the little town. On the east side of the square was

Mann's Mercantile, which carried clothing and boots and tools and bolts of yard goods and kitchenware — and even (in the back room, on a secret shelf behind the horse harness and saddles) bottles of corn whiskey. Bessie wasn't in the market for moonshine, but everybody in town knew where to get it when they wanted it.

On the north side was Musgrove's Hardware, which had everything you needed if you were building something or fixing something up — plumbing, roofing, lumber (stacked out back), and fence wire; baby chicks and ducklings and turkey poults in the spring, trucked in from the hatchery over at Monroeville; and seed potatoes and green onion sets for gardeners. Next to Musgrove's was the Diner and the Exchange, owned by Myra May and Violet, which was the unfortunate focus of Darling's discontent these days. Next door to the Diner was the Darling Dispatch, where Ophelia Snow was a reporter and sold advertising. And upstairs over the Dispatch was Mr. Moseley's law office, where Liz Lacy worked. Bessie always smiled when she thought that on the north side of the square, five Dahlias were blooming in a row: Myra May, Violet, and Raylene at the diner; Ophelia at the Dispatch; and Liz at the law office upstairs.

Next door to the Dispatch was Hancock's Grocery, Darling's only grocery store. Mrs. Hancock was sometimes rude and short-tempered, and she liked to give you her Temperance lecture while she was getting your order together and figuring up how much she was owed. But she would also give you credit if you asked for it, or trade a dozen fresh eggs from your backyard chickens for two pounds of flour or a pound of your fresh-churned butter for a half-pound of Hills Bros. ground coffee. And if your grocery bags were heavy, Mrs. Hancock would ask Old Zeke to load them in his red wagon and deliver them to your kitchen door.

Before the Crash, Bessie had heard talk about the possibility of the A&P putting one of those new-fangled self-service grocery stores — a *supermarket,* it was called — on the vacant lot on the south side of the square, where Sevier's Stationery had burned down back in the summer of 1927. People said it would be the kind of store where you carried a metal shopping basket over your arm and collected what you wanted, rather than waiting while Mrs. Hancock did it for you. Then you took your basket to a girl who sat behind a cash register at the front of the store, where you paid for everything and then carried it home yourself.

But Bessie thought this was just talk, with the economy so shaky. At least she hoped so. If the A&P came to Darling, that would likely mean the end of Hancock's. But while self-service might be convenient, the A&P wouldn't give you credit. You'd have to pay every time you needed groceries, which might mean going without sugar or tea or coffee until Friday rolled around and you got your paycheck. The A&P wouldn't take your eggs and butter, either — they had plenty of their own. And no delivery. Old Zeke would be out of a job and you'd be toting your own shopping bags.

When Bessie got to Dunlap's, she saw that something new had been added. Up to now, the front window had been a hodge-podge of whatever items had come in recently, displayed without any attention to making it pretty. Now, the window itself was sparkling, and the display — an attractive arrangement of Halloween witch masks and pirate masks and even a skeleton costume for little kids to wear when they went door-to-door for candy — was eye-catching. There were also a couple of carved jack-o'-lantern pumpkins and twisted streamers of orange and brown crepe paper, with toy brown mice and a stuffed squirrel peeking out of drifts of colorful maple and sweet gum leaves.

Bessie paused to admire the display, thinking that the store's appearance had definitely perked up since Mr. Dunlap (a widower with two grown-up girls) had married Audrey Lacy. The wedding had come as a big surprise to everyone in Darling, but especially to Liz — Audrey's daughter — and to Bessie, who had known her since Mrs. Dribble's elementary class in the old two-room schoolhouse on Chestnut Street.

In fact, Bessie could not for the life of her understand how mild-mannered Mr. Dunlap — a small, timid man, thin-shouldered, gray-haired, with thick, round spectacles — could have summoned the courage to propose to the redoubtable Widow Lacy. But there must be more to the man than met the eye, Bessie decided, for he had proposed and been accepted. After the wedding, the newlyweds had driven down to Mobile for a week at the Wild Beach Motor Inn, right on the beautiful blue Gulf. Bessie had even gotten a postcard from the bride, with a heart drawn around the picture of the honeymoon cottage and a row of little hearts across the bottom to indicate that she was having a romantic time. When they returned from their honeymoon, Audrey had confided to Bessie that her new husband was a "tiger."

But the refurbished display window was just the tip of the iceberg, so to speak. Inside the store, the new Mrs. Dunlap had worked other miracles, scrubbing and waxing the wooden floors, reorganizing the messy countertops, and building attractive displays that showed off the merchandise. There were racks of men's neckties and leather belts and bins of socks and underwear and handkerchiefs. There were displays of women's rayon and cotton hosiery and silk scarves and costume jewelry and sparkling tiered glass shelves of Cutex and Revlon nail polish in the latest match-your-dress colors of emerald green, mulberry, and cornflower blue, with a poster that showed you how to paint your nails in the popular new style: half-moons and tips left bare, with only the center of the nail polished. There was Maybelline makeup, too: mascara in tiny red boxes with little brushes; eye shadow in brown and black and even (gasp!) green. There was Tangee lipstick, which was advertised to change color, depending on your skin tone. Oh, and those precious little heart-shaped bottles of Blue Waltz perfume.

For boys, there were kites, of course, plus

218

the new green-and-red Duncan yo-yos, an orange-painted Amos 'n' Andy Fresh Air Taxi (with Amos and Andy riding in it, right out of the radio show!), and Marx balsawood airplanes with rubber-band windup propellers. Girls could cuddle the latest Flossie Flirt doll (with real shoes and a blue ribbon in her shiny brown hair) and the new Bottletot baby doll that drank out of her bottle, wet her diaper, and closed her eyes when she was put down. There were rolls of brightly colored hair ribbons for a nickel a yard and plastic barrettes and jacks and jumping ropes. And for girls and boys, games of Authors and Old Maid and Dr. Quack, and books in the Nancy Drew and Hardy Boys series, all neatly arranged on a shelf where the kiddos could reach them.

In fact, the whole store looked especially nice, Bessie thought — and Audrey Dunlap got all the credit. Mr. Dunlap ought to be very grateful, although she had to wonder whether he might repent of his bargain when Audrey got tired of managing the store and began managing *him.*

This morning, though, Mr. Dunlap was nowhere to be seen, and Audrey herself — a large, heavy-bosomed woman with a penetrating voice — was waiting on a customer in Housewares. Specifically, Bessie saw, she was urging Leona Ruth Adcock to spend sixty cents for a new skillet instead of putting a new wooden handle on her old one. Bessie had to smile. Leona Ruth, who was wearing a purple dress with purple gloves and a purple hat with shimmering cockade of peacock feathers perched on her tight gray curls, hated to be urged to do anything. She was more than a match for Audrey and was putting up quite a fight.

By the time Bessie found the lace Leticia Wiggens wanted (ecru, scalloped, seven-eighths of an inch wide, seven cents a yard), Audrey had given up battling with Leona Ruth. She hurried over to Dry Goods to measure out Bessie's three yards against the wooden yardstick that was nailed to the counter. (Dry Goods was *not* self-help, since customers might yield to temptation and help themselves to an extra half-yard or so.) She rolled up the lace neatly and fastened it with a pin.

"Here you are, Bessie," she said. "That will be twenty-one cents."

"I have a few other things to look for," Bessie said, and offered a compliment. "That front display window looks right pretty, with that crepe paper and leaves and those cute little mice. You did it all yourself, Audrey?"

Audrey pressed her lips together. "If I'd had any idea I'd be doing store windows when I agreed to marry Mr. Dunlap, I might have told him no." She gave an ironic little chuckle to show that she was joking, then glanced over her shoulder to see whether Leona Ruth — Darling's most notorious gossip — was loitering nearby. Leona Ruth had wandered from Housewares to Brooms and Mops, but Audrey leaned closer and lowered her voice anyway.

"I have something to tell you." Her voice was apprehensive, and her round face was flushed and worried. "Something serious, I mean."

"Really? What sort of something?" Bessie was surprised at the anxiety she heard, for in her experience, Audrey usually preferred to put on a show of being firmly in control. "Apprehensive" was not a word you would naturally think of when you thought about the large and domineering Audrey. Bessie suspected that something serious really *was* going on.

"You know Mr. Whitworth, I'm sure." Without waiting for Bessie's answer, Audrey went on, almost breathlessly. "Well, he came over to our house yesterday evening, late, to talk to Mr. Dunlap — about the Clovers, he said. Mr. Whitworth sings bass, you know, and Mr. Dunlap sings tenor, and the two of them are on the arrangements committee for the Dixie Regional competition next week." She took a breath. "But that wasn't what they talked about."

"It wasn't?" Bessie asked. Now that she understood that this was about Mr. Whitworth, she was deeply curious. It sounded as if Audrey wasn't aware that Mr. Whitworth hadn't made it home last night. That he had been *kidnapped*.

"No," Audrey said, in a wavering tone. "It was about their *partnership*!" Her voice rose and her lips trembled. "They were downstairs in the parlor and I was in the bedroom upstairs. The hot air register in the bedroom floor is as good as an open window, you know, and I couldn't help hearing everything they said."

Privately, Bessie suspected that Audrey probably went upstairs on purpose so she could listen to what the men were saying. Audrey always liked to be fully informed. But she only said, "It's too bad that they upset you." Impulsively, she added, "I didn't know they were partners."

It was true. As Darling's unofficial town historian, Bessie had written an article for the *Dispatch* a few years back, on the history of the businesses around the court-

222

house square. As she remembered it, Mr. Dunlap had opened the Five and Dime in 1912, the same year that Woodrow Wilson beat President Taft *and* Teddy Roosevelt for president. And as far as she knew, Mr. Dunlap had been the store's only owner ever since.

"I didn't know it either, Bessie!" Audrey said. Her eyes widened and her heavy jowls quivered. "That's what's so *alarming* about all this! I thought Mr. Dunlap owned this store free and clear. In fact, I asked him, point blank, *before* we got married." Defensively, she added, "I mean, it's something a wife should *know,* isn't it? Of *course* I asked him what kind of business obligations he had. You wouldn't expect me to jump into marriage *blind,* would you? At *my* age?"

"No," Bessie replied slowly. She had never been married, but she could see the wisdom in that. "On the other hand —"

"But there's more, Bessie," Audrey went on. "Mr. Whitworth says that Mr. Dunlap signed a paper saying that he got one thousand dollars from Mr. Whitworth — something called a limited partnership. And for that paltry amount, Mr. Whitworth gets half the profits, *forever.*"

"I'm afraid I don't understand." Bessie frowned. "Isn't that a rather unusual —"

"Of *course* it's unusual," Audrey said, with an impatient wave of her hand. "The problem is that Mr. Dunlap has to buy a new oil heater before winter sets in, because the old one has completely quit. And it's not just the heater, but the heat pipes, too. They have to be replaced." She gestured toward the ceiling, where an overhead duct ran the length of the store. "The whole thing is going to cost over fifteen hundred dollars. Mr. Dunlap was asking Mr. Whitworth to split the cost with him."

"That sounds reasonable," Bessie said. "Shoppers expect —"

"They expect to shop in comfort," Audrey snapped. "But Mr. Whitworth said he wasn't going to give Mr. Dunlap any money, and there was this huge argument." She shook her head. "A fight, actually."

"A *fight*?" Bessie was shocked. "You don't mean it, Audrey!" Mr. Dunlap might be a tiger in certain circumstances, but he was not a large man — not nearly as large as his wife — and he didn't look very strong. Bessie could not imagine him trading blows with Mr. Whitworth, who outweighed him by forty or fifty pounds.

"Well, pushing and shoving, anyway," Audrey said. "And lots of shouting. Mr. Dunlap got mad — *really* mad, I mean — and told Mr. Whitworth to get out. When Mr. Whitworth left, he banged the front door so hard that he broke the glass. And my poor husband —" Her chin quivered. "Mr. Dunlap was so upset that he had to go for a long drive, just to calm himself. He wouldn't let me go with him, either. He didn't come home until nearly midnight, and when he did, he was still terribly upset. He paced around the house for half the night and he refused to eat any breakfast this morning, not even Sally-Lou's apple pancakes, which are his favorites. This is terribly hard on him, Bessie. *Terribly* hard. If he doesn't get the money, we might have to close the store!"

"Audrey, I am so sorry to hear all this," Bessie said. "I wish I could help, but —"

"It gets even worse," Audrey went on. "Sheriff Norris came into the store this morning. He had this very serious look on his face, and he and Mr. Dunlap went into the office and talked for nearly half an hour. When he came out, he asked me what happened after Mr. Whitworth left last night, and I said that Mr. Dunlap went out for a drive. And then he asked what time he got home and I said midnight. And then he told Mr. Dunlap not to leave town!" She pulled in a ragged breath. "I don't understand what this is all about, Bessie, but I have the feeling that the sheriff thinks my husband is guilty of something. And Mr. Dunlap won't tell me what it is!"

Bessie suspected that Audrey was frustrated because she was being kept in the dark. She would probably feel better if she knew that none of this had anything to do with her husband.

In a comforting tone, she said, "I wouldn't worry if I were you, Audrey. I imagine this is about what happened to Mr. Whitworth."

Audrey frowned. "Something happened to Mr. Whitworth?"

"Apparently," Bessie said. "People are saying that he's been —"

But at that moment, Leona Ruth (who had moved from Brooms and Mops to Stationery and Greeting Cards, beside the big front window) exclaimed with great excitement, "Well, I *swan.* Just look at that, will you, Bessie! What d'you reckon . . ."

Bessie hurried to stand at the front window beside Leona Ruth and saw an odd cavalcade of vehicles parading slowly along the street. The black Ford roadster at the head of the procession was driven by Mr. Springer, the new sheriff's deputy, with a raincoat-clad fellow in the rumble seat — a drunk, Bessie guessed, the way his head was bent forward. Behind the deputy's car clanked a heavy, steel-wheeled tractor, pulling an ivory-colored automobile with a smashed-in roof. And behind that came a black Ford sedan, bearing the Alabama insignia and the words *Jericho State Prison Farm.*

Audrey came to the window and pushed herself between Bessie and Leona Ruth. "Why, I recognize that wrecked car they're towing!" she exclaimed. "It's Mr. Whitworth's Pierce-Arrow! He was driving it when he came to our house last night. He —" She pressed her hand to her heaving bosom.

"Gracious sakes alive, it *is* his Pierce-Arrow!" Leona Ruth's voice was rising. She was so agitated that the peacock feathers on her purple hat quivered. "And that fellow in the deputy's car, in the rumble seat —" By this time, she was practically screeching. "Why, I'll be blessed if it isn't Mr. Whitworth *himself*! He must have had too much to drink and wrecked his car and —"

"But he *isn't* drunk," Bessie said, drawing in her breath. She was dizzy with the understanding that Mr. Whitworth had not been kidnapped, after all — or maybe he had been kidnapped and then he had wrecked his car when he tried to speed away from

227

the people who had snatched him. "Just look at all that blood on his head! Why, Mr. Whitworth is —"

"Bessie, I do believe you are *right,*" Leona Ruth shrilled excitedly. "Mr. Whitworth is dead. He is *dead*!"

Between the two of them, Audrey let out her breath. Bessie turned to see that her eyes were as big as coat buttons and her face was white as a hanky. "Oh, no, Mr. Dunlap, *you didn't*!" she cried.

Leona Ruth stared at her. "Didn't *what?*" she demanded. "Audrey Dunlap, you are surely not thinking your husband had anything to do with Mr. Whitworth being *dead,* are you?"

But Audrey's eyes had rolled up into her head so that only the whites were showing. Before Bessie could grab her, her knees had buckled and she was flat on the floor.

CHAPTER FOURTEEN:
CHARLIE IS BUFFALOED

While Bessie and Leona Ruth were getting Audrey back on her feet, Charlie Dickens was rushing into the Dispatch office, his tie pulled loose, his fedora pushed to the back of his head, his Rolleiflex in his hand.

Ophelia looked up from her typewriter in surprise. "My goodness," she said. "What's happened to you?"

"I'm not the one it happened to," Charlie said breathlessly. The deputy had wanted his photos in a hurry, so he had driven as fast as he could from the accident scene back to town. But he'd had to stop at the Standard station to pick up that flat tire. He shrugged out of his seersucker jacket and hung it beside his desk.

"It's Whitney Whitworth," he added, turning around. "He's dead."

"Dead?" Ophelia stared at him, shocked. "Oh, my golly. Dead — *really*?" She leaned forward over her typewriter. "How did it happen? When? Are you writing the story?"

"Unmistakably, undeniably dead. Car wreck. Accident. Ran off the road at the bottom of Spook Hill sometime last night. And yes," he added firmly, "I am writing the story." Ophelia was always eager to cover events outside her usual women's page stuff and he tried to accommodate her when he could. But there was no way he was giving her *this* story. It was his, along with those photographs.

She was frowning. "Spook Hill? What in the world was he doing out *there*? He didn't have business at the prison farm, did he? That's the only thing on that road."

Charlie shrugged. "No idea," he said. He wasn't surprised by the question — it was what everybody would want to know.

"Was he alone?" Her frown intensified. "His wife wasn't with him, I hope."

"Nope. He was the only one in the car." Charlie raised his camera. "Gotta get this film developed and over to the sheriff's office right away." He was more than glad to be of service. If you did a favor for the sheriff, you could claim a favor in return: next week, next month, next year. That's how a real newspaper reporter operated — cashing in on favors when payoff time rolled around.

"Oh, dear," Ophelia said sadly, shaking her head. "Oh, poor Mrs. Whitworth. I hope she has a friend with her when she learns about the accident. She's sort of . . . well, she's fragile right now. I'm afraid she's going to feel guilty."

Halfway to the curtained-off corner he used for a darkroom, Charlie turned. "You know Whitworth's wife?"

"Yes, of course I know her," Ophelia replied. "She and I have been on the decorating committee for the Ladies Guild for a couple of years. On Friday, it was our turn to put up decorations at the Retirement Haven, the old folks' home over on Rayburn Road. We needed some orange and brown crepe paper and some red construction paper to make autumn leaves, and Mrs. Dunlap had used everything the Five and Dime had on her window display. So Mrs. Whitworth and I drove over to Monroeville to get it. Or rather," she added, "*she* drove." She gave a delicate shudder. "To tell the truth, it was pretty nerve-wracking. She's been taking driving lessons in her new car, but she needs a lot more practice." She blinked. "Gosh, was *that* the one that got wrecked? Mrs. Whitworth's new car?"

"No. The one that got wrecked was the Pierce-Arrow. The car Whitworth always drives around town. Drove, I mean," Charlie corrected himself. He turned to regard Ophelia. "Wait a minute. You said she's going to feel guilty." He frowned. "Why? Why should Mrs. Whitworth feel guilty about her husband getting killed in an automobile accident?"

Ophelia sat back in her chair. "Forget I said that." She held out her hand. "Please, Charlie. I shouldn't have. I'm just guessing, really."

"But you did say it." Charlie leaned toward her, scowling. "Come on, Ophelia. Out with it. Why in the hell should the wife feel guilty about the husband's *accident*?"

Ophelia didn't say anything for a moment. Then she sighed. Obviously reluctant, she said, "Because she's planning to get a divorce. That's why she bought the car. She wants to be independent."

Charlie stared at her, mystified. "And that makes her feel guilty?"

Ophelia rolled her eyes. "*You* know, silly," she said, as if she didn't understand why he was asking. "It's because she was thinking of getting rid of him and now —" She turned up her hand. "Well, now she's a widow. Wouldn't *you* feel guilty, under those circumstances?"

"Not in the slightest," Charlie said. Really,

he thought, he would *never* understand women, especially when it came to this independence thing. He paused. "She told you about the divorce?"

"Yes, she did." Ophelia sounded a little defensive. "We stopped for a couple of root beers on the way home and she told me why she bought the car. I think she just needed somebody to talk to, and I happened to be handy."

"Did she tell you why she wanted a divorce?" Charlie asked curiously. "Was he seeing another woman, maybe?" Whitworth hadn't struck him as the type who would keep a sweetie on the side, but you never could tell. Even the most conventional people sometimes did unconventional things. He once knew a pastor and a church secretary who ran off to Mexico together, leaving five children and two bewildered spouses behind. On the other hand, a woman of Mrs. Whitworth's social status and pedigree wouldn't consider a divorce unless she had a substantial reason. The guy must have been getting up to *something.*

"Well, did she?" he demanded.

Ophelia lifted her chin. "No, she didn't say why, and I didn't ask. A divorce is a very personal thing. It was none of my business." She looked him straight in the eye and added, quite firmly, "It isn't any of your business, either, Charlie Dickens. It doesn't belong in the *Dispatch,* especially now that Mr. Whitworth is dead." She shook her head sympathetically. "Oh, *poor* Mrs. Whitworth! She's going to feel just dreadful. And she has no family to lean on. Her parents are dead and she has no brothers or sisters. No support at all."

Charlie was thinking fast. Ophelia was certainly right on one score. He couldn't include anything about a possible divorce in his story. The Methodists and Baptists went up in flames whenever they saw the word in print. And as Ophelia said, the issue was moot anyway, now that Mrs. Whitworth was a grieving widow — or a guilty widow, although the logic of that still escaped him. But the divorce angle aside, maybe he could soften up the story with a little human interest.

He gave Ophelia a long look. "So far as I know, Mrs. Whitworth hasn't been notified yet. What would you think about going with the sheriff to break the news? Are you *that* kind of friend?"

"I don't know exactly what you mean by '*that* kind of friend,'" Ophelia said cautiously. "But if Buddy Norris thinks I can help, I'll be glad to go along." She glanced up at the clock. "Of course, if I do that, I won't be able to cover the meeting of the Share the Wealth Society, but —"

"There'll be another meeting," Charlie cut in. "This is more important. I'll call Norris right now." He went to the phone on his desk and asked the Hello Central girl to speak to the sheriff's office. A few moments and a brief conversation later, he hung up the receiver.

"The deputy has taken Whitworth's body to Noonan's Funeral Parlor," he said. "Noonan will need time to clean him up before the widow sees him. Buddy Norris is leaving for the Whitworth house now. He says he'll be glad to have a woman go along — especially a friend of Mrs. Whitworth. He'll pick you up on his way over there." He frowned. "Where's your notebook?"

"My *notebook*?" Ophelia stared at him "You mean, you want me to —"

"You're damned right I do," Charlie said impatiently. "You're going as a friend, but don't forget — you're a reporter. If you pick up any details about the accident or about Mrs. Whitworth's reaction to it, make a mental note and write them down as soon as you can. Bits of human interest will go a long way to soften the story of the accident. *My* story," he added quickly, in case Ophelia might be getting ideas.

"I don't know if I like this," Ophelia muttered. "It isn't the kind of situation where I can just whip out my notebook and —"

"Doesn't matter whether you like it or not," Charlie said flatly. "I'll say it again, Ophelia. You're a *reporter.* This is your job. Got it? Be a friend and help Mrs. Whitworth get through this, but stay objective, listen hard, and keep your reporter's eye on the situation — on everything that goes on. Remember, human interest is what you're after. Don't get involved. It'll be a good test for you."

With a sigh, Ophelia picked up her notebook and dropped it into her bag. "What sort of things are you looking for?" Frowning, she shrugged into her pink sweater. "Is something going on here that I need to know about, Charlie?"

Charlie had been asking himself that very same question. "I don't think so," he said, pursing his lips. "But that business about the divorce has got me thinking. And the deputy was pretty definite about getting photographs. I'm wondering if he spotted something that —" He broke off.

"Spotted what? Didn't you say it was an accident?"

"That's what I said." A car horn sounded

on the street outside. "There's the sheriff. You pay attention, you hear? And you're a reporter, looking for human interest. A *reporter*. Don't get involved. Remember that, while you're busy being a friend. Don't get involved!"

Ophelia rolled her eyes.

Charlie had never been very good at developing film, but when he turned out the red light and pulled the curtain aside, there were two dozen photos hanging from the line. It would be a little while before they were dry enough to take down. In the meantime, he rearranged them on the line so they were in order. Not the order he had taken them in, but from the top of the hill to the bottom, following the tracks of the heavy Pierce-Arrow from the moment Whitworth topped the hill to his summersault at the bottom. At the far end of the line were the photos of the wreck as it lay on the embankment and a couple he had taken of the car's rear end, after it had been towed up to the road.

Charlie studied the photos for a few moments, his eyes narrowed, brow furrowed. Then he went to his desk, took out a magnifying glass, and went back to the photographs, starting at the beginning, leaning close, peering at details, and moving slowly from one photograph to another. The problem was that there were several sets of tracks, and they intersected, but . . .

After a while he straightened, shaking his head. He was buffaloed. He could be wrong, of course. But judging from the tracks, it looked like something had happened on the way down that hill, before the Whitworth's Pierce-Arrow had gotten to the bottom and flipped. But he'd be damned if he could figure out what.

However, this wasn't the only mystery Charlie had on his mind. All morning long, whenever he stopped thinking about whatever he was thinking about at the moment, his thoughts had returned to the question that was painfully lodged at the back of his mind. It was the mystery of Fannie's money — those monthly fifty-dollar checks she was sending to somebody (or something) with the initials JC. It was like having a tiny thorn stuck in the ball of your foot: it hurts, but you can't find it to pull it out. Fifty dollars a month, six hundred dollars a year. *Six hundred dollars a year!*

What was the story on those checks? What kind of secret was his wife concealing? Why hadn't she told him what she was doing? Was it because she didn't trust him? Or

238

because whatever she was hiding was so terrible that she feared that he would . . .

Charlie made himself stop. He couldn't let his brain whirl around and around the problem like a kid's toy top, spinning this way, then that. He had to *do* something — good, bad, or indifferent, it didn't matter, so long as he was doing it.

And at that moment, he decided what he was going to do. The photos were dry enough now so that he could take the copies to the sheriff's office and leave them with the deputy. Then he would walk across the street to the bank. What he wanted was a look at one of those canceled checks, to see if the endorsement gave any clue to the identity of the person who had cashed it.

Of course, Charlie reminded himself, it was Fannie's account, and there were probably bank rules against letting anybody else take a look. But he was her husband, after all, and he and Al Duffy had gotten to be pretty good friends over the year that Al had been president of the bank. He figured Al would go along with what he wanted to do, although he would have to add one important condition: that Fannie not learn anything about this.

His wife would be *really* angry with him if

she found out he was snooping in her business.

CHAPTER FIFTEEN:
THE SHERIFF GETS
THE WRONG IDEA

Buddy Norris wasn't any too happy as he walked up the steps to the front door, Ophelia Snow right behind him. When he had been here earlier that morning, Mr. Whitworth was a missing person. Now the man was dead, and announcing that tragic news to the next of kin was not a favorite part of Buddy's job. But it was his to do, for although he hadn't been out to the accident scene yet, his deputy had told him what had happened. So he had the story — as much of it as Wayne was able to put together at this point, anyway. There were some loose ends to be tied up, but it was time to notify the new widow.

When he rang the Whitworths' doorbell for the second time that day, the sheriff felt pretty well prepared. And because Ophelia Snow had come along, he also felt quite a bit easier in his mind. If there was to be any fainting, Ophelia could handle it. She had

241

smelling salts in that handbag of hers, along with the reporter's notebook he had glimpsed.

When he saw that, he had frowned and said, "No notetaking while we're in there, Miz Snow," and Ophelia had rolled her eyes and said, "Yes, Buddy," in the tone adults use to little kids when the kid is being a nuisance.

Ophelia Snow was one of the Darling people who called him Buddy in the way he didn't like. The Snows remembered him from when he was fourteen or fifteen and had been smitten by one of the daughters of their next-door neighbor. They had seen him riding his old rusty bicycle or hanging out at the swimming hole on Pine Mill Creek, where pretty much everybody in town went to cool off on a hot August Saturday afternoon. They had no doubt heard about him getting into trouble — stealing smokes, catching a ride on an L&N freight car, smacking a baseball through old Mr. Newkirk's dining room window — the things boys do when they don't have a momma to ride herd on them and make sure they do what's right.

And now here he was, the sheriff of the town he'd grown up in, which meant that he always had something to prove to folks like the Snows who knew him from back when. And quite a few things to live down, because people in Darling seemed to remember the most embarrassing stuff — like the time somebody stole his britches and shoes at the swimming hole and he'd walked home barefoot and humiliated in nothing but his long-tailed shirt.

Thankfully, Regina Whitworth had not known him when he was a kid. While she wasn't much older than he was, she had grown up on her grandmother's plantation on the Alabama River, where she had been privately schooled. For once, he would be starting with a clean slate.

When the maid showed them into the parlor, Buddy was relieved to see that Mrs. Whitworth had settled down some since the morning. Clutching a hanky and wearing a long-sleeved navy silk dress that emphasized her delicate throat and slender shoulders, she was seated on a garnet velveteen love-seat in front of two tall, graceful parlor palms, under a large gilt-framed oil portrait of a heavily jeweled woman with a formidable bosom and an autocratic look. Buddy didn't have to guess who *that* was: the wealthy Helene Marie Vautier, who (he'd heard) had died and left her plantation and her fortune to her granddaughter Regina, shortly before she became Mrs. Whitworth.

Buddy took a chair — gingerly, because it looked like a rickety antique and he wasn't sure it would hold his weight. Ophelia lingered in the doorway, whispering to the maid that it would be a good idea if she brought in a pot of very strong tea. Then she sat down on the loveseat close to Mrs. Whitworth. Buddy leaned forward, put his elbows on his knees, and broke the news as gently as he could.

"He was killed instantly," he said at the end, hoping that would be a comfort. "Doc Roberts is over in Monroeville this morning and hasn't yet had a look," he added. "But we think that's a safe assumption."

There were tears and sobbing, of course, but Ophelia put her arms around Mrs. Whitworth and stroked and patted and soothed, and to Buddy's relief, the worst of the crying was over fairly quickly. The maid appeared with a polished silver teapot and delicate china cups on a silver tray. Ophelia forced a cup on Mrs. Whitworth and poured for herself and Buddy. While they sipped their tea, Buddy was able to ask the question that had been bothering him all morning, ever since he'd heard where the accident happened.

"The car went off the road at the foot of

Spook Hill," he said. "Do you have any idea why your husband was out there on that road last night?"

Mrs. Whitworth pressed her lips together tightly. She looked down at her fingers, twisting her white handkerchief into a tight knot. When she looked up again, her hair swung back, and Buddy saw something he had missed when he'd talked to her earlier: a dark purplish bruise on her jaw, and an abrasion.

And then her hair swung forward again, concealing the injury. Hesitantly, in a low, slow Southern-lady voice, she said, "I don't know for sure, but he might have been on his way to meet Bodeen Pyle."

Buddy was genuinely startled. "Bodeen Pyle? You mean —" He thought immediately of what Violet had told him earlier that morning: that Mr. Whitworth might be in the bootleg business with Bodeen Pyle.

"I should try to hide this, to save his reputation," Mrs. Whitworth said, sounding resigned. "But I suppose you ought to know. I do hope you'll keep it to yourself, though. It doesn't have anything to do with . . ." She twisted the handkerchief again. "With how he died, I mean. Since it was an accident."

"What is it you want me to know, exactly?"

Buddy asked, feeling his way.

She untwisted her handkerchief and smoothed it out. "That he invested money — some, I don't know how much — in Bodeen Pyle's liquor business. If I'd had any say in the matter, I would have said no," she added. Buddy thought he heard a note of something like bitterness in her voice. "But I didn't. It was all his doing." She added in a low voice, as if to herself, "With my money."

Ophelia leaned forward. "Was that the reason for the divorce?"

"Divorce?" Buddy straightened, blinking. "You and Mr. Whitworth were thinking of —"

"No, not at all," Mrs. Whitworth said quickly. She looked at Ophelia, her eyes dark. "I don't know where you got that silly idea, Mrs. Snow, but it's not true!" Her voice went up a notch. "Really. Not in the very *slightest.*"

Ophelia looked startled, then contrite. "Oops, sorry." She ducked her head, embarrassed. "The gossip in this town is just . . . well, there's enough to drown a horse, that's for sure. Listen long enough, and you'll hear just about everything under the sun, no matter how ridiculous. I do sincerely apologize."

"Thank you," Mrs. Whitworth said softly, and leaned over to pat Ophelia's hand. "It's not one bit important, really. I . . . I just wouldn't want the sheriff to get the wrong idea, that's all."

Buddy looked from one of them to the other. He had always been a pretty good reader of people's reactions. He would swear that Ophelia had been right in the first place and Mrs. Whitworth was pretending she was wrong and Ophelia was pretending to agree. And that both of them understood exactly what was going on. But he was more interested in her remark about Mr. Whitworth's business arrangement with Bodeen Pyle, because he knew that Pyle's moonshine camp was somewhere in Briar Swamp, not more than a couple of miles from where the accident occurred.

Buddy cleared his throat. "How long had your husband been Pyle's partner?"

"I don't know. I only found out about it a couple of weeks ago." Mrs. Whitworth took a cigarette out of a silver bowl on a table beside her. "I think it had something to do with Pyle wanting to expand his business after that other man was arrested."

"That other man?" Buddy asked, frowning.

And then he understood. Mrs. Whitworth

was talking about Mickey LeDoux, who for years had run a highly professional moonshine production and distribution business out of a wooded hollow on Dead Cow Creek, in the hills west of Darling. LeDoux's moonshine had generally been vouchsafed the best in this part of the state. But Mickey had been put out of business by Chester P. Kinnard, a revenue agent who had made it his mission to shut Mickey down. It was a sad story. Mickey's youngest brother was dead, shot by the revenue agents in Kinnard's posse, and Mickey had been sentenced to the Wetumpka State Penitentiary.

But Mickey's loss had been Bodeen Pyle's gain, and it wasn't more than a few days before Cypress County had another supplier. Pyle had long been Mickey's fiercest competitor, and he used whatever tricks came handiest to gain a bigger piece of the market. His whiskey didn't pack the notorious LeDoux punch, but it didn't cost as much, and for folks who had to choose between a new pair of boots and a couple of bottles of white lightning, a cheap drunk was as good as a pricey one. When Mickey was hauled off to Wetumpka, Pyle had expanded his operation. In fact, Darling whispered that Pyle was getting some investment money somewhere, although nobody knew exactly where. And nobody really wanted to guess, because the less you knew about Bodeen Pyle's business arrangements, the better off you were.

"Ah," Buddy said, feeling that he was moving toward an understanding of something, although he wasn't sure what it was. "Did Pyle ever come here to discuss this with your husband?" The skin on the back of his neck was prickling, but he made his voice light and casual. He didn't want her to think that his questions held any special significance.

"Once," Mrs. Whitworth said. Not looking at him, she pulled on her cigarette. "But my husband preferred to meet him . . . somewhere else. People talk, you know."

He understood what she was not saying. Whitworth wouldn't have wanted his ritzy neighbors on Peachtree Street to see a known moonshiner dropping in every so often. It would make more sense for him to meet Pyle out at the Briar Swamp operation. Which might explain what Whitworth was doing on that road.

"I see," he said again, but in a different tone. Mrs. Whitworth had a lot to deal with right now, and he didn't want to upset the lady. But what they were talking about was against the law — against several laws, actually. Roy Burns had done what he could to keep foreign moonshiners — nonlocal bootleggers — from setting up shop in the county. They brought in crime and violence, he said, and it was true. But Roy had been a man of compassion and he'd left the locals pretty much alone. It was, after all, a simple matter of economics. Corn was selling right now for no better than fifty cents a bushel, less than it cost to raise it. But that bushel of corn would yield three gallons of shine, which would sell for twelve dollars a gallon. Twelve dollars a gallon! Buddy could remember Roy's exact words: "They can cook up whatever the hell they want out there in those camps so long as they live decent and don't bother me none. Some of 'em couldn't feed their kids if they couldn't shine."

Of course, the shiners and their families were Cypress County voters, so Buddy suspected that there was more to Roy's tolerance than simple compassion. But that wasn't *his* approach. In the short time he'd been sheriff, he had already arrested Pootie McKay and dumped out the eighty gallons of bootleg tiger spit he was carrying. Prohibition had been repealed but that didn't make unlicensed and untaxed moonshine legal. And the key word here was "tax," for the feds were collecting a whopping two-dollar tax on every gallon of whiskey. The eighty gallons that Pootie was hauling amounted to $160 that didn't find its way into Uncle Sam's pockets. Of course, dumping out all that perfectly fine shine hadn't made Buddy many friends, but a lawman who worried too much about votes probably wasn't doing his job.

Nervously, Mrs. Whitworth blew out a stream of smoke. "I wouldn't want you to think that my husband's arrangement with Pyle was something I . . . encouraged." She seemed to be choosing her words carefully. "I . . . wasn't any too happy about it when I found out. I wouldn't want anyone else to know."

"I can imagine," Ophelia said quietly.

"I'm sure it must have bothered you," Buddy said, feeling that this was a substantial understatement. He cleared his throat. "Say, is it okay if I use your phone? I need to call Lionel Noonan and find out when you can go over there and see your husband."

Mrs. Whitworth's eyes widened. "Do I . . . do I *have* to see him?" she whispered faintly. She held out an appealing hand to Buddy. "I am so sorry, Sheriff, but if you made me go over there, I'm afraid you would just have to carry me out. I couldn't bear to look at my grandmother when she was laid out in her coffin." She closed her eyes and brought her hand to her forehead. "Just the thought of it makes me feel —"

Alarmed, Buddy said, "No, of course you don't have to see him. Not if you don't want to." He wondered if Ophelia could locate that bottle of smelling salts in a hurry.

"And please don't feel sorry about it," Ophelia said quickly. "You just do whatever you can do." She gave Buddy a cautioning glance and put an arm around Mrs. Whitworth's shoulder. "Mr. Noonan will be glad to come over here and discuss funeral arrangements with you any time you feel up to it," she added soothingly. "Give him a call and let him know. And if I can do anything for you, let me know."

"Thank you," Mrs. Whitworth said in a muffled voice. "You're terribly kind, both of you. I appreciate it more than I can say."

A few minutes later, Buddy and Ophelia were in his sheriff's car, heading back into town.

"My goodness," Ophelia said, puffing out her breath. "*That* was informative, wasn't it?"

"What sort of information did you get out of it?" Buddy asked, sliding a glance at her.

252

One thing he had learned about women. They saw things a whole lot differently than he did. He could be in the same room with a woman, listening to the same conversation, but then come to find out, the conversation she heard wasn't the same one *he* had heard.

"Well, for one thing," Ophelia replied thoughtfully, "she didn't seem too surprised when you told her about the accident. I mean, she was upset, of course. And maybe she was sort of expecting something, since he hadn't been home all night." Without hesitating, she added, "And she told a lie — just a little one, but it was still a lie. I wasn't going to contradict her to her face, but she *did* tell me she planned to get a divorce."

"Did she really?" Buddy said, interested.

Ophelia nodded. "We drove over to Monroeville the other day — in her new car, actually. We stopped for something to drink and she told me about the divorce. In fact, she even said she had talked to Mr. Moseley about it. He's advising her."

Buddy wasn't terribly surprised — people seemed to be getting divorces awfully easily these days. But he found himself puzzled. "She said she didn't want me to get the wrong idea — but you're saying she lied. Why? If she was planning on getting a divorce, why did she say she wasn't?"

"Because she didn't want you to wonder whether she might have a motive."

"A motive for *what*?" Buddy asked, now more puzzled than ever. He felt like a schoolboy who knew he was missing an essential part of the lesson but had no idea what it was or what page it was on. If there was a right idea, he hadn't got it.

With a wave of her hand, Ophelia went on as though she hadn't heard his question. "And because now that he's dead, she'd like us — or maybe just me — to think that her reason for wanting a divorce is irrelevant. Just a little piece of history that doesn't matter any longer." She tilted her head thoughtfully. "Which of course might not be true. It might actually be important."

Buddy still felt puzzled. "Well, I don't exactly —" He stopped. "Why *was* she getting a divorce?"

Ophelia thought about that. "She didn't say why, actually, and I didn't ask. A divorce is awf'ly personal, don't you think? And I don't really know her well enough to be her confidante. She was talking to me because she felt she just had to talk to someone, and I happened to be handy." Another pause. "But she said something that made me think it might have to do with money. She had a lot of it, you know. From her grand-mother — that fierce-looking lady in the portrait over the loveseat."

Buddy slowed to let Mr. Snipp's ancient black and brown coonhound amble across the road in front of him. You had to be careful in Darling, where there were as many dogs as there were people, and some of the dogs were old as Moses and blind as bats. If he damaged that coonhound, Mr. Snipp would never forgive him. When the hound was safely on the curb, Buddy accelerated again.

"I guess I heard word of an inheritance," he said cautiously, "a long time ago. You say she *had* money. She doesn't have it now? Did she lose it in the Crash?"

In Buddy's admittedly limited experience, that was the main reason for Darling folk going broke. And even if you didn't have money invested in the stock market, Black Tuesday changed your life. Any American citizen who had been alive on that day and in the weeks right afterward would remember it forever.

"The Crash?" Ophelia pursed her lips. "I have no idea, honestly. But that house doesn't look like a lot of money, do you think? I mean, it's nice enough, but it's really pretty dinky — nothing like the Vautier plantation. And of course, she *did* buy that new Dodge from Kilgore's. But if I had her kind of money, I'd have a bigger house, over by the country club. And more help in the house. She's just got DessaRae, who does everything but the laundry. You'd think she could afford more, wouldn't you?"

"Well, I —" Buddy was about to say that the house looked like a million dollars to *him,* although he didn't have a lot of familiarity with the price of real estate. And he had absolutely no idea how many maids a woman ought to have, or how much she ought to pay them.

But Ophelia was rattling on. "Come to think of it, I wonder why the Whitworths aren't living on the Vautier plantation. Her grandmother's place, you know. I've seen pictures of that mansion — it's fabulous, really *fabulous.* I've never heard that she sold it, but I suppose she did." She rolled down the car window and let the breeze blow through her hair. "Why don't you ask Mr. Moseley, Buddy? Like I said, he's her lawyer."

"Ask Mr. Moseley what?" Buddy said helplessly, feeling as if he had totally lost track of the conversation.

Ophelia turned to face him, both eyebrows raised. "Why she wanted a divorce, of course. And what happened to the money. I wasn't curious before, but I am now. I think you should ask him. See what he says. I'll bet it would be interesting."

Well, if that was what she was talking about, Buddy had an answer.

"No," he said firmly. "I am not going to ask Mr. Moseley. I don't see how Mrs. Whitworth's wanting a divorce — because of money or any other reason — is connected to Mr. Whitworth's accidentally killing himself by going too fast down Spook Hill."

"Mmm," Ophelia said. "Well, you just never know, you know." She put her hand on his arm. "Watch out, Buddy. There's Mrs. Vanderoy, poor old thing. I'll bet she doesn't know where she is."

He slowed again. Mrs. Vanderoy was standing uncertainly at the corner, clutching her sweater, her gray hair hanging down over her shoulders like a tangle of fuzzy wool yarn. The old lady had a habit of wandering off whenever she was able to get out of the house by herself. But then he saw her daughter hurrying after her, so he figured she would fetch her mother home. He and Ophelia waved at the pair and he drove on.

"Anyway," he said to Ophelia, "Mr. Moseley can't talk to people about his clients' business. There's some sort of rule about that." He knew that sometimes the rule could be broken, but he didn't know why or how and he wasn't going to bother Mr. Moseley by asking.

Ophelia wasn't listening. "I happen to know that he's in Montgomery this week," she went on. "But Liz Lacy is in the office. She might know something about this money thing. Why don't you talk to *her,* Buddy?"

Buddy sighed. Some women just couldn't take no for an answer. They were approaching the courthouse square, and he changed the subject. "A minute ago, you said that Mrs. Whitworth's lying about the divorce business was 'one thing.' What was the other thing?"

Ophelia gave him a look. "You mean to say you didn't notice?"

"Notice what?"

"That bruise on her face — and the scrape."

"I saw it," Buddy said, "but I didn't —"

"She covered it up with makeup," Ophelia said knowingly. "A *lot* of makeup."

"Really?" Not only did women hear different things than he did, they saw different things. He had noticed the bruise, of course, but he hadn't thought much about it.

"Really. If it weren't for that, it would look much worse. Just looking at the bruise, I'd say that somebody hit her a good lick," Ophelia said. "On the other hand, that scrape — maybe she fell. And she was wearing long sleeves, so we couldn't see what her arms look like." She chuckled wryly. "Listen, Buddy, whatever you do, do *not* get in an automobile with that woman under the wheel. She is the worst driver I have ever seen. She's been taking driving lessons from that salesman at Kilgore's, but you certainly can't tell it. She drives like a maniac."

"I'll try to remember that." Buddy turned the corner at Hart's Peerless Laundry. "Do you want to go back to the newspaper office, or are you headed home?"

"The office will be fine," Ophelia said. She squinted at him. "You're not going to talk to Liz?"

"I don't have a reason to talk to her," Buddy said firmly. He pulled up in front of the Dispatch. "I'm going to the sheriff's office and see if Wayne is back from Noonan's yet."

One way or another, he and his deputy spent a fair amount of time with Lionel Noonan, who owned the only funeral parlor in town. Banks could fail, stores could go

259

bankrupt, even the county could go broke and you might not know until a bridge went out and nobody came to fix it. But the funeral parlor was probably the most essential business in the entire town. Everybody who died had to go there, like it or not. And folks always said that Lionel Noonan could be relied on to do the right thing by a funeral, with the corpse looking as nice as possible under the circumstances, and flowers and music and all the rest. Lionel always said that a funeral was a once-in-a-lifetime occurrence. He never wanted to disappoint any of his clients.

"Well, if you won't, maybe I will." Ophelia opened the car door. "Thanks for letting me go along, Buddy. Like I said, it was informative."

Buddy nodded. He thought she was probably right, although he wasn't sure exactly what he was going to do with the few scraps of information he had picked up.

CHAPTER SIXTEEN:
DEPUTY SPRINGER
OFFERS A THEORY

The sheriff's office was located a few doors west of the courthouse square, in a converted house behind Snow's Farm Supply. The dilapidated old place had been repossessed by the Darling Savings and Trust a couple of years before, then sold to Cypress County so the sheriff would have someplace to hang his hat, as Roy Burns had put it. If nothing else, the office had a convenient location. It was next door to the Darling jail — two shoebox-sized cells upstairs over Snow's Farm Supply. If Buddy wanted to climb the outside stairs and see if old Pete Peevy had recovered from his weekend drunk, it was handy.

Buddy parked the sheriff's car in front of the office and went up the front porch steps. The resident tomcat, black as the pit, stared balefully at him from the railing, eyes glowing like burning copper. Nobody knew where the cat had come from, and nobody

261

remembered seeing him around town. Which was strange, since most of the town's cats belonged to somebody — or to several somebodies, since philandering tomcats are generous with their patronage. This one, the scarred veteran of many wars, had shown up the day after they hauled the late Roy Burns out of Horsetail Gorge. In a quavering voice, Jed Snow had joked that the cat was Roy's ghost, "come back to ha'nt us." But Buddy thought that it was unlikely that mere haunting was involved. He thought it more probable that Roy had arranged for the animal to watch the new sheriff and report back when he didn't do things right. He had named him the Beast.

Buddy opened the screen door, which was loose on its hinge and crooked. "You comin' in?" he asked the Beast, holding the door. The cat considered, stretched (deliberately dragging it out to make Buddy wait), then leaped lightly down to the floor and went inside.

To get a little more space, Buddy and Wayne had knocked out the plaster wall between the small living room and the minuscule dining room, turning them into a single reception area with a couple of wooden folding chairs against a wall and a pine-topped counter across the middle.

They hadn't gotten around to painting the walls all one color yet, and the red-and-blue checked wallpaper in the back section clashed with the pink cabbage roses in the front. One door opened onto the small bedroom that was Wayne's office; another led to the front bedroom, now Buddy's office. The kitchen was their meeting room and workroom.

The deputy's job paid peanuts, so besides being their office, the house did double duty as Wayne's living quarters. There was an icebox and a little electric Fidelity Rangette in the kitchen where Wayne made grilled cheese sandwiches and cooked his supper — Buddy's too, sometimes. As a bachelor cook, Wayne's preferences ran to corned beef hash, Wolf Brand chili, and canned hominy with sausage and onions liberally laced with catsup, molasses, and a glug of cider vinegar.

Buddy had ordered a folding cot ($2.89 from the Sears and Roebuck catalogue) and Wayne slept on it in the pantry, which Buddy thought was a pretty good plan, all things considered. Having Wayne sleeping on the premises meant that he was handy to answer the telephone or go to the door if a citizen came banging on it in the middle of the night. Which almost never happened, because most Darling folks went to bed early and stayed there, barring emergencies. But it allowed Buddy to brag that the Cypress County Sheriff's Office was staffed around the clock.

As Buddy tossed his uniform hat onto the peg beside the door, he heard the clackety-clack of a typewriter. "That you, Springer?" he called.

The typing stopped. "Not me," Wayne said. "It's some guy from the Infernal Revenue Service. He's here to arrest you for skipping out on your income taxes. I'm letting him use my typewriter to type the summons he's going to serve on you." The typing resumed.

"He'll have to prove I have an income first," Buddy countered. He went into the kitchen and filled a white china mug with coffee from the percolator on the back of the stove. Being sheriff might sound like a glamorous job, and Roy Burns had never seemed to hurt for money. In fact, he lived in a very nice house, his wife had a full-time cook and housekeeper, and they owned a vacation cottage down at Oyster Bay, where Roy kept a thirty-foot fishing boat with a monster Evinrude outboard motor.

Buddy wasn't so lucky. After he paid Mrs. Beedle for his upstairs room (breakfast included, hot bath once a week, laundry twice a month), there was just enough left to take Bettina to the Darling Diner for Friday night supper and then to the Palace for a movie. Or a movie plus popcorn and a box of Jujubes and two orange Nehi sodas and skip supper at the diner. (Bettina offered to pay half but the thought of such a thing scandalized him. Other guys could mooch if they wanted to, but he had more self-respect. *His* girl would never pay one red cent out of her pocket.) The night before, they had gone to see a real thriller-diller, *King Kong.* Buddy figured that the climb all the way to the top of the new Empire State Building had to involve some pretty slick camera trickery, but he couldn't dope out how they managed to film the fight between the ape and that dinosaur. Bettina had hid her pretty face against his arm all the way through that scene, which was worth the price of admission all by itself.

He took his coffee into Wayne's office. A small Silvertone battery radio sat on the shelf behind the desk, playing Rudy Vallée's hit recording, "Brother, Can You Spare a Dime." Wayne had stopped typing and was leaning back in his chair, his eyes closed, doing a pretty good Vallée imitation. *Once in khaki suits, gee we looked swell, full of that*

Yankee doodly dum. Half a million boots went sloggin' through hell —

"Not exactly the most cheerful song in the book," Buddy said. He had once heard Wayne singing "Old Man River" while he stirred a pot of fatback, beans, and cabbage and had thought he was good enough to sing on the radio. Come to think of it, "Old Man River" was melancholy too, in a different way. *Tote that barge, lift that bale, get a little drunk and you land in jail* —

Wayne broke off. He opened his eyes, dark in his sunburned face, those high cheekbones giving him an enigmatic look. His glance flicked to Wayne, standing in the doorway. "Hey," he said. "Just heard on the radio that the feds finally got Pretty Boy Floyd."

Buddy whistled in surprise. After the Kansas City Massacre the year before, J. Edgar Hoover had named Floyd Public Enemy Number One. Ordinary folks, though, admired Pretty Boy's lawless ways. In Oklahoma, where he grew up, some newspaper reporter had called him the "Robin Hood of the Cookson Hills," and the name had stuck. He gave money away, and when he robbed a bank, he also destroyed the mortgage files, effectively shutting down its foreclosures.

"They cornered him in some woods in Ohio," Wayne said. "Shot him dead." He looked down at the Royal typewriter on the table in front of him. "I'm working on the Whitworth auto crash report. Give me ten minutes and I'll have it on your desk."

"Turn up anything interesting?" Buddy asked, sipping his coffee. He grimaced. He wasn't crazy about Wayne's coffee, which was strong enough to stop an elephant. But he didn't dislike it enough to go to the trouble of making another pot just for himself.

"Maybe." Wayne gestured to a short stack of photographic prints. "Charlie Dickens brought these over. Pictures he took at the wreck site this morning." He quirked an eyebrow. "Foot of Spook Hill. I understand you know the place."

"Yeah. There've been several accidents out there, over the past couple of years." Buddy frowned. "How did Dickens come to find out about the wreck?"

He liked Charlie, and sometimes he was a help. He'd put notices and such in the *Dispatch* for free, and it helped to have the local newspaper on your side when it came to an unpleasant story, like the time he'd dumped Pootie's load of shine. But he wouldn't tell you where he'd heard some-

267

thing. "Protecting my sources" was the way he put it, which was frustrating when Buddy thought he really ought to hand that information over. And he could be a nuisance. When something important was happening, he didn't mind getting in the way.

"Lucy Murphy called it in to him," Wayne said. "She called here first, then the newspaper." He pulled a flat can of Prince Albert out of his hip pocket and a pack of cigarette papers out of his shirt pocket. Deftly, he began to fashion a cigarette. "Gotta say I was glad he showed up. He had his camera with him. Caught some things we might've missed."

"Yeah? Like what?"

"Ruts in the road. They give a clue as to how come Whitworth went over the embankment." He shook tobacco into his folded cigarette paper. "And the crease in the rear end of his Pierce-Arrow."

"Crease?" Buddy frowned.

"Yeah. A fair-sized dent, actually." Wayne finished rolling, licked the length of the cigarette to seal it, and stuck it in his mouth. He reached across the table for the stack of photos, leafed through them, and pulled one out.

"There," he said, and jabbed a finger at the photo.

"Huh," Buddy said. He bent over it, frowning. He was looking at a picture of the rear end of the once-stately old automobile, no longer the proud beauty it had been. It was sitting upright on all four wheels, but the top was smashed against the top of the seats. He shivered. No chance for the driver to survive.

And there it was. A shallow horizontal dent — a crease, as Wayne put it — a couple of inches above the rear bumper.

"You think . . ."

But Buddy didn't need to finish the sentence. He knew what Wayne thought. That somebody had driven up behind the Pierce-Arrow, whacked it smartly, and sent it careening down that steep hill. He looked again.

"This dent could've been made any time, you know. Last week. Last month. Before. Not necessarily last night. And not on that hill. Could've happened anywhere."

"Don't think so." Wayne scratched a match against his boot heel and lit his cigarette. "It was pretty muddy out there. There's mud splatters all over that car. But when I've seen him driving around town, that baby has always been clean as a whistle, sparkly and shiny as a new penny." He pulled on his cigarette. "In fact, Whitworth paid Jake Pritchard to keep it washed and polished. Like he was goin' to a wedding every day of the week, Jake says."

"So you talked to Jake." That was what Buddy liked about Wayne. He was an independent thinker. When he got an idea, he followed wherever it took him without anybody having to tell him to do one thing or another. Old Roy Burns, he hadn't liked that in a deputy. He liked a man who didn't do a thing until he was told to do it, which had frustrated Buddy.

Wayne nodded. "Yeah. I gave Jake a call a little while ago. He washed that car yesterday afternoon — himself. Shined up that old Pierce Arrow real pretty. Swears there was no dent. Says a dent in that precious auto of Whitworth's would've made him blow a fuse."

"So your theory —"

"There's more." He took another photo from the stack. "That road out there was nothin' but Alabama mud and slick as the devil. See these ruts? Looks to me like somebody braked hard right here and skidded sorta sideways. Could've happened when it hit that Pierce-Arrow hard enough to send it downhill and down the embankment." He paused. "That's my theory, anyway. For what it's worth."

Buddy looked. "I see what you're saying, Wayne. So you think we're looking for another car." He was leaving to call on Mrs. Whitworth just as the tractor towing the wreck had arrived. He had directed them to the alley. "They park the wreck out by the fence?"

"Yeah. It was there when I got back from dropping Whitworth off at the funeral parlor." He paused, shaking his head. "Poor fella's face is pretty much of a mess. Smashed against the steering wheel, from the looks of it. His best friend probably wouldn't know him. Lionel doesn't think he can fix him up decent," he added. "Says it'll have to be a closed-casket funeral."

"Folks won't like that," Buddy said. Darling folks liked to see their friends and loved ones laid out face up, just to make sure they were burying the right one. They were superstitious that way. He looked down at the photo of the crease in the car's rear end. "Any other damage to the car? Bullet holes?"

It sounded like a frivolous question, maybe, but it wasn't. If another vehicle had been pursuing Whitworth, there might have been shooting. He thought of what Mrs. Whitworth had said. If Bodeen Pyle had been involved, shooting wouldn't surprise

271

him. He guessed that half the homicides in Alabama were related to bootlegging. Moonshine was a violent business. Stick your nose in where it wasn't wanted, you'd get it shot off.

"Nope, no bullet holes in the vehicle," Wayne said. "I also took a good look at Whitworth when Noonan got him on the mortuary table. Doc Roberts will tell us for sure, but I couldn't see any bullet holes in him, either." Wayne squinted through the smoke of his cigarette. "You're thinking of Bodeen Pyle, I reckon."

"You read my mind." Buddy gave him an appraising look. "How'd you know?"

"Charlie Dickens passed on some rumors when he brought the photos over here. He's heard that Whitworth was a partner in Pyle's moonshine operation." He quirked an eyebrow. "How'd you find out?"

"Heard it mentioned at the diner this morning," Buddy said. "I wasn't sure I believed it — Whitworth always looked like a straight-up citizen to me. But Miz Whitworth confirmed it. She doesn't much like the idea."

"I don't wonder. Husband involved in a shady racket. Doesn't look good for her." Cigarette dangling from one corner of his mouth, Wayne restored the photos to the

272

stack and put the lot into a manila envelope. "Did you take her to Noonan's to identify her husband?"

"She didn't want to go." Buddy frowned. "Jed Snow's wife told me that Miz Whitworth was thinking about getting a divorce. She's apparently already talked to Moseley about it."

"Interesting," Wayne said briefly. He jerked his head. "Car's out back, on the alley."

The wrecked Pierce-Arrow squatted forlornly in a corner of the yard, under a green canvas tarp. Wayne pulled it off and Buddy shook his head sadly. Up close and personal, the damage looked worse than it had in Charlie's photo. The elegant old car was completely wrecked, and there was a good deal of blood mixed with the red mud splashed on the driver's door. No bullet or buckshot damage, though, just that unmistakable crease.

And looking at that dent, Buddy decided that Wayne's theory was quite reasonable. At some point, somebody had driven up behind the car and given it a right smart smack. Had it been done carelessly or deliberately? A bad driver or somebody with a grudge? But however it had happened, the impact could have sent the Pierce-Arrow careening out of control and over the embankment. Which could turn an accidental death into manslaughter, at a minimum. The question was *who*?

Back in the office with a second cup of coffee, Buddy sat down at his desk and took his notebook out of his shirt pocket. The Beast followed him in, jumped gracefully onto the windowsill, and began washing his right paw with a bright pink tongue.

Buddy regarded the cat for a moment. Gravely, he said, "You go back down where you came from and get Roy Burns to tell you who was driving that car — the one that hit Whitworth's Pierce-Arrow last night."

The Beast put his paw down and stared at him with those burnt-copper eyes. He didn't say anything. After a moment, he began washing his left paw.

With a sigh, Buddy turned to a clean page in his notebook and wrote *Pile* at the top of the page, and *moonshine.* Under that he wrote *Warden.* He frowned, thought, and wrote *Bufford,* although he wasn't sure that was how the man spelled his name. Then he thought some more, remembered the widow's lie about the divorce and wrote *Miz Whitworth.* He frowned, remembering something else Ophelia Snow had told him, which hadn't really registered at the time.

After the name, he wrote *new car* and added a question mark. And hadn't Ophelia also said something about Mrs. Whitworth being a terrible driver? He added another question mark.

He was still considering this list when the front screen door slammed and a sharp female voice shrilled, "Yoo-hoo! Sheriff? Is anybody here? It's *me.*"

Buddy sighed. He knew who *me* was, and he fervently wished she would go away. But he also knew she wouldn't, so he closed his notebook and raised his voice. "I'm in the office, Miz Adcock."

The woman who came in — a sharp-chinned woman with a prissy mouth and squinty gray eyes — was wearing a bright purple dress, purple gloves, and a purple hat. Over the past few months, Leona Ruth Adcock had taken a liking to the new sheriff and had gotten into the habit of bringing him "tips" that she hoped might help him "solve crimes." Indeed, one of her tips had resulted in the return of four disgracefully overdue library books to a grateful Miss Rogers at the Darling library, which Buddy didn't count as much of a crime.

As a tipster, Leona Ruth was only marginally useful. She was a sponge. Everywhere she went, she soaked up bits of this and that and mixed and mingled (and mangled) all of it with her own imagination. When she came to him with a story, it was impossible to tell what part of it — if any — was factual. Still, he had to listen to her. It was his job.

"How are you today, Miz Adcock?" Buddy said with a phony heartiness, and waved his hand toward a chair. "Sit down and rest yourself a bit."

"B'lieve I will, thank you," Leona Ruth said, and settled herself on the other side of Buddy's desk. "This won't take long, Sheriff. I just stopped in to tell you that Mr. Whitworth didn't get hisself killed in any accident. It was deliberate." She gave a sharp nod and the peacock feathers fluttered on her hat, their markings looking remarkably like a pair of large, iridescent blue eyes, encircled in green. "I know it for a *fact*."

"You do?" Normally, Buddy would have been skeptical. In this case, however, the lady might be onto something. So far as he knew, he and Wayne were the only ones aware of that dent in the back of Whitworth's wrecked car.

"Yes, I certainly do," she said emphatically. "Mrs. Audrey Dunlap thinks her husband killed him."

Buddy's jaw dropped. "Mrs. Dunlap? You mean, Liz Lacy's mother? The one who —"

"Exactly," Leona Ruth said with satisfaction. "Mrs. Dunlap, who recently married Mr. Dunlap, from the Five and Dime. I learned this just a little while ago, and I've been thinking about it ever since. I finally decided that it was my duty as a concerned citizen to tell you." She gave a nervous look at the Beast, who was staring at her with a fixed concentration. "That cat — he is certainly a *malevolent* creature."

"He's just an old cat," Buddy said. "A stray. Don't pay any attention to him. Why would Mr. Dunlap —"

"Because Mr. Whitworth was his *partner,* that's why." Leona Ruth leaned forward and lowered her voice. "Which Mrs. Dunlap just found out about."

"I see," Buddy said. Armed with Myra May's tip, he had already been down that road. He had talked to Mr. Dunlap that morning, while Mr. Whitworth was still just a missing person. Dunlap had told him that Whitworth had come over for a few minutes the evening before to talk about the upcoming barbershop competition. Nothing suspicious there. He cleared his throat. "Did Mrs. Dunlap say why she thought her husband might have wanted to —"

"Because there was a *fight,*" Leona Ruth said with relish. "It seems that a ways back, Mr. Dunlap signed a paper saying that the thousand dollars he got from Mr. Whitworth for his store was all he was ever going to get, while Mr. Whitworth would get his share of the profits forever. Doesn't seem right to me, but that's the way it is."

Buddy nodded. It was the situation that Myra May had described that morning. "It's called a limited partnership."

"Whatever." Leona Ruth waved her hand. "Doesn't make it *right.* Anyway, Audrey — that's Mrs. Dunlap — she told me that when Mr. Dunlap asked Mr. Whitworth to chip in on a new heating system, Mr. Whitworth said no, he wasn't putting in any more money. They got into a big argument — worse than that, there was pushing and shoving, Audrey said. After Mr. Whitworth left, Mr. Dunlap was so upset that he went for a long drive, to calm himself. He wouldn't let Audrey go with him, and he didn't get home until midnight — and after that, he paced around the house all night and wouldn't eat Sally-Lou's apple pancakes for breakfast, which Audrey says he has never done before."

"I understand," Buddy said, "and I'm glad to know all that. But does Mrs. Dunlap have any concrete evidence that her husband actually —"

"We didn't go into that," Leona Ruth said, very prim. "Poor Audrey was *terribly* upset, and I didn't feel I should make it worse by asking questions." She looked down at her purple-gloved hands folded in her purple lap. "Of course, she would never tell you a word of this herself," she added righteously, "but I felt *I* had to. It was my civic responsibility!" The peacock feathers on her hat trembled with the force of her conviction.

Buddy took a deep breath. "Well, I'm glad you did, Miz Adcock," he said. "I'll be sure and check into it."

Leona Ruth raised her head and fixed him with her eyes. "But I sincerely hope and trust that you won't tell dear Audrey that *I* was the one who told you. I mean, I wouldn't want her to think —"

But that was as far as she got. For as Leona Ruth raised her head, her peacock feathers shimmered, their eyes twinkled enticingly, and the Beast launched himself into the air, closing the gap between himself and Leona Ruth's hat in one powerful leap, its force carrying both him and the hat halfway across the room.

It took quite a while to calm Leona Ruth's hysterics, rescue her battered, de-feathered hat, and banish the Beast. Afterward, Buddy escorted her out to the sheriff's squad car and drove her home, still sniffling into her handkerchief. He walked her to her door, took off his hat, and solemnly thanked her again.

"Speaking as the sheriff," he said, "it's just real good to know that the law in this town can count on people like you."

"Thank you," she said. "I consider it my duty."

Back in the office, he opened a fresh can of tuna fish, whistled for the Beast, and watched while the cat made short work of an extra-large helping.

CHAPTER SEVENTEEN:
OPHELIA, LIZ, AND CHARLIE

Ophelia's husband Jed was always cautioning her against poking her nose into things that weren't her business, but she had never been able to corral her curiosity once it got a bit between its teeth. And while she felt downright sorry for Regina Whitworth — even if the poor thing *was* planning to divorce her husband, it must have been terrible to lose him in the blink of an eye, as it were — she was still puzzling over several unanswered questions.

Which was nothing new, of course, for Ophelia often spent whole days trying to unravel variously twisted skeins of thought that led her here, there, and everywhere. She had never been what anybody would call an organized thinker — although in her own considered opinion, this was an asset, because it sometimes led to conclusions that a more orderly thinker might miss.

And for another thing, Ophelia had not

once during her expedition with the sheriff taken her reporter's notebook out of her handbag, and she had almost no little bits of human-interest story to soften Charlie Dickens' report of the accident. While there was that intriguing business about Mr. Whitworth's being a silent partner in Bodeen Pyle's moonshine operation, that didn't exactly qualify as human interest, did it?

And Regina's little white lie about the divorce — well, that didn't count, either. The sheriff was right when he said it wasn't related to Mr. Whitworth's accident. At least, not on the surface and not in any way that Ophelia could easily see. And anyway, Charlie couldn't use it. *Divorce* was one of the words Darling didn't like to read in its newspaper.

So when Sheriff Norris let her out of his car in front of the Dispatch office, Ophelia stood for a moment on the sidewalk, trying to decide what to do next. She hated to confess to Charlie that her errand — for which she had given up that meeting with the men of the Share the Wealth Society — had not been as productive as he hoped. She needed to talk this over with somebody who could help her think this through. Liz Lacy. That's who she would talk to!

And having made up her mind, she

turned, crossed the street, and headed straight for the bed of bright fall annuals — purple asters, orange marigolds, red zinnias, and yellow chrysanthemums — blooming with a burst of color in a corner of the courthouse lawn. As a Dahlia, she had helped plant that bed, along with Aunt Hetty Little and Bessie Bloodworth. She had weeded it, too. Which made them her flowers more than anybody else's.

She bent over and began to pick a bouquet.

Upstairs at her desk in Mr. Moseley's law office, Lizzy was talking to Mrs. Ellie Sue Slimm, who had a legal problem.

"I'm so sorry you've had this trouble," she said soothingly. "I've written down everything you've told me, and I'll let Mr. Moseley know about it the minute he gets back to town. But in the meantime, maybe you could have a talk with the sheriff."

The woman seated in the chair on the other side of Lizzy's desk was wearing a plain cotton housedress and no gloves, and her going-to-town straw hat was trimmed with a wilted-looking red crepe paper rose.

"I did that yestiddy," Mrs. Slimm said. "The sheriff says it's a civil matter, which ain't the same as criminal, so he can't do anything about it. Or won't," she added with weary resignation. "Which amounts to the same thing, I reckon. The sheriff says I should take Tom Jerkins to court to make him pay what he owes me for that mule. He's a good mule with a lot of years left in him." She unsnapped her pocketbook. "I've got a bill of sale right here, with Tom Jerkin's name on it and the date, all legal. There's more than half owing on that mule, and I purely do need that money."

Tom Jerkins. The name rang a bell, Lizzy thought. Mr. Moseley had dealt with him earlier, when he had tried to skip out on another debt. "It's good that you have the bill of sale," she said. "You hang onto it until you've talked to Mr. Moseley. How can he get in touch with you?"

The woman looked down at her chapped, work-worn hands. "Don't have no phone. But he can call my near neighbor, Stella Parnell, and she'll send her little girl across the road to get me. Her number is Evergreen 237."

"Thank you." Lizzy wrote it down: *EV 237.* "I'll tell him."

Mrs. Slimm's complaint against Tom Jerkins was typical of the things people asked Mr. Moseley to do for them — drawing up property deeds, making wills, collecting debts, mediating disagreements. Small-time, small-town work, but Mr. Moseley preferred it, he said, to the big-city clients he had in Montgomery and Mobile, who were often intentionally crooked and hired him to clean up their criminal messes.

But the trouble was that Mr. Moseley's Darling clients didn't always have cash to pay their legal bills. Which meant that they paid in whatever they had of value. The week before, a farmer in bib overalls had brought in two fat Rhode Island Red hens.

"These'll make real good chicken and dumplings," he said, handing them to Lizzy. Mr. Moseley, with an eye to a more durable reward than a Sunday dinner, donated the hens to Lizzy's backyard flock, where they would lay eggs for breakfasts for the two of them, with plenty left over for the Darling Blessing Box. The unfortunate thing, of course, was that people who paid their bill in chickens weren't paying Lizzy's salary — which was why Mr. Moseley was thinking of reducing her hours.

The door opened and Lizzy saw that it was Ophelia. "Oh, hello, Mrs. Snow," she said brightly. "I'll be with you in just a minute."

Mrs. Slimm stood. "You tell Mr. Moseley." Her crooked smile showed a missing tooth. "I'll sure thank him if he can help me get the rest of the money. That mule is a *good* mule."

Lizzy stood and held out her hand. "You'll hear from him soon," she promised with a smile. When the woman had gone, she turned to Ophelia.

"Hey, Opie. Nice to see you." She gave her friend an appreciative glance. Ophelia didn't spend much money on her clothes, but she always looked neat and fresh. Today, her pink-and-white belted seersucker dress and pink sweater looked both feminine and professional, and she was carrying a small bouquet of bright flowers.

"For you," Ophelia said, holding them out. "For your desk."

"Oh, how lovely!" Lizzy exclaimed. "Thank you!" She buried her nose in the flowers and breathed deeply. The marigolds had a distinctive fragrance that always reminded her of a summer garden on a hot, sunshine-blessed day. "What's the occasion?"

"No occasion." Ophelia gave a little shrug. "You know what Aunt Hetty always says. 'All it takes to be happy is good health and a little bunch of flowers.' " She raised an eyebrow. "And I just might have a question or two that you could answer, if you have a few minutes."

Lizzy smiled. "I do. But I'll put these in water first." She got up. "Would you like some coffee?"

"I'd love a cup," Ophelia said, and took the chair Mrs. Slimm had vacated.

Lizzy filled a small crystal vase with water and arranged the flowers. With coffee, the flowers, and a tin of cookies, she went back to her desk. "I want you to try one of my Chocolate Crunch cookies." She opened the tin. "They've got little chunks of chipped chocolate in them."

"Chipped chocolate?" Opie took a cookie.

"Right. The story goes that a lady named Ruth Wakefield, somewhere up in Massachusetts, invented the recipe by accident a couple of years ago. She planned to make some chocolate cookies, but she was out of baking chocolate. She did have a chunk of semi-sweet chocolate, though, so she chipped off some little pieces, about a cup or so. She expected the chips to melt into the dough the way regular baking chocolate would, but they didn't. Instead, they mostly stayed the way they were, little chips of chocolate, but sort of soft and gooey. She called it the 'Chocolate Crunch cookie.' I heard the recipe on the *Betty Crocker* radio program a couple of weeks ago." She paused to nibble a cookie. "What do you think?"

"It's swell!" Ophelia said delightedly, munching. "Little chips of chocolate. I know my kids would love it — Jed, too. Will you give me the recipe?"

"Of course," Lizzy said, and picked up her coffee cup. "So what's going on?" She eyed the flowers on the corner of her desk. She wanted to ask — again — what they were for, but she figured that Opie would get around to telling her.

Ophelia held up her reporter's notebook. "Actually, I'm working on the Whitworth story for Charlie. I've just been talking to Regina Whitworth. With the sheriff," she added importantly.

The sheriff? Lizzy frowned. This sounded serious. "Then he hasn't turned up yet? Mr. Whitworth, I mean."

"Turned up?" Ophelia frowned. "I guess you haven't heard, then."

"I've been behind this desk for most of the day," Lizzy said. "I brought my lunch, so I haven't been out. I —" She broke off. "Heard *what,* Opie?"

"Why, Mr. Whitworth is dead, Liz. He was killed in an automobile crash out on Spook Hill. His body was found this morning."

"Dead?" Lizzy set her coffee down so hard the coffee almost sloshed over. "Oh, no!"

she exclaimed, feeling breathless. "How terrible! Was he . . . had he been kidnapped?"

"Kidnapped?" Ophelia asked quizzically. "My gracious, Liz — why in the world would you think *that*?"

"I didn't, exactly," Lizzy said. "Mrs. Whitworth brought it up when I talked to her this morning."

"*You* talked to her?"

"Yes," Lizzy said. "She called here quite early, wanting to talk to Mr. Moseley. She seemed upset, so I gave her his number in Montgomery. After he talked to her, he called to tell me that Mr. Whitworth hadn't come home last night. He wanted me to go over there and see if I could help."

I must tell Mr. Moseley about Mr. Whitworth, she thought. *But I don't suppose there's any huge hurry. Now that her husband is dead, Mrs. Whitworth won't be getting a divorce.*

Aloud, she said, "So you're writing the story for the *Dispatch*?"

Ophelia shook her head regretfully. "You know Charlie. He always keeps the best for himself. But the sheriff thought he ought to take a woman along when he went to tell Mrs. Whitworth what had happened, so Charlie suggested me. He asked me to collect some human-interest bits that he can use in the story." She looked glum. "I didn't do so well with that assignment, I'm afraid."

Lizzy leaned forward, feeling concerned. "How did Mrs. Whitworth take the news? Is she okay? Is anyone with her?" She took a breath, thinking out loud. "Mr. Moseley will probably want me to go over there again and offer to help with arrangements."

"She must be Mr. Moseley's client, then," Ophelia said quickly. "I suppose she consulted him on the divorce."

Lizzy was surprised. "You know about *that*? How did you find out?"

"She told me herself, last week," Ophelia said. "We had to go to Monroeville on an errand for the Ladies Guild. She drove her new car — that gorgeous pumpkin-colored Dodge she bought from Kilgore's."

Her new car? "Ah," Lizzy murmured, remembering. She had glimpsed that car in the Whitworth's garage that morning. But she hadn't known it belong to *Mrs.* Whitworth.

Ophelia went on. "Anyway, she wanted to talk about the divorce when we stopped for root beer. I got the impression that she was looking forward to a new life, maybe even to getting out of Darling." She frowned. "But it was odd, Liz. When I mentioned the divorce in front of the sheriff, she denied it. Heatedly."

"That *is* odd," Lizzy said. "I wonder why she did that." She bit her lip. Maybe she shouldn't be discussing this with Opie. But now that Mr. Whitworth was dead, there wouldn't be a divorce. Maybe Mrs. Whitworth was no longer a client. If that was true, was the subject still covered by client privilege? Anyway, Ophelia seemed to know all about it.

"That's exactly what *I* said." Ophelia was emphatic. "She's wrong — or more accurately, she's lying." She added, "If you ask me, she didn't want the sheriff to suspect that she might have a motive."

"A motive for what?" Lizzy asked blankly.

Ophelia gave her a defensive look. "Well, her husband did die rather suddenly."

"But you said it was an accident," Lizzy pressed. "An automobile crash. Crashes tend to happen suddenly, don't they?"

"Yes, but —" Ophelia waved a hand. "Accidents do have a cause, you know."

Lizzy frowned. "Are you accusing Mrs. Whitworth of *causing* her husband's accident?"

"Well . . ." Ophelia sat back, looking deflated. "Not really, I suppose. I just thought maybe — I mean, I have a feeling that . . ." Her voice trailed away.

"What?" Lizzy asked.

"Oh, I don't know," Opie said testily. "But there's another thing, Liz. It turns out that Mr. Whitworth was in partnership with Bodeen Pyle, which certainly doesn't make him look good." She took a breath. "Regina Whitworth was pretty upset about that. I had to wonder if that was her reason for wanting the divorce. She surely wouldn't be happy if word got around that she was married to a bootlegger."

"Bodeen Pyle?" Lizzy frowned. She was surprised by this, for Mrs. Whitworth hadn't said anything about a partnership with Pyle in last week's interview with Mr. Moseley. Perhaps she hadn't known it at the time. But the woman had told Mr. Moseley something else about her husband, something equally illegal and incriminating — something that had spurred her to consider divorce — and Lizzy thought about it now.

Regina Vautier had been just nineteen when she married Whitney Whitworth. "I was a wide-eyed innocent," she'd said, "just a baby, really, and all alone in the world." She had known next to nothing about financial matters — and cared even less. She was far more interested in romance. In fact, she had believed that her new husband — older than she, experienced and romantic — was a wealthy man, and that he was paying all their bills with *his* money. She had simply assumed that hers was still in the bank and she could take it out and spend it whenever she wanted.

But recently, she had discovered to her dismay that this was not the case. All this time, they had been living on *her* inheritance, not his income. When she learned this, she had begun to think about divorce.

And there was another part to the story, which Regina Whitworth had told Mr. Moseley only because he had warned her that she had to tell him *everything* or he couldn't represent her. She said she had always wanted to learn to drive but Mr. Whitworth wouldn't let her. Women were too scatterbrained to drive, he'd told her, and anyway, the Pierce-Arrow was too large an automobile for her to manage. *He* would drive her where she needed to go.

Finally, in an act of rebellion, she had gone to the bank to withdraw the money to buy a new car. That's when she discovered that her husband had nearly depleted her account. Angrily, she had taken what was left and bought a car for herself. Frank Harwood, the Kilgore salesman, was teaching her to drive — and she had fallen in love with him.

"We are *not* having an affair," she had said

quickly and insistently, as if anticipating Mr. Moseley's question. "I could never do such a thing. But Frank wants me to marry him, and I've told him I will consider it, after Whitney and I are divorced."

That was the full story, and as Lizzy thought about it, she could see why Regina Whitworth hadn't wanted Sheriff Norris to know that she had been planning a divorce. If there were any questions about the cause of that car wreck, *she* would be the first one to fall under suspicion.

"Well, then," Lizzy said quietly. "I think I'd better call Mr. Moseley and fill him in on what's happened. The fact that Whitworth was involved with Bodeen Pyle raises some other questions."

"I'm sure it does." Ophelia got up, smoothing her dress around her hips. "Well, I'd better get downstairs and give Charlie what little I've got for his story." She hesitated for a moment, biting her lip. "I wonder . . ." She fell silent.

"Wonder what?" Lizzy asked, reaching for the telephone on the corner of her desk.

"About that car," Ophelia said. "Regina Whitworth's new car, I mean. I'll bet it's in the Whitworths' garage, Liz. Do you suppose we should go over there after dark tonight and take a look at —"

"No," Lizzy said emphatically. "We should *not.*" If Mr. Moseley asked her to check out that car, that was one thing. Going there with Ophelia was quite another.

Opie sighed. "I suppose you're right. Well, see you later, Liz. Enjoy your flowers."

The minute she was gone, Lizzy lifted the receiver. She was about to dial the Exchange to place a long-distance call to Mr. Moseley's Montgomery office when the telephone rang.

"Law offices," she said pleasantly. "How may we help you?"

The woman on the other end of the line was shrill and imperative. "Your Mr. Moseley can keep Mr. Dunlap from going to jail, Elizabeth. *That's* how you can help!"

"Mama?" Lizzy felt chilled. "Mama, is that *you*?"

"Of course it's me," Mrs. Dunlap snapped. "I want you to send Mr. Moseley over to the Five and Dime right now, Elizabeth. Right *now,* do you hear me? That sheriff's deputy is back there in the office right now, questioning my husband!"

Trying to be calm, Lizzy said, "Mr. Moseley is in Montgomery, Mama. He won't be back for a day or two." She hesitated. "The deputy is questioning Mr. Dunlap about *what*? What's happened?"

"About killing Mr. Whitworth, *that's* what! And if somebody doesn't do *some*thing, he is going to haul my dear Mr. Dunlap off to jail." She took a breath. "And it's all because of Leona Ruth Adcock, that wretched old busy-body! When I get my hands on her, I'm going to —"

"Killing Mr. Whitworth?" Lizzy was aghast. "But *why,* Mama? I understand that Mr. Whitworth died accidentally, in a car wreck. What could Leona Ruth possibly know that —"

"She doesn't 'know' anything, Elizabeth." Her mother's voice dripped acid. "She is making it all up."

"Well, of course she is," Lizzy said, trying to be comforting. "I'm sure Mr. Dunlap won't be going to jail."

"Well, I'm not," her mother snapped. "If you're not interested in helping us, I will call Gerald Cankron. He did some legal work for Mr. Dunlap last summer. I'm sure *he'll* be glad to see that Mr. Dunlap is released."

Lizzy sighed. She had learned through long, frustrating experience that there was no use in trying to argue with her mother, who was very good at twisting what people said to make them think that they were in the wrong. And as far as Leona Ruth Adcock was concerned — well, that old woman made it her business to *put* people in the wrong, all for the momentary glory of feeling herself in the right.

"Whatever you think, Mama," Lizzy said quietly. Gerald Cankron was one of Darling's other two lawyers, and not a very good one. At least, that was Mr. Moseley's opinion, and it must be accurate, since he regularly bested Mr. Cankron when they ended up on opposite sides of a case.

"Well, then, good*bye,* and no thanks to you, Elizabeth," her mother retorted angrily, and banged down the phone.

Lizzy sat for a moment, thinking. She knew her mother well enough to discount her dramatic exaggerations. Nothing was ever as bad (or as good) as her mother said it was. But if Mr. Dunlap was being questioned, the sheriff must think there was something to Leona Ruth's accusation. What was it?

She couldn't reveal what she knew. That would be to violate Mr. Moseley's confidentiality rule. But the rule didn't have to keep her from learning more, if she could. And she felt that to be an obligation, now that Mr. Dunlap was somehow involved. She pulled the phone toward her and dialed the Exchange.

First, though, she had to tell Mr. Moseley that Mr. Whitworth was dead, and find out what further instructions *he* might have.

Charlie Dickens walked confidently into the Darling Savings and Trust, expecting to see Alvin Duffy sitting in his glassed-in office, keeping an eye on the goings-on in the lobby. Charlie knew for a fact that while Al might look like your ordinary mild-mannered banker, he was a crack shot and kept a loaded revolver in the top drawer of his desk. It was just a commonsense precaution, Al insisted, given the rash of bank robberies that had plagued the nation since the beginning of the Depression.

"Nobody's going to rob *my* bank," he said, whenever the subject came up. All of Darling believed him and felt a little safer when they took their money out from under the bed and entrusted it to Mr. Duffy's bank.

But Al Duffy was not at his desk when Charlie went in. "He's in Atlanta this week," Alice Ann Walker explained. She had recently been promoted from teller and was now Mr. Duffy's secretary. "Can *I* do something for you, Mr. Dickens?"

Charlie hesitated. What he had come for was a look at Fannie's canceled checks, to see if he could figure out who (or what) JC was and why his wife was sending this person (or company or organization) fifty dollars every month. Al was a friend of his, so he figured that — man to man — he could ask that little favor.

But Alice Ann and Fannie were both Dahlias, and they were pretty friendly. Even if she let him have a look, she might very likely tell Fannie about it. Charlie was planning to keep his little investigation out of sight. So no, on balance, he didn't think Alice Ann could help him.

"He's out *all* week?" he said. "When will he be back?"

Alice Ann tapped her pencil on the calendar on her desk. "Well, he originally said Friday. But then he mentioned going down to Jacksonville after Atlanta. I'm sorry, but I really couldn't tell you exactly when." She smiled pleasantly. "Speaking of travelers, have you heard from Fannie yet? When is she due to get to New York?"

"Tomorrow," Charlie said, glad that he hadn't mentioned his errand to Alice Ann. "It's a long trip, with a couple of changes."

"Well, when you talk to her, tell her I'm thinking about her. I had a peek at some of her hats before she packed them up. I *know* she'll do very well." Alice Ann wrinkled her forehead. "Are you *sure* I can't help you, Mr. Dickens?"

"I'm afraid not," Charlie said. "But thanks."

It looked like he was going to have to live with his puzzle a little while longer.

CHAPTER EIGHTEEN:
THE SHERIFF AND
THE BOOTLEGGER

When Mrs. Adcock had gone, Buddy Norris went into Wayne's office and told him what she had said about the bad blood between Dunlap and Whitworth.

"I don't think it amounts to anything much," Buddy said. "Leona Ruth is bad about getting things mixed up. But Dunlap lied to me this morning when I talked to him about Whitworth. So we need to check it out."

"I'll do it." Wayne pulled a page out of his battered Royal typewriter. "Here's what I've got on the accident." He nodded toward the stack of photos. "And there are Dickens' photos."

Buddy took the report and picked up the photographs. "Thanks. Bodeen Pyle lives with his mother on the other side of town. I'm headed over there to see if I can talk to him. I want to find out where he was last night, and who was with him."

Wayne arched an eyebrow. "With his momma?"

"Yeah. The Pyle boys may come down on the wrong side of the liquor laws, but they take good care of their own. Bodeen was supporting two grandmothers up until last year, when both of them died."

Wayne nodded. "How about a sandwich before you go? Got some baloney in the icebox if you're hungry." He grinned. "Bottle of cold beer, too."

"Sounds good to me," Buddy said, thinking again that he'd hired himself the right deputy.

Bodeen Pyle lived with his mother and his brother Beau on Pleasant View, which was anything but. The red-dirt street, ankle-deep in red mud when it rained, was lined with junky front yards, dilapidated houses set on piles of bricks, and scrawny trees. The small gardens and chicken yards were unsuccessfully fenced against rabbits, deer, and the neighborhood boys, who made a habit of snatching ripe sweet corn, watermelons, and fresh eggs. The Pyles' house was as ramshackle as the rest, its white-painted wood siding weathered to a defeated gray, with a sagging front porch and a rusty tin roof.

Inside, though, it was a different story.

Buddy had been there a time or two and had seen the new Frigidaire and Magic Chef gas range, the chrome kitchen dinette set with shiny red chairs, and the plush sofa and matching armchair in the parlor. Bodeen's momma refused to move out of the old house where she'd lived her whole life, but she allowed her son to use his moonshine profits to make things easier and more comfortable for her.

The front steps were guarded by a pair of coonhounds too lazy to do more than lift their heads when Buddy pulled up in front. A stripped-down 1932 black Ford that belonged to Bodeen's younger brother Beau was parked just ahead of him on the street. A fast car, it could easily outrun the old Model T four-door sedan that Buddy had inherited from Roy Burns.

That is, it could until Buddy had bolted on a high-compression cylinder head and installed a high-speed camshaft and a bigger carburetor. On the door, he had painted a six-pointed star around the words "Cypress County Sheriff," and added a red light and an ear-splitting siren, rigged to run off the battery. He'd also anchored a sturdy strip of hog wire across the back of the front seat, so if he had to haul a prisoner, the guy couldn't grab him from behind and get him in a choke-hold. Although he was still itch-ing for an opportunity to prove its merits, he was confident that his souped-up Model T could now outrun almost anything on the road.

Dispiritedly, the coon hounds left the steps and flopped down under a cotton-wood tree at the edge of the yard, displac-ing a red rooster and a couple of squawking hens. As Buddy rapped on the screen door, he could hear a soothing male voice an-nouncing that it was time to tune in to "Oxydol's own Ma Perkins." The announcer was abruptly throttled when somebody switched off the radio.

Bodeen's mother answered Buddy's knock. Her gray hair was wound on top of her head and fuzzy tendrils frizzed around her face. She wore a green-checked cotton dress and a flour sack apron that still bore the washed-out brand name, Sunbonnet Sue Flour. She glanced at the badge on Buddy's shirt pocket. Her tone was re-signed. "Which one you lookin' for this time?"

"Bodeen, ma'am," Buddy said, taking off his hat respectfully.

The Pyles had three sons: young Beau, a rakishly good-looking troublemaker; Bodeen; and the older boy, Rankin, who'd joined a gang over around Atlanta and was said to keep busy robbing banks. Old man Pyle had just been released from Wetumpka (also known as "The Walls") where he had served a five-year sentence for knifing a man in a fight in a speakeasy in Monroeville.

Of the lot, Bodeen showed the most self-discipline and industry, although the industry he was involved in was generally considered illegal. His still had already been shut down once by that pesky revenue agent, Chester P. Kinnard. But that had been a temporary setback, and it wasn't long before he had relocated from the south end of Briar Swamp to the north. Following Roy Burns' lead, Buddy had so far considered Bodeen's bootlegging as none of his business. That is, it was none of his business until Bodeen got up to something *else* illegal, like thieving or murder, in which case, he'd have to do something about it.

"Well, Bodeen ain't here," Mrs. Pyle said in a resentful tone.

Buddy wondered whether she ever got tired of defending her kin or worrying about what they were up to. "Happen to know where I can find him?"

Somewhere in the house, a male voice shouted, "Ma, you made my sandwich yet? I'm hungry."

Mrs. Pyle shook her head. Over her shoulder, she yelled, "You fix it, Beau. I'm busy."

"Bodeen's out at the swamp, I reckon," Buddy hazarded.

Mrs. Pyle regarded him darkly. After a moment, she replied, "I ain't sayin'. You can find him your own self."

Buddy sighed. "You know, you'd save me a goldurned long drive if you'd just tell me he's *not* out at the swamp. I could be in a better mood when I get there."

She gave him a narrow-eyed look. "Ain't sayin' he ain't," she said at last.

"Thank you, ma'am." Buddy put his hat back on. "What I needed to know."

The male voice came again, plaintively. "Ma, there ain't no cheese!"

Unless Darling folk had important business in Briar Swamp — hunting, fishing, or hiding out — they mostly stayed away. Briar Creek flowed deep and dark there, and the swamp itself was embraced by a series of wide oxbow bends of the Alabama River, which snaked slowly along on its muddy way to Mobile Bay and the blue Gulf beyond.

The swamp's bottomland was thick with trees and underbrush and even thicker with mosquitoes and snakes — cottonmouth, copperhead, coral snake, diamondback rattlesnake. The few houses along the river weren't houses at all but houseboats, tin-roofed and shanty-like and liable to be swept from their moorings when the river flooded, which it did often. The CCC boys at Camp Briarwood had been cutting trees and digging ditches along the eastern margins of the swamp, attempting to drain the land and claim it for agriculture. In Buddy's view, that was a waste of time — make-work, really — an opinion shared by many Darling people. They liked Briar Swamp the way it had been in their long memory, deep and dark and free, a nearly impenetrable refuge for those who needed a place to hide out. Like General Bedford Forrest's Confederate boys, on the run after the Battle of Selma, near the end of the war.

When he was a kid, Buddy had spent a fair amount of time in the swamp, playing hooky from school, mostly, but also getting to know the place, which had a strange, almost hypnotic hold on his imagination. Long narrow fingers of shallow bayous reached into the swamp on the river side, their shores bordered with bald cypress, their waters home to some pretty fine gators and longnose gar lazing among the lily pads and water willow. Where the land rose up a few feet, the trees were mostly tupelo and gum, mixed with southern red oak, sweet gum, yellow poplar, and beech. And the waters and shorelines and trees were home to an astonishing variety of birds: dabblers like the Canada geese, mallards, gadwalls, and blue-winged teal; waders like the herons, bitterns, egrets, ibises, and wood storks; raptors like the osprey, kites, eagles, hawks, and owls.

Buddy knew where a wooden skiff was tied to a swamp cottonwood and had occasionally borrowed it to fish the bayous for largemouth or spotted bass, catfish, crappie, pickerel, and sunfish. Sometimes he'd pole to a place where the water shallowed over a clean gravel bottom and hunt for freshwater mussels — southern fatmucket, yellow sandshell, Alabama orb — or for crawdads and frogs, to be cooked over a campfire while the sky darkened down to night and the ivory moon lifted above the trees.

Buddy hadn't been down to the swamp since he'd been elected sheriff, but he still knew his way around. What was more to his present purpose, he knew the way to Bodeen's relocated moonshine camp, although he hadn't been there for a while, either. He had a choice. He could drive in past the prison farm on the Jericho Road, then take the dirt two-track that curled and twisted through the trees for several miles. Or (and this would be quieter and give no notice of his coming) he could pole up Snipes Bayou, if the skiff was still moored to that swamp cottonwood.

It was, although he had to disturb a great blue heron and a small flock of hooded mergansers and buffleheads fishing in the dark, still waters nearby. He had to bail the skiff out, too, using a rusty coffee can he found in the gunwale. But by midafternoon, he had poled his way up the narrow bayou to the point where he could smell the smoke from Bodeen's moonshine camp and hear the dull thud of an ax.

He pushed the skiff onto the bank below a tangle of tree roots and got out. He had left his holster and gun locked in the car — he'd never been very keen on firepower, feeling that having a revolver on his hip increased the likelihood of rash behavior on both sides of the law. When he walked up to Bodeen's camp in a large cleared space in the middle of a dense wood, he made it easy for anybody he met to see that his hands were empty and he was unarmed.

The center of the clearing was taken up with three large boilers set up on stacks of bricks. Off to one side was a storage shack, with a row of wooden barrels and smaller kegs along one wall and a shanty bunkhouse nearby, with an iron pot of something — squirrel stew, maybe, or fatback and beans — perched over a campfire.

At a quick glance, Buddy counted three men in the clearing. An old man, gray-bearded and gaunt, was stacking empty cans — the square five-gallon metal cans bootleggers used to haul their moonshine, instead of the glass jugs that were easily broken. A young boy in ragged overalls, shirtless, was splitting short lengths of firewood with a heavy ax as long as he was tall. Seeing Buddy, the boy stopped in mid-swing.

"Look sharp, Bodeen," he said loudly. "We got us some comp'ny."

Bodeen Pyle was bent over, shoving firewood under a four-hundred-gallon blackpot boiler. He straightened up quick as a nervous cat and turned around, a stick of firewood in his hand. When he saw Buddy, he relaxed and dropped the firewood. He nodded at the boy and old man, and they went on with their work.

"A little out of your usual territory, ain't you, Sheriff?" Bodeen said.

Buddy always wondered if Bodeen had a different daddy than his older and younger brothers, for while Randall and Beau were dark-haired, sultry, and slouchy, he was red-haired, blue-eyed, and freckled, with the straightforward, no-nonsense manner of a born businessman. He was wearing a dirty denim work shirt and jeans, and he had a red bandana tied around his head to keep the sweat out of his eyes. Bodeen had never been one to shirk hard work.

"Maybe so," Buddy allowed affably. "Still in my county, though." It was true. The entire swamp was in Cypress County, for whatever that was worth. If you asked the county commissioners, the swamp was more a liability than an asset. It didn't produce anything but some timber and a lot of mosquitoes.

"You got time to talk?" he added, as if this were a casual meeting in front of the courthouse or at the diner. "Don't mean to take you away from your work."

"Hang on a minute," Bodeen said, and reached for a wooden paddle fashioned out of a piece of beech. He climbed up on top of the boiler and took off a lid. "Fire's about to take hold. Have to give this here batch a good stir."

If you were making corn liquor or peach or plum or apple brandy for your family or your neighbors (and plenty of Darling folk did), you probably used what was called a "turnip pot" — a copper boiler about the size of a half-barrel, small enough that a man could carry it on his shoulder. All you needed was your turnip pot, forty or fifty pounds of fruit and twice that much sugar, plus a source of clear spring water. Once you had all that, you were cookin'. One or two runs and you'd have enough for the whole year.

But if you were in the business of making moonshine for money, you'd have a black-pot still — or several of them — that held up to eight hundred gallons of fermented mash apiece. Cobbled together from boards and sheets of metal, the blackpot boiler was set up above a fire pit on stacks of brick and filled with the makings of mash: corn-meal, usually, or a varying mix of corn, rye, and barley meal; sugar, yeast, and water. The quantities were daunting. For each big blackpot, you'd need a hundred pounds of grain meal, eight hundred pounds of sugar, some yeast, and enough water to top it off. You might also want to pour a couple of eighty-pound sacks of wheat bran on top of the mash to hold in the heat of fermenta-tion. Getting the supplies without getting caught required some skilled advance plan-ning.

Once it was all in the blackpot, the mash

was left to ferment, with an occasional stir. Then a fire was lit under it and the mash was boiled, releasing the alcohol in the form of steam. The steam was run through a coil of copper pipe (the worm) in a vat or box of cold water, cooling it into a liquid. At its most potent, what came out of the worm was 150 proof — 75 percent alcohol, with a knife-edged, explosive jolt. White lightning. White dog. Tiger spit. Hooch.

After the blackpot had been run once, more sugar could be added to the mash and the process begun again. Shiners could get as many as six or seven runs of tolerable liquor out of one pot of mash, although they might have to settle for less potency in the later runs. Buddy had heard it said that blackpot moonshine didn't have the fine taste of liquor produced in smaller quantities. But it was cheaper to make and most drinkers didn't care what it tasted like, as long as it had plenty of firepower. Corn whiskey was never aged, the way bourbon whiskey was, up in Kentucky and Tennessee. It was simply siphoned off into metal cans, packed into a fast car, and run down to Mobile or up to Montgomery.

Buddy sat down with his back to a nearby sweet gum tree, keeping an eye on the boy and the old man. Bodeen, whistling "Dixie,"

313

finished stirring, climbed down from the pot, and hunkered Indian-style beside him. He stopped whistling and reached into his shirt pocket for a crumpled pack of Camels and a matchbook.

"Heard you busted Pootie McKay," he said.

Buddy shrugged. "Just doin' my job."

"You ain't busted none of my haulers."

Buddy thought about that. "Haven't crossed my path yet, I reckon."

The boy had gone back to his splitting, and the silence was broken by the solid *thunk* of his ax. Bodeen swatted a mosquito on his neck.

"Tell the truth, I've been expecting you, Sheriff," he said. "I've been wondering why you ain't showed up out here sooner — to pick up where old Sheriff Burns left off. Pick up his cut, I mean."

Buddy was puzzled. "His . . . cut?"

"Sure." Bodeen rubbed his thumb and first finger together. "Moolah. Gravy." He pursed his lips. "I paid him ten dollars a week plus five dollars a load protection fee. Reckon that'll work for you?"

Protection fee? And then Buddy understood — and wondered why in the hell he'd been so oblivious for so long. No wonder Roy Burns had been live-and-let-live about

Bodeen's moonshine — and probably Mickey LeDoux's, too, before Mickey got busted. And maybe the small local shiners, as well. The sheriff had his hands in their pockets. Folks had been paying him to turn a blind eye.

For a moment, Buddy was surprised. And then he wasn't. He was just mad at himself for not cottoning to the racket sooner. Burns' nice house, his wife's cook and housekeeper, their vacation cottage, that big motor boat on Oyster Bay — all the signs had been there. He just hadn't been smart enough to put the picture together.

But being dumb in the past was no excuse for not being smart now.

"Give me a minute to think on this," he said.

Bodeen bent a match against the matchbook striker, lit it with a jab of his thumb, and held it to the tip of his cigarette. He narrowed his pale blue eyes, and when he spoke, his voice was colder.

"You figure on askin' for more?" He paused, frowning. "Bear in mind that I got other obligations, Sheriff. If I pay you more, word'll get out, and I'll have to come up with more for them. Then I'll have to add that to the price of the shine." He shook his head. "Drives up the cost for ever'body."

Buddy wanted to ask what those other obligations were, but now didn't seem like the right time. He turned this new and surprising situation over in his mind, trying to sort through all the ramifications. But it wasn't easy. Bootleg operations were one thing, an ongoing bribery racket was another. And there could be more he didn't know about.

Finally, hesitantly, he said, "I reckon what you gave Roy will be okay for me. I don't want to upset the applecart." He frowned. "For now, anyway. We can talk about it again later, after I've had a chance to see how things are going."

"Swell," Bodeen said. He reached for his wallet. "How about if we start right now?" He took out five tens and handed them over. "This is for the last two weeks plus the six loads that've gone out in that time. Which somehow didn't cross your path." With a grin, he added a twenty. "And this is for good faith, because we're pals. We got a deal, Sheriff?"

Buddy folded the bills into his shirt pocket and buttoned it shut. This thing was too damned complicated for him to dope out on the spot. He felt like he had just stumbled into a nest of angry rattlers, and every single one of them was buzzing around his

316

feet. The arrangement between Roy Burns and Bodeen Pyle might have been a small-time, short-term private transaction, one man to the other — or it might be something bigger.

Bigger than what? Buddy couldn't even begin to guess. And starting from where he was right now — a position of total and complete ignorance — it might take weeks to figure out.

And in the meantime, he knew one thing. He was between a rock and a hard place. It didn't feel good, and he didn't see any way out. But there was something that had to be said, right here and now, before Bodeen got any other ideas.

"Yeah, we've got a deal, Pyle. I'll overlook what goes on out here — for the moment, anyway. But that doesn't mean you get a free pass in town. Long as you do right, stay out of sight, and don't give me any heart-burn, we're pals. Give me or my deputy a bad time, and the deal's off." He gave the other man what he hoped was a steely glance. "You got that?"

Bodeen didn't look pleased, but he nod-ded. "Yeah. I got that. Anything else?"

"I need to know where you were last night."

"Last night?" Bodeen seemed surprised.

317

"I was over at Pete's Pool Parlor, playing pool. Most of the night, anyway." He flicked the ash from his cigarette. "How come you're askin'?"

"Who else was there?"

"Well, Pete, o'course. That little tattooed guy who works at the prison farm. Bragg, his name is. The warden's fair-haired boy." Bodeen blew out a stream of smoke. "A couple of officers from the CCC camp. Archie Mann — he's a regular. A few others, in and out. Pete could tell you, I reckon. There was a poker game in the back."

The warden's fair-haired boy? "How long were you there?"

Bodeen hesitated. "Went in around eight, I guess. Stayed until just before eleven."

"Then what?"

"Then I went over to the Exchange. My girl, Lila Jean, gets off work at eleven. I walked her home and we sat on her front porch swing."

Buddy refrained from inquiring what they were doing there. "How long?"

Bodeen gave him a crooked grin. "Until Miz Crisp — Lila Jean's mama — came out and ran me off. Half-past midnight, I guess, maybe a little later. Shame, too. Lila Jean and me was just gettin' warmed up." More cautious now, he slid a glance at Buddy.

"How come you're askin'?" he said again, more emphatically.

"So you weren't here last night?" Buddy said, watching him. "Or out on the Jericho Road?"

"Nope," Bodeen said promptly. "Pokey over there" — he jabbed a thumb in the direction of the old man — "Pokey was out here all night, minding the fires. Gotta keep the heat steady, you know. Can't let the fire go out, can't let the pots boil dry."

Buddy leaned back against the tree, remembering Wayne's report — and thinking of what Mrs. Whitworth had told him. "You said Bragg was there, from the prison farm. What time did he leave?"

Bodeen frowned. "I don't know. Pretty early, I reckon. He played one game and then quit." He took a drag on his cigarette. "I'd still like to know —"

"How come I'm asking," Buddy said evenly, "is because Whitney Whitworth went off the Jericho Road at the foot of Spook Hill last night. When he was found this morning, he was upside down under his Pierce-Arrow. Dead."

"Whitworth? Aw, hell." Bodeen's eyes widened and his jaw dropped. "You're kiddin'."

"Not," Buddy said. "You didn't know?"

319

"Naw. First I heard. I was over in Mon-roeville all morning, gettin' supplies." Bodeen pulled the red bandana off his head and threw it on the ground. "Bad news." He sucked on his cigarette. "Damned bad news," he muttered.

"Why?" Buddy asked. "What's Whitworth got to do with you?" When Bodeen didn't answer, he made his voice hard. And loud.

"What's Whitworth got to do with *you,* Pyle? Come on — let's have an answer."

Somewhere, a crow squawked. The boy stopped splitting wood, and the old man turned around to look. After a moment, Bodeen said, "Look, sheriff, you and me, we're partners now, so I've got no reason not to level with you. I got a business to run. I've got markets down in Mobile and up in Montgomery, asking — begging — for more. I need experienced haulers. I need cars." He made a sweeping gesture that included the entire clearing. "I need more boilers and condensers. I need more boys out here workin' for me. And I can't get any of that unless I got more *capital.* With-out capital, I'll always be just a damned two-bit backwoods operation. That's what Whit-worth was to me. The damn goose that laid the golden egg."

If that was true, it pretty much canceled

Bodeen out as a suspect, Buddy thought. He looked around the camp. "So how long had he been in on this?"

"He was one of my earliest investors," Bodeen said. "Came in with some cash three-four years ago. Last week, he told me he was ready to come in with more. I was counting on him." His voice was bleak. "Nobody else in this county has money that he's willing to invest in the bootleg business. With Whitworth gone, I'm back to where I was, operating on a shoestring."

"You didn't see Whitworth yesterday?" Buddy asked. "Did he have any reason to be coming out here?"

Bodeen shook his head. "Ain't seen him since the middle of last week. And no, he was only out here a time or two. He didn't like me visiting his house, neither. Didn't want his wife knowing what he was up to, I guess. So we met out by the old airfield to do our business." He pulled down his mouth, looking glum. "Hate to say it, Sheriff, but if you were thinkin' to make some extra money out of our partnership, you're gonna be disappointed. Would've been a whole lot more for you if Whitworth was still around."

Buddy couldn't argue with that. Anyway, he had the feeling that Bodeen had said all he was likely to say. He stood up. "I guess that does it for me, then. At least for now."

Bodeen got to his feet and stuck out his hand. "Let me know if there's anything else I can do for you, Sheriff. Always glad to help a partner out, when I can."

Partner. Buddy had a sour taste in his mouth, but he managed to dredge up a small smile as he shook Bodeen's hand.

He thought it was a good time to leave.

CHAPTER NINETEEN:
LIZZY TAKES PICTURES

The Exchange operator couldn't connect with long distance, and it was past three by the time Lizzy was able to reach Mr. Moseley in Montgomery. He listened to her report, expressed dismay at the news of Whitworth's death, and said, "Let me think about this for a few minutes, Liz — and make another call. You stay there at your desk. I'll get back to you as quick as I can."

When he did, he began with a request for the Exchange operator, in his most sugary voice (the one he used with difficult female witnesses). "Mabel, honey, I need to talk to Miss Lacy private-like, if you don't mind. I'd appreciate it if you'd get off the line now."

When they heard the audible *click,* he spoke briskly. "Liz, I've just spoken to Wayne Springer, over at the sheriff's office. He says they have evidence that another vehicle might have been involved in Whitworth's crash."

"Another vehicle?" Lizzy was surprised. "But what —"

"It's not clear, but Springer thinks there may have been a rear-end collision somewhere on that hill, and it could have sent Whitworth's car out of control and down the embankment. With that in mind, I need you to do something. I would do it myself, if I were there, but I won't be there until tomorrow. I want it done right away, before the sheriff thinks of doing it. Are you game?"

"Of course," Lizzy said. And then added, more cautiously, "I'll do what I can."

"Good. My Brownie camera is my right-hand desk drawer, along with an extra roll of Kodak film. I want you to get it."

Camera? Lizzy frowned. *Now what?*

But when Mr. Moseley had explained, she felt a little better. She looked down at her notes and said, "This thing that you want me to do — it sounds like we're assuming that Mrs. Whitworth is still our client. Is that right?"

"She's our client until she tells me otherwise — in writing," Mr. Moseley replied firmly. "She may be upset when you tell her what I've asked you to do, so make sure she understands that we're doing it to protect her interests. As her attorney, I need to know the extent of her culpability in this case — and she may not be willing to tell us everything."

"It sounds like you don't trust her," Lizzy hazarded.

"Every client has something to hide." His voice was flat. "I don't trust Regina Whitworth to tell us everything I need to know to defend her, if it comes to that."

Lizzy was startled. "Defend her against —"

"At worst, against a charge of vehicular homicide. There are no witnesses. We don't really know what happened on that hill."

"Oh, *dear,*" Lizzy whispered.

"Hang on," Mr. Moseley said. "I don't believe she's a suspect — yet. But Norris and Springer may get around to that, after they've had a while to think about it. I have to know everything there is to know, just in case." He added, more sharply. "You keep your lip buttoned, Liz, especially when it comes to that young sheriff. He's easy to talk to, and you may have to guard against being too chummy with him. Client privilege, remember."

"I will," Lizzy promised. She hesitated, wondering if she should tell him about DessaRae's note and the meeting with Fremon that Sally-Lou had arranged for that evening. But there wasn't anything to tell, not really. She would wait until after she'd heard what Fremon had to say — if anything.

"Good girl. You go on and do what I said, then call me and let me know what you find out." His voice softened, warmed. "I'll be home tomorrow. But in the meanwhile, it's awfully good to know I can count on you, Liz. You're always right there when I need you."

Pleased, Lizzy found herself smiling. "Thank you, Mr. Moseley. I appreciate that."

He cleared his throat. "But when I get home, we're going to have to talk about your hours." He sounded uncomfortable and unhappy. "I took another look at the office accounts this morning. We're owed a quite a bit of money by a lot of people, with no way to collect, given the economic situation. We obviously have a problem, and I'm afraid it's much worse than I thought."

Hearing the unhappiness in his voice, Lizzy felt suddenly cold. Was he trying to tell her that she would have to leave? She didn't have many bills, but she didn't have many savings, either. Nadine Fleming had made it clear that she couldn't count on royalties from her new book, which was likely to earn her almost nothing. Every job in Darling was already taken. Where could she find work? How would she manage without a regular salary coming in? Would she have to move somewhere else to find another job?

But she kept her apprehension out of her voice. "I understand," she said. "We'll work it out. Don't worry." She said goodbye, hung up the phone, and went into Mr. Moseley's office to get the camera.

She was trying not to think what her life would be like if she no longer worked for Benton Moseley.

The front door of the Whitworth house was already draped in black crepe, the usual symbol of mourning for the homes of the Darling bereaved. Lizzy knocked and DessaRae opened the door. She had changed her white apron for a black one, and her white maid's cap now bore a black ribbon.

"Why, Miz Lizzy," she said, surprised. "Wasn't expectin' to see you back again so soon."

"I'm here for Mr. Moseley," Lizzy said. "I need to speak to Mrs. Whitworth. Is she . . . is she seeing company?"

"No, but she'll see *you*," DessaRae said. She stepped back, holding the door open.

"She layin' down right now, but I'll tell her you're here." Discreetly, she dropped her voice. "You an' Fremon gone git together, like I said?"

"Tonight," Lizzy replied in a near-whisper. "Sally-Lou is bringing him over to my house after supper." She frowned. "Really, DessaRae, I do wish you'd tell me —"

"You jes' talk to him," DessaRae said. She raised her voice cheerfully. "You go on into the parlor. I'll fetch Miz Wentworth."

Lizzy sat down on the garnet loveseat in the darkened parlor, took the Brownie out of her handbag, and put it on the walnut coffee table. When she got it from Mr. Moseley's desk drawer, she saw that the film in the camera was completely exposed — she could tell by the red number in the camera's little window. So she had stepped into the closet and loaded the new film, hoping she was fitting it properly into the take-up spool. Brownies were easy to manage, but it sounded like these photos might be terribly important, and she didn't want to make a mistake.

She waited for ten minutes or so, listening to the canary singing cheerfully in the neighboring room. The faint fragrance of rose potpourri hung on the still air. In the corner of the room was a piano, with a piece of sheet music — "Stormy Weather" — open on the rack. Lizzy remembered that Mr. Wentworth had been one of the Lucky Four Clovers, and that she had heard them sing "Stormy Weather" just the week before. Who would replace him in the quartet, she wondered. It would be a challenge, especially with the barbershop competition coming up in just a few days.

Finally, Regina Whitworth came downstairs. She had changed into a black dress that emphasized her slimness, with long sleeves, a bit of lace at the cuffs, and a simple lace collar. It made her look fragile and vulnerable and young — too young to be a grieving widow. But beautiful, like a rose that has been crushed by an early frost. Her dark brown hair was still worn down to her shoulders and pulled forward. Presumably, Lizzy thought, to conceal the bruise, and she wondered again how it had happened.

Mrs. Whitworth sat in the upholstered club chair on the opposite side of the coffee table. DessaRae came in with a tea tray — a china pot, two cups, sugar and lemon — and went out again, careful not to glance at Lizzy.

Mrs. Whitworth poured tea and handed a cup across the table. "DessaRae says you have something important to talk to me about, Miss Lacy."

Lizzy added sugar to her tea and stirred. "I'm sorry to disturb you," she said sympathetically. "I know this is a difficult time, and you must have a lot on your mind. However, I've been in touch with Mr. Moseley, and he's asked me —"

But Mrs. Whitworth didn't let her go on. "There's not going to be a divorce," she interrupted, "so I've decided I don't really need a lawyer." She picked up her teacup and sipped. "I can ask Mr. Duffy, over at the bank, to help me go through my accounts, so I won't need Mr. Moseley for that, either." She put her cup down again. "He's been very kind. But please thank him for what he's done and ask him to send me a bill for his services."

Lizzy had been expecting this. "I'm afraid that's something *you'll* have to tell him," she said. "In writing. Until he receives that notice, he's still your attorney. And because that's the case, he feels duty-bound to look out for your welfare." She paused. "In fact, that's why I'm here, Mrs. Whitworth." She set her cup on the table. "He spoke with the deputy sheriff this afternoon. He asked me to tell you that it's likely that the sheriff will come here and ask to take a look at your car. The one you recently bought from Kilgore's," she added, just so there was no misunderstanding.

"*My* car?" Mrs. Whitworth stared at Lizzy. "But why in the world would the police want to look at my car?"

"Because the sheriff has reason to think that another vehicle might have been involved in your husband's accident," Lizzy said gently. "Perhaps even *caused* it." She gestured toward the camera on the coffee table. "Mr. Moseley has asked me to take a few photographs of your car. He feels that we should document the fact that it hasn't been involved in an accident. That there is no damage."

"No . . . damage?" Mrs. Whitworth's eyes widened and she shrank back into the cushions of her chair. "But I'm afraid there is . . . I mean, I . . . Well, to tell the truth . . ." Her voice trailed away.

Lizzy frowned. "Mrs. Whitworth, do we have a problem?"

There was a tense silence. "I hope not," the other woman said at last. She hesitated, then pulled her hair back, exposing the bruise and abrasion on her cheek. "Actually, I did have a bit of an automobile accident yesterday, I'm afraid." She spoke apologetically. "That's how I got this horrible scrape on my face." She rubbed her left sleeve. "And on my shoulder and arm, too, so I'm wearing long sleeves. I'm still a little sore."

Uh-oh, Lizzy thought. So *that* was the explanation behind the mysterious abrasion. Mr. Moseley would not be pleased to hear this. Aloud, she said, "What kind of accident, exactly?"

"Well, I . . . I'm not a very good driver, you see. I'm still learning. Frank says I was very lucky not to be hurt worse."

"Frank?" Lizzy asked blankly.

"Mr. Harwood." Coloring, Mrs. Whitworth hastily corrected herself. "Perhaps you've heard that Kilgore's has been offering free driving lessons with the purchase of a new car. I bought mine several weeks ago." She shifted uneasily in her chair. "Mr. Harwood is my driving instructor. He was in the car with me when the accident happened."

Lizzy stared at the woman, suddenly remembering the confession in her interview with Mr. Moseley — the one she had typed just that morning. Frank Harwood, who was as good-looking as Mrs. Whitworth was beautiful, was more than just her driving instructor. When pushed, she had admitted that she had fallen in love with him and was thinking of marrying him after she and Mr. Whitworth were divorced. No doubt that was why (as Ophelia had noticed) she hadn't wanted the sheriff to know about the divorce, and why she was so uncomfortable right now. But was there something else?

Lizzy took a breath and confronted the question straightforwardly. "Mrs. Whitworth, I hope you're not telling me that you were involved in your husband's accident — you and Mr. Harwood."

Mrs. Whitworth pressed her fingers to her lips and shook her head violently. "Oh, no! No, really, Miss Lacy! Please believe me — I don't know *anything* about that what happened to Whitney! But my car . . ." She swallowed. "What I'm trying to say is that . . . well, I'm afraid it's damaged. Yes, it certainly is, and I'm sorry. I mean, I didn't intend to . . . It was an accident, really. And it has nothing to do with Whitney, I swear!"

"I see," Lizzy said evenly. "Well, why don't you just tell me what happened."

"Yes. Yes, of course. Frank — Mr. Harwood, I mean . . . Last night, Mr. Harwood and I were out on the Monroeville Road, on that long, straight stretch just past the old sawmill."

"Last night?"

"Yes. I . . . I'm afraid I didn't quite tell

the truth, before. I didn't go right to bed after Whitney left. I went out with Mr. Harwood. I was practicing driving, and probably going just a teensy bit too fast." She smiled, then realized she was smiling and stopped. "But it felt so good, you know? Just *so* good. The top was down and the wind was blowing my hair. I felt freer and happier than I've felt since before . . . well, since before Grandmamma made me marry Whitney. When I was young and still had everything to look forward to." She glanced up at the portrait of her autocratic grandmother, staring down her patrician nose. "Sorry," she muttered. "Forget I said that, please. I shouldn't have."

Lizzy was remembering that Regina Whitworth had been just a teenager when she married the much older Whitney Whitworth. It was understandable that she would like to recapture some of her earlier freedoms. The car, *her* car, may have represented that. But what was this business about her grandmother making her marry Mr. Whitworth? She was tempted to ask, but Mrs. Whitworth was hurrying on with her story.

"Anyway, it was dark, and I was maybe going a little too fast. A deer ran across the road and instead of trying to stop, I swerved to miss it. I fell against the door — it's one of those silly things that have the hinges on the rear. It flew open, and I tumbled out onto the road. That's how I got this scrape on my face." Mrs. Whitworth gingerly touched her cheek. "And on my left shoulder and arm. The sweater I was wearing was completely shredded."

"Oh, dear," Lizzy said. "Mr. Harwood is right. You *were* lucky." That is, if she was telling the truth. Lizzy wanted to believe her, but Mr. Moseley's doubt was still fresh in her mind.

Mrs. Whitworth nodded. "If Frank — Mr. Harwood — hadn't been so quick, the car would have been wrecked and *he* might have been killed. He managed to get it stopped, but not before it sideswiped a tree and the door — it was still open — was ripped off its hinges. I hope the sheriff doesn't look at it and decide that I had anything to do with Whitney's accident." She paused, biting her lip. "But if they don't believe me, Mr. Harwood can tell them what happened. He was with me."

Lizzy started to reply and then stopped. If the matter came to court, Mr. Mosely would be reluctant to call Frank Harwood as a witness, since his relationship to Mrs. Whitworth would likely come out and his credibility would be questioned. But Mr. Moseley should be the one to share that with their client — *after* he had talked to Harwood.

She leaned forward and picked up the Brownie. "I think I'd better have a look," she said. "And Mr. Moseley asked me to get some pictures of the car. I hope you won't mind," she added.

Mrs. Whitworth stood, clearly unenthusiastic. "If you want to take pictures, I'd better back it into the driveway where there's more light. I'll get the key."

Lizzy helped Mrs. Whitworth push the garage doors open, revealing her convertible, a sleek, beautiful pumpkin-colored Dodge, parked inside. As far as Lizzy could tell from where she was standing, the car was undamaged — except for the door on the driver's side. It was completely missing. The door itself, which appeared to have a few scratches, was propped against the garage wall.

"Frank — Mr. Harwood — says it won't cost much to put the door back on," Mrs. Whitworth said. "I was going to ask him to get that done today, but then Whitney turned up missing and . . ." She sighed heavily. "Well, fixing the door somehow didn't seem important. But now that Grandmamma's Pierce-Arrow is wrecked, I suppose I'll have to get it replaced so I can drive this car. Wait here and I'll back it out."

It was obvious from the cautious way Mrs. Whitworth handled the car that she was still a novice driver and a little nervous about backing up. She got out, giving the car a rueful glance.

"The poor thing looks odd, without that door," she said. "I really don't know why they make doors like that. They're dangerous."

Camera in hand, Lizzy agreed. "Mr. Moseley says that those rear-swinging doors are called 'suicide doors.' If the inside handle is accidentally flipped, the door can be ripped open by the wind and the passenger, or the driver —"

"Tumbles out," Mrs. Whitworth said.

"Exactly," Lizzy said. At the front of the car, she bent over to examine the bumper and grill, as Mr. Moseley had asked. But as far as she could tell, the chrome-plated trim was brand-new. It wasn't scratched. It wasn't even muddy. And the sheriff would have to notice that there was no mud elsewhere on the car — as there surely would have been, if it had been driven on the Jericho Road after the recent rains.

Lizzy aimed the Brownie at the bumper

and grill and took several photographs, watching the numbers in the camera's little window and being careful to advance the film each time. Then she took a picture of each front fender and, for good measure, the missing door — eight altogether.

"Well, that's that," she said, when she had finished the roll. "Thank you for letting me do this. I'm sure Mr. Moseley will be relieved to know that you weren't terribly injured when you fell out of the car." *And that he won't likely have to defend you in court,* she thought.

Mrs. Whitworth looked penitent. "Please thank him for me, Miss Lacy. And I would appreciate it if you didn't mention that I thought of letting him go. It feels very good to know he's looking out for me. And you've been helpful, too." She frowned apprehensively. "You don't *really* think the sheriff is going to . . ." Her voice trailed off.

"I think you should be prepared for that," Lizzy said. She made her voice sound confident. "But as far as I can see, there's nothing here that would suggest that your car was involved in your husband's accident." She thought of something she had heard Mr. Moseley say on occasion and went on. "Still, it would be a good idea if you didn't see or talk to Mr. Harwood until after the sheriff has finished his investigation. That might just complicate things."

Mrs. Whitworth's face fell, and Lizzy suspected that she had been planning to see him that night — or at least talk to him on the phone.

"Do you really feel that's necessary?" Mrs. Whitworth asked plaintively.

"I'm afraid I do." Reassuringly, Lizzy added, "But just as a precaution — and only until the sheriff figures out what really happened last night. I don't think you have anything terribly serious to worry about."

"I hope not," Mrs. Whitworth said fervently, wrapping her arms around herself. "It's bad enough to have to deal with my husband's death. Being accused of causing it would be just too much!"

Lizzy liked Mrs. Whitworth and found herself hoping so, too. When she called Mr. Moseley to report what she had seen and heard, that's what she told him.

"I don't believe she'll have a problem with the sheriff," she said. She wondered whether she should tell him about the odd remark about her grandmother making her marry Mr. Whitworth. But maybe it wasn't so odd, after all. The Vautiers had been an old, traditional family, and Regina's grandmother was the matriarch. Perhaps she had realized that she was nearing the end of her life and felt she needed to find a husband for her young granddaughter.

"Unless, of course," Mr. Moseley put in cautiously, "there's something she's not telling us." His voice darkened. "And this business with Frank Harwood bothers me, Liz. I'll be back in town about eleven tomorrow. I'll drop in at the Dodge dealership and have a little talk with Harwood. I want to hear his side of the story."

Lizzy felt relieved. She'd been half-afraid Mr. Moseley was going to send her to interview Frank Harwood, and her evening was already spoken for. Fremon and Sally-Lou were coming over.

CHAPTER TWENTY: LIZ HAS VISITORS

Daffodil — Lizzy's orange tabby cat — was waiting on the porch swing when she walked up the four front steps to her butter-yellow house. He jumped down and followed her as she unlocked her front door (recently painted a playful green) and went inside, feeling the quiet pleasure that always settled over her as she stepped into the front hall. She took off her sweater and hung it on one of the brass-plated hooks where she kept her straw garden hat and her raincoat and umbrella.

Daffy rubbed her ankles, purring, and she bent over to pet him, then let him lead her into the kitchen. There, as he did every day, he supervised her preparation of his supper. Daffy was especially fond of a bit of mashed cooked chicken livers served with his tuna fish. Lizzy always asked Mrs. Hancock to save her some when fresh chickens arrived at the grocery. At five cents a pound, livers were cheaper than tuna, which had recently gone from eight to ten cents for a small can.

While Daffy was enjoying his feast, Lizzy hurried upstairs to change into comfortable slacks and her favorite green plaid blouse, then went out to the chicken coop to gather the day's eggs. There were eight jumbo-sized brown eggs in the nests, contributed by her mixed flock of Rhode Island Reds, Barred Rocks, and a white Leghorn. She paused to stroke Caruso, her mild-mannered Buff Orpington rooster, who joined the other neighborhood roosters in a daily dawn chorus. On Lizzy's block, it was impossible to sleep past sunrise.

Heading back to the house, she stopped in the kitchen garden to pick a large ripe tomato and the last green bell pepper, grown from seed Bessie Bloodworth had given her. In the kitchen, she sliced the tomato and pepper and whipped up an omelet with two of the fresh eggs, along with a bit of leftover ham and some onions. She added several soda crackers and a helping of cottage cheese to her plate, poured a glass of cold apple cider, and sat down to her supper, feeling extraordinarily lucky and *rich*.

She wasn't rich, of course. Nobody was rich these days, with the Depression howling at the door like a hungry wolf, and she was increasingly anxious about the situation in Mr. Moseley's office. But if she set aside the fear of getting her hours cut back, she had everything she needed to keep her comfortable and content. She had friends, especially the Dahlias, and her pretty house and garden and chickens, and her *real* work, her writing. Even if she had to find another job, she would be content — wouldn't she? And being content was better than being rich.

But there was Grady, and the unresolved question brought her a tiny nibble of something like . . . was it guilt? Yes, she was enjoying her life and was contented with what she had. But was it selfish to be focused so entirely on herself, on what *she* wanted to do with her time — with her days and nights, with her life?

Her mother thought so, and seized every opportunity to remind her that it was a woman's job to create a comfortable home, please a husband, and take care of the children. Grady thought so, too. He had never made any secret of his opinion. She certainly understood his point of view and could even sympathize, especially now that he had to think about little Grady, about making a life — and finding a mother — for his motherless son. A man couldn't raise a child by himself. Well, she supposed that it might be *possible,* but she had never known one who had tried.

She got up and carried her supper dishes to the sink, frowning. Why was it so hard to imagine herself as Mrs. Grady Alexander? She had loved Grady once — not passionately, perhaps, but warmly. She was sure it would be easy to love him again. Her heart had been touched by his pain and his need and by his desire to pull her back into his life. She knew she could count on him to love enough for the both of them.

There was something else, too, something that hadn't occurred to her until just that moment. Mr. Moseley spent more and more time in Montgomery these days. Was he keeping her on at the office just to give her a job? Perhaps he would be glad if she announced that she was planning to quit and get married. Grady had a good, secure job that paid enough to support a family, especially if they lived in his house and found somebody to rent hers. And surely she could find a couple of hours in the day — perhaps when little Grady was napping — when she could sit down at her typewriter. When she thought of the possibility of losing her job, the idea of marrying

Grady seemed more attractive, although the thought of somebody else living in her beautiful little house was an unpleasant taste in her mouth.

She rinsed off her supper dishes, left them on the sink to dry, and went back down the hall. On her right, polished wooden stairs led up to the two small bedrooms with steeply slanted ceilings and gable windows. In the front bedroom: her bureau and dressing table and a single bed covered with a home-crafted pink-and-yellow quilt and yellow ruffled pillows, with a window overlooking the shady front yard and the oak-lined street. In the back bedroom: a worktable, a chair, a bookcase, her typewriter, and a window overlooking the back yard and garden. Under the window were shelves that held her quilting fabrics and tools and baskets of knitting yarn.

She hesitated, thinking that she might go upstairs and put in an hour's work on the manuscript before Sally-Lou and Fremon arrived. But she didn't like to get started when she couldn't devote several hours to the task, so she went into the parlor to make sure it was ready for company. Like the two rooms upstairs, it was small, with just enough space for a Mission-style leather sofa, the old armchair she had reupholstered in brown corduroy, a Tiffany-style lamp with a stained-glass lampshade, and bookshelves on both sides of the small brick fireplace.

She turned on the lamp, plumped the cushions, and brushed a bit of Daffy's orange fur off the armchair, where he liked to lie and keep an eye on her as she knitted or read the newspaper. A copy of the weekend's *Mobile Press Register* was lying on the floor, with the headline "Woman Kidnap Victim Feared Dead!" staring up at her. This one was a wealthy young socialite from Louisville, Kentucky. Her family had already paid $50,000, and the victim had not yet been returned.

Lizzy picked up the newspaper and was folding it when she heard the front doorbell ring, just once, briefly and authoritatively. Startled, she glanced at the banjo clock on the fireplace mantle. It was much too early for Sally-Lou and Fremon — and they were coming to the back door. It wouldn't be Grady, either: he'd had a funny *shave-and-a-haircut-two-bits* knock that always set the two of them laughing — unless he'd decided that things had changed and the knock was no longer appropriate. Or it might be her mother, coming across the street, loaded with a barrage of complaints about Mr. Dunlap's encounter with Deputy Springer.

Guiltily remembering their phone conversation that afternoon — sometimes she really *wasn't* a very good daughter — Lizzy stuck the newspaper under her arm and hurried to the door.

But it wasn't her mother. It wasn't Grady, either.

On the other side of the screen door stood a man in a slim-fitting gray three-piece business suit, a crisply pressed white shirt, a steel-blue tie the color of his eyes, and a gray fedora with a rakish tilt. He was tall, well over six feet, and well built, and he held himself with the easy confidence of an athlete. He wasn't handsome; his features — a hard mouth, high cheekbones, pale eyes — were too rugged for that. Behind him, parked on the street, was a racy-looking blue roadster with the top folded down.

"Miss Lacy?" He took off his hat. Sun-bleached hair fell across his tanned forehead. His voice was firm and clipped, a business-like Yankee voice. "Elizabeth Lacy?"

"Yes," Lizzy said hesitantly. Her first panicky thought was to slam the door and lock it, but reason quickly prevailed. A kidnapper wouldn't be driving a roadster with the top down — and while he looked strong enough to make off with her under one arm, she doubted that kidnappers went around in a dapper-looking suit and tie. Anyway, it was still daylight, and old Mr. Perkins was sitting on his porch on the other side of the street, watching.

But just out of caution, she waved and smiled at Mr. Perkins, letting the man know they were being watched. "I'm sorry," she said, directing her attention back to the man. "Who did you say . . . ?"

He held up his wallet and displayed an identification card. "My name is Ryan Nichols. I'm with the WPA — the Works Progress Administration — in Washington, D.C." He quirked an eyebrow. "You've read about us in the newspapers?"

Lizzy leaned forward and looked at the card. There was his photograph, his name, and the rest of it. "Yes, of course I've read about the WPA," she said.

The Works Progress Administration was an ambitious companion to the popular Civilian Conservation Corps, which had constructed and was managing the CCC camp a few miles outside of town. The WPA employed workers to build public roads and highways, construct dams and airfields, and erect public buildings all over the country. Established by President Roosevelt and run by FDR's right-hand-man, Harry Hopkins, the WPA was the government's answer to the hated "dole." People didn't want relief, they wanted to work. They wanted to earn their money, rather than take a government handout. The WPA was already helping nearly two million unemployed men find work that would enable them and their families survive these lean years.

"I know about the WPA," she repeated. "But I don't know what the WPA wants with me. I have a job." *At least, I have a job right now,* she thought, *although that could change at any moment.* She added dryly, "And I'm a woman."

"Ouch." There was that quirky eyebrow again, and a quick, disarming grin that eased the lines of his craggy face. Lizzy thought suddenly that he looked as if he'd be more at home in a flannel shirt, blue jeans, and work boots than in that three-piece suit.

Nichols folded his wallet and put it back in his pocket. "You've got a point, Miss Lacy, unfortunately. So far, the WPA's projects have been mostly heavy construction — buildings, roads, airfields, docks. We employ mostly men. But that's about to change. The WPA is in the process of creating a new federal project that will support writers, editors, historians, teachers, and librarians — many of them, maybe *most* of them women. They'll be compiling and writing tourist guides for every one of the forty-eight states, collecting local history and folklore, doing social research, that sort of thing. They're going to need program directors and administrators to manage their assignments — those people will likely be women, too."

"Well, that's good news," Lizzy said decidedly. "There are plenty of women who need work. But I don't understand why —"

"The project hasn't been funded yet," Nichols went on. "But when it's up and running early next year, it will be part of a group of New Deal arts programs known as Federal Project Number One. I'll be in charge of the Southern Region, based in Montgomery." He tilted his head, regarding her. "You've been recommended to me, and I'd like to tell you more about the project. May I come in?"

"*I* was recommended to you?" Lizzy was astonished. "But I don't know anybody in Washington. Who in the world —"

"You know people in New York. In fact, I think it's fair to say that they're big fans of yours."

Lizzy shook her head. "I don't . . ." She paused. "I think you must be mistaken, Mr.

Nichols. The only people I know in New York are my agent and my editor, and I've never met them, except through the mail."

"But they know *you.*" Nichols grinned. "It happens that I was in the city last week, and both Nadine Fleming — your agent — and your editor, Max Perkins, spoke to me about you. They told me that you have a book coming out with Scribner's in a few months. Historical fiction, Max Perkins said, about the Civil War. Both he and Miss Fleming seemed to think that you know quite a lot about this area and the people here. And that you're the kind of person who could help us with this important project."

Lizzy's apprehensions eased somewhat, even though the man was still very large and almost — but not quite — physically intimidating. But she couldn't turn away a friend of Miss Fleming and Mr. Perkins, even if he was a Yankee.

She opened the screen door. "Well, I suppose you should come in, then, Mr. Nichols." She added, "I'm expecting someone in a little while, but perhaps you'd like a cup of coffee."

"I would," Nichols said, stepping inside. "I had a swell supper of meatloaf and mashed potatoes and gravy at the diner —

good down-home food. Another cup of coffee would hit the spot. And I promise not to take up too much of your time."

Ryan Nichols looked no smaller sitting down. For the next twenty minutes, he occupied a good half of Lizzy's small parlor sofa. Over coffee and a plate of Chocolate Crunch cookies, he talked with energy and excitement about Project One. When it was in full operation, he said, it would eventually employ some six thousand workers — three-quarters of them women — across the United States. Field workers, most of whom would have done white-collar work, would be drawn from the local unemployment lists. They would be trained and managed by an editorial staff, people (again, mostly women) with experience in writing and management. For the editorial staff, there would likely be some regional travel, overseeing fieldworkers and attending meetings with other managers.

Nichols leaned forward, gesturing, his face animated, its lines eased. "Our biggest goal, of course, is to put people to work — get them a job, put money in their pockets, give them a future to hope for. But we're also expected to produce useful projects that will help local communities and states. Not buildings or roads, but a better understanding of their local landscape, a clearer sense of local history."

"Mr. Nichols," Lizzy said carefully, "here in Darling, we are *steeped* in history. Sometimes I think we are drowning in it. This is the South, you know. The Confederate South."

"Yes, of course it is. And that's why it's important." He set his coffee cup down and reached for another cookie. "Once the project is up and running, we'll be collecting oral histories from citizens who haven't yet told their stories — older citizens, especially, who remember what life was like in the old days, before our modern times. People whose parents and grandparents settled an area. Immigrants from foreign countries. Colored citizens, too, some of whom may have slave stories to tell."

Slave stories? *Uh-oh,* Lizzie thought wryly. *This Yankee doesn't know what he's getting into.* But she only said, "Well, there are plenty of those stories around here."

"We're also hearing from the folklorists," he added. "Some of them are interested in documenting local folklore." He popped the rest of the cookie into his mouth. "Say, this is *good.*"

"That one happens to be a Yankee recipe," Lizzy said with amusement. "But we have plenty of wonderful Southern cooks here. Maybe the government would be interested in compiling a book of Alabama recipes."

He regarded her with mock sternness. "Don't laugh, Miss Lacy. That might just happen. Food and drink can tell the history of an area, can't it? I'm sure the food here in Darling is part of Darling's story."

Suppressing a chuckle, Lizzy thought of the secret ingredient in Aunt Hetty's pecan pie and wondered what Mr. Nichols would say if she told him about it. But he was going on.

"Federal One will also include projects on music, theater, and art and handicrafts. Just last week, I met Harriet Clinton, who directs our WPA program in Milwaukee. She's planning a work project that will employ women to make and sell toys, dolls, furniture. They're even setting up a weaving studio to make rugs. She says it's a way to preserve traditional crafts while creating jobs for people — for women, mostly." He grinned. "You can bet that Mrs. Roosevelt is interested in that one. In fact, she's behind the whole thing."

There was a current of excitement in Ryan Nichols' voice, and Lizzy found herself studying him closely. He was a Yankee, which certainly made him different from the other men she knew. He was also very good-looking, with an easy manner that was at once friendly, engaging, and confident. And he was clearly enthusiastic about what the federal government was doing: creating jobs for people who needed them, jobs that would put money in their pockets and raise their sense of self-worth. What's more, he obviously believed that this was the right thing for the government to be doing in the current desperate situation.

There were people who didn't like the idea of the government making work for people, but Lizzy wasn't one of them. Over the last year, she had seen how Darling had been helped by the CCC camp. The boys from Camp Briarwood spent their pocket money in Darling stores, and people in Darling who worked at the camp or sold their farm produce to the camp spent *their* money in town, too. Darling was more prosperous and Darling folk were beginning to feel better. She wanted to believe that the federal arts programs would have a similar impact.

"As I said, we don't have the funding right now," Nichols went on. "But we're asking for five billion dollars, with the money to come as soon as we get congressional approval. FDR is a man in a hurry, as you probably know. He's told us that he wants

355

us to be ready to hit the ground running as soon as the money is available. I'm starting now. I'm lining up people who might be available to work as program administrators, full or part-time." He gave her a serious look. "I know it's too soon to ask for a commitment, Miss Lacy. And I understand that you're currently employed. But people's situations change, especially these days. And if the position is out of the question for you, perhaps you can recommend someone — someone local — who might be available."

And then, suddenly, it all came together for Lizzy. She had been fortunate so far, but times were hard right now, and she couldn't count on keeping her full-time job with Mr. Moseley. Perhaps she wouldn't even have a part-time job. And while she might very well decide that she loved Grady, it would be wrong to marry him just because she had lost her job and he still had his. Really, she ought to be ashamed of herself for even thinking of it! This proposal from Mr. Nichols — it was like a bolt out of the blue, and a very lucky bolt, at that. It might be exactly what she needed, at exactly the right time.

She leaned back in her chair and spoke as evenly as she could. "To tell the truth, Mr. Nichols, things are a little rough in the office right now. I work for a lawyer here in town, and the people who need him can't afford to pay him. He's been talking about reducing my hours. If things don't improve, I'm afraid he might have to let me go altogether."

The words were a hard slice at her heart. But hearing them, she felt suddenly, surprisingly relieved. Spoken out loud, in that even, factual tone of voice, they didn't seem nearly as menacing as they had when they were screaming in the dark corners of her mind.

"I'm sorry," Mr. Nichols said gravely. "Unfortunately, I've been hearing that all too often. And I've felt the pinch myself. It's hard to make plans when you can't see past the end of the week." He gave her a crooked smile. "But if you're facing a layoff — or worse — maybe I came along at the right time."

She managed a half-smile in return. "Maybe so. Anyway, please do put my name on your list, and when you're ready to get started, let me know. If I can help, I will." She gave him the office number and her home number too, and added ruefully, "If you can't reach me at the law office, it probably means I don't work there any longer, or that my hours have been reduced. I'll be here at home, working on my book."

Mr. Nichols wrote down her numbers on a card. "Thanks," he said. "I'm grateful to Miss Fleming for giving me your name. And to you for giving me your time tonight — and coffee and cookies, too. Even a Yankee cookie." There was that grin again. "You'll be hearing from me as soon as I have news."

He slipped the card into his suit jacket pocket, then paused and took something out. "Hey, I almost forgot. When I got out of the car out in front of your house, I happened to look down and noticed this. It was growing in your yard, so it belongs to you. But since I'm the one who found it, maybe it means good luck for both of us."

He was holding out a four-leaf clover.

When Mr. Nichols had gone, Lizzy took their coffee cups to the kitchen, where she refilled the plate of cookies. She had just set the plate on the kitchen table when there was a soft knock at the kitchen door. It was Sally-Lou, with Fremon behind her. Sally-Lou was wearing a dark cotton skirt and blouse and a dark brown sweater, clutched around her against the October night chill. Fremon was dressed in bib overalls and a blue cotton work shirt, and a striped denim railroad cap.

"Hi, Sally-Lou," Lizzy said, smiling. "Gosh, Fremon, it's good to see you again."

Fremon looked down at her. When they were kids, she'd been the tall one. He was taller than she by a full head now, and broad-shouldered rather than skinny. But he still had that quick, shy grin. "Same here, Miz Lizzy. You still go fishin' down at Spook Creek?"

"No, but I remember when we used to do that, on hot summer days." Lizzy matched his grin. "You still have Myrtle the turtle?"

He shook his head. "Nope. Took her out to the swamp and turned her loose so's she could find some friends. But my kids got a goat name of Gen'ral Grant. They go fishin' at Spook Creek ever' chance they get."

Lizzy laughed. "I guess kids don't change much, do they? Shall we take our coffee and go into the parlor?" She gestured toward the plate of cookies. "We have something to munch on, too."

Sally-Lou frowned. "We ain't stayin' long, you know. This ain't exactly a parlor call." She pointed to the table. "Y'all can sit right here and have your talk. I'll go out on the po'ch."

"Spoken like a big sister," Lizzy said.

"Yeah," Fremon said, sounding disgruntled. "Sally-Lou, she jes' can't stop orderin' people around. Come here, go there, git those chores done." He pulled out a chair and sat down. "But this here's good enough for me. And if I know Sally-Lou, she'll put her ear to the do' if she goes out on the po'ch. Far as I'm concerned, she can sit right here and listen." He gave his sister a pointed look. "Long as she don't talk too much or try to act like she smarter 'n' us." He turned the look on Lizzy. "And long as somebody tells me how come I'm here."

Sally-Lou sat down, too, and Lizzy poured coffee. "Sally-Lou didn't tell you?"

"Uh-*uh,*" Fremon said, shaking his head. "She just told me I gotta come see you."

Lizzy reached into the pocket of her slacks and took out DessaRae's penciled note. *Tell Sally-Lou you need to talk to Fremon right away. Tell him I told you to ask him what he saw last night. And don't take no for an answer.*

She handed the wrinkled paper to Fremon. "I was at the Whitworth house this morning, and DessaRae slipped me this note. Do you know what it means?"

Fremon read it silently, pushing his lips in and out. "Don't take no for an answer, huh?" He scowled. "Means you all are fixin' to get me in trouble."

Sally-Lou frowned. "You got to tell what

you seen, Fremon," she said firmly. "If you didn't do nothin' wrong, you won't get in trouble."

"Oh, yeah?" Fremon was caustic. "Lots you know about it, Sister."

Lizzy pushed the plate of cookies across the table. "Does it have something to do with Mr. Whitworth's accident?"

Fremon took a cookie. "Less said, the better," he muttered.

"Uh-uh, Fremon." Sally-Lou narrowed her eyes. "What you know, you gotta tell. So get to it."

Fremon looked at his sister as if he were measuring her authority. Finally, reluctantly, he gave in. "Well, for starters, wa'n't no accident. Doobie and me, we was there. We seen it."

"Doobie?" Lizzy asked. "Who's he?"

"A no-count scallywag is what he is," Sally-Lou muttered, taking a cookie.

Fremon frowned at his sister. To Lizzy, he said, "Doobie Jenkins. We go fishing together, some Sundays. He works some for Mrs. Forenberry, tidying up her garden. He had to run an errand over to the Whitworths' house this mo'ning. We'd agreed we wasn't goin' to tell, but I reckon he could've said something to DessaRae. She got a nose about as long as a rake-handle." He sounded disgruntled. "Doobie, he likes to brag on hisself. Shoulda known I couldn't trust him to keep his goldurned trap shut."

Sally-Lou scowled. "Fremon, I want you to stop talkin' 'bout Doobie. Tell what *you* saw. Straight out, right now. And we don't need none of your cursin'. You hear?"

Fremon put both hands flat on the table, and for a moment, Lizzy thought he was going to get up and march out. But Sally-Lou had practically raised her younger brother, and her old command over him was too strong. He sighed, sat back in his chair, and gave in. With an obvious reluctance, he began his story.

He and Doobie Jenkins had spent Sunday afternoon and evening fishing underneath the railroad bridge over Spook Creek. The fish were biting — each of them had a hefty string of catfish and stripers — and they hated to leave. But it would be dark soon and they were on foot, so they thought they'd better head back to town. They were halfway up Spook Hill when they saw Mr. Whitworth's Pierce-Arrow, coming over the top.

"He was comin' right smart," Fremon said, "and the road is kinda narrow right there." So he and Doobie jumped the ditch on the uphill side and climbed a little way into some trees. They were waiting to let him pass when they saw another car — a black Ford — coming down the hill behind him, fast. The Pierce-Arrow was halfway down the hill when the other car rammed it in the rear.

"*Pow!*" Fremon said, smacking his right fist into the flat of his left palm. "Just like that. And then *pow!* Damned fool revved his engine and did it again." He slid a glance at Sally-Lou, who was narrowing her eyes at him. "Sorry," he muttered.

"Wait." Startled, Lizzy held up her hand. "You say the Ford hit Mr. Whitworth's car *twice*? On purpose?"

"On purpose?" Sally-Lou echoed. "Lordy me!"

"Yes, on purpose." Fremon's face was grim. "That hill was muddy, and once could've been an accident. Not twice. Made two big, loud clangs, like a freight car couplin'. Doobie and me, we 'bout jumped out of our skins."

"And then what?" Lizzy asked.

"And then that old Pierce-Arrow, it sailed down the hill like a big bird and flipped off the road at the bottom." Fremon illustrated a somersault with his hands. "And then went flyin' down that big steep bank."

"And the car that hit him? The Ford?

What did the driver do?" Lizzy asked excitedly. "Did he stop? Did he get out?"

"Nope." Fremon shook his head. "He speeded up and jes' kept on going down the road. Didn't get out, didn't even stop. Jes' kept on drivin' like nothin' had happened."

"He left the scene," Lizzy murmured. Even if it couldn't be proved that he deliberately caused the accident, it was a crime to drive away. One of Mr. Moseley's clients had gotten into some pretty serious trouble doing just that.

"Lord sakes, Fremon," Sally-Lou said, leaning forward. "So that bad man jes' up and drove off? What did you and Doobie do?"

"Us? Why, we dropped our fish and our poles and we run fast as our legs'ud carry us down the hill to see if we could do anything for poor old Mr. Whitworth. But the good Lord done took him — or the devil, one." Fremon's eyes went to Sally-Lou, as if he was expecting her to correct him. When she didn't, he went on. "I'm here to tell you there was no way on God's little green earth that me and Doobie could've got that car back on its wheels, the two of us. And even if we could've, there was nothin' at all we could do for that man. He was squashed flat as a bug under that car.

He was *dead.*"

Sally-Lou regarded her brother fixedly. "So *then* what did you do?"

Fremon looked away, unwilling to meet her eyes. "Me an' Doobie?" he said innocently. "Why, we picked up our poles and our fish and we hot-footed it back on home, fast as we could."

Lizzy frowned. "You didn't call the sheriff?" No, of course he didn't. That's why nobody knew what had happened until well into the next morning, when the wreck was discovered.

"Don't got no phone," Fremon muttered.

Sally-Lou's voice oozed sarcasm. "You two grown-up men couldn't *find* a phone? Or walk across the courthouse lawn to the sheriff's office and tell him face to face what you seen?"

"I guess maybe we could've." Fremon twisted his mouth. "But you gotta take the whole situation into account, Sally-Lou. Doobie's been arrested twice, see. He's scared of the law. And we . . ." He ducked his head. "Well, we had us a bottle of shine down there under the bridge, and —"

"So you was *drunk.*" Sally-Lou's tone was withering.

"Not very," Fremon protested. "Not by that time, anyway." He turned to Lizzy, his

365

hands out. "Miz Liz, I swear, I was sober enough to see what happened. And so was Doobie. We jes' wa'n't sober enough to tell it to the sheriff. At least, that's how Doobie saw it. He made me promise."

"Sure he did," Sally-Lou growled. "And then he done went and told it hisself, to DessaRae. So you can forget that promise."

Doggedly, Fremon shook his head. "Sis, I give Doobie my word that I —"

"Fremon," Lizzy said, "you witnessed a crime. Not an accident, a *crime.* If the person who did it isn't caught and punished, he could do it again. A man is dead. It's your duty to help Sheriff Norris get to the bottom of if." She could see the dogged expression on Fremon's face, but she took a breath and plunged ahead. "The car that hit Mr. Whitworth's car — did you recognize it?"

Fremon hesitated. His eyes were half shut and he was pushing his lips in and out. He wasn't looking at Sally-Lou, but that didn't stop her.

"If you know that car, Fremon," she said grimly, "you gotta tell. You got no choice."

Fremon laced his fingers around his coffee cup.

"You hear me, little brother?" Sally-Lou raised her voice, and Lizzy recognized the tone. She had heard it often enough herself when she was a girl. Sally-Lou wasn't a big person, but she had a big voice and a way of making you do the right thing, whether you wanted to do it or not.

Fremon pulled at his bottom lip. "It was the warden's car from the prison farm," he muttered. "The one that's got the state seal painted on the side."

Sally-Lou let out her breath with a loud *whoosh.* "The *prison* farm car?"

Lizzy felt completely confused. Why would anybody at the prison farm want to kill Mr. Whitworth? But maybe . . . "Could you see who was driving?" she asked. "Maybe the car was stolen." But that still didn't explain what happened.

Fremon made a face. "Yeah, we could see. And no, it wasn't stolen. It was Jimmie Bragg behind the wheel. He drives that car all the time. Works for the warden as an assistant or something. Doobie and I know him from Pete's. He hangs out playin' pool there."

Lizzie stared at him, beginning to understand just how serious this was for Fremon and Doobie. Jimmie Bragg was known around town as a troublemaker. Not very long ago, Archie Mann had asked Mr. Moseley to call Warden Burford to report that Bragg had started a fight that had resulted in some damage to merchandise in the back room at Mann's Mercantile. Even though the warden had made Bragg settle with Mann, he'd denied having any part in it — just as he was likely to deny this far more serious accusation. If he were indicted and the case went to court, Fremon and Doobie would be called as witnesses for the prosecution. And colored men as witnesses — colored men who had been *drinking* — well, it wasn't hard to predict the outcome. It was no wonder that Fremon and Doobie had decided they didn't want to get involved.

Sally-Lou was obviously thinking the same thing. "You're *sure* it was deliberate, Fremon?" she asked hopefully. "It wasn't accidental, like? Maybe a little game that got out of hand?"

Fremon gave his sister a long look. "What you want me to say, Sally-Lou?" he asked thinly. "Jimmie Bragg — he hit that car *twice*. Then he drove off without stoppin' to see what he'd done or how bad Mr. Whitworth was hurt. Even if it was some kinda game, it was wrong." He hunched his shoulders. "And now I'm the one who's in trouble. Me and Doobie both."

Lizzy understood how he felt and the

jeopardy he was in. But she also knew what she had to do. "Mr. Moseley will be back in town tomorrow, Fremon. I'm sure he'll be able to help. But in the meantime, we need to call Sheriff Norris." She stood. "I'll do that right now. I'll ask him if he'll come over here and talk to you, instead of you going to the office."

"No!" Fremon cried, his voice anguished. He started to get up from his chair. "No, please!"

"Yes," Sally-Lou said, clamping her hand on Fremon's arm and forcing him to sit back down. "You call the sheriff, Miss Lizzy. Me and Fremon will wait right here."

CHAPTER TWENTY-ONE:
THE SHERIFF GETS HIS MAN
— AND THEN HE DOESN'T

The day had been a long one and it wasn't over yet.

But the half hour Sheriff Buddy Norris had spent with Fremon Hawkins in Liz Lacy's kitchen had given him the information he needed (as well as several very good cookies and a fine cup of coffee), and he felt better and wiser than he had all day. Now he knew who had caused Whitworth's wreck and how. And he had the word of an eyewitness, and perhaps two, if Doobie Jenkins agreed to testify to what he had seen.

There were still some things Buddy didn't know, though. He could not for the life of him figure out how Liz Lacy had managed to persuade Fremon Hawkins to speak up — especially since Hawkins had nothing to gain and plenty to lose by helping the police. Most colored folks weren't willing to come forward and say what they'd seen for fear of being called as a witness and, afterward, threatened (or worse) by friends of the accused. Buddy didn't blame them for being afraid. If he was colored, he'd be scared too. But however Miss Lacy had managed to pull it off, Buddy was grateful to her for convincing Hawkins to tell what he had seen. His reluctant story (which certainly had the ring of truth) explained what had happened on Spook Hill.

But even when Buddy put Hawkins' story together with what he had learned from Mrs. Whitworth and Bodeen Pyle, the *why* of it still eluded him. He could see several possible explanations branching out in several different directions, but if they made sense at some point, it was beyond his immediate understanding. When it came to motive, he was baffled. And when he left Liz Lacy's house, his relief at knowing *who* was darkened by the twin shadows of *why* and *what next*. Buddy was not in the mood for doing what came next. It was the part of the job he liked least.

Thinking about that without enthusiasm, he drove back to the sheriff's office and went inside. He found Wayne, who was a serious reader, deep in the pages of an old issue of *Popular Science,* with Zane Grey's *Sunset Pass* at his elbow. Buddy hadn't read the Western but he and Bettina had gone to see the movie, which starred Randolph Scott and Tom Keene, when it came to the Palace. Tonight, he wished he was as good with a gun as Randolph Scott.

"Get your weapon, Wayne," he said with resignation. "We're going out to the prison farm on this Whitworth business, and I don't know what kind of situation we'll walk into."

"Oh, yeah?" The deputy shot him a surprised look, and then glanced up at the clock. It was nearly nine.

"Yeah. And bring the cuffs. We'll likely need them."

Wayne closed his magazine. "So I guess you figured out who dunnit."

"Tell you on the way," Buddy said tersely.

But before they went out to the prison farm, they had to stop at Jed Snow's house. Jed was a justice of the peace and could give them the warrant that would allow them to examine the car Fremon Hawkins claimed to have seen — and seize it, if they wanted to. Under ordinary circumstances, Buddy might not have bothered with the warrant. But in this case, they were dealing with the warden of the prison farm, who might not take kindly to yielding up a state car.

Buddy didn't ask Jed for an arrest warrant, though. He wanted to hear what Bragg had to say for himself first, and get a sense of whether he was telling the truth. If he figured he had probable cause after that — well, he could arrest him then.

The Jericho State Prison Farm had been where it was since Buddy was a boy, its main buildings clustered in a compound behind an intimidating seven-foot fence that was topped with barbed wire. Its nearly fifteen hundred acres of open pastures and farm fields spread out far beyond, to the Alabama River on the west and Briar Swamp on the south, both significant barriers, in case a prisoner took it in his head to try to escape. Most preferred a bed, meals, and a roof to gators and copperheads.

Like other prison farms across the country, Jericho was designed to be self-supporting. That is, the three hundred or so inmates were supposed to produce enough food — vegetables, meat, milk, eggs — to feed themselves and their keepers. They also baked their own bread, cooked their own meals, operated their own laundry, produced their own clothing, built their own buildings, and repaired and maintained their own vehicles. They even ran their own sawmill. The only thing they didn't make,

Buddy thought with some irony, was their own booze. That, they were buying from Bodeen Pyle.

But prison farms weren't judged on their self-sufficiency alone. They were expected to turn a profit, the bigger the better, and Jericho had long had the reputation of being the most profitable in the entire Alabama system. Lumber, corn, sorghum, cotton, cattle, pigs, and even chickens were substantial cash crops, and the profit they earned was returned to the state (minus the bonus paid to the warden for productivity and efficiency). The inmates, too, were a source of profit, for they were hired out as farm workers and lumberjacks and on road gangs. Warden Burford, who had been in charge of Jericho for over a decade, regularly won the state award for operating the most profitable prison in the entire state. Every November, he went up to Montgomery to collect his trophy at the big banquet, and Charlie Dickens always ran his picture on the *Dispatch* front page.

It was full dark by the time Buddy and Wayne drove up to the compound gate, a short distance off the Jericho Road. To the south, ominous flickers of lightning lit the sagging belly of a thundercloud, and an erratic breeze stirred the grass and trees along the road. Buddy hoped they could get their business done and get their suspect back to town before the storm hit.

Late as it was, he worried that they might have some trouble getting into the prison compound, since the front gate was usually locked at dark. But to his surprise, there was a uniformed guard in the kiosk, and when he saw the sheriff's star on the side of the Ford, he hurried to open the gate. Buddy recognized the guard, a heavy-set guy named Leonard, whom he remembered as a skinny, pock-marked senior who was the star forward on the Darling high school basketball team when Buddy was a freshman. Now, he looked like he'd keel over if he had to run more than twenty paces.

The guard lumbered up to the car and Buddy rolled down the window. "Wasn't expecting you so quick, Sheriff," Leonard said. "How in the hell did you *do* it?"

"Do what?" Buddy asked.

"Why, get here so fast. Couldn't have been more than twelve-fifteen minutes ago that the warden called your office." Leonard shook his head admiringly. "Reckon you've more under that hood than old Henry Ford put there." He grinned. "Take me for a ride sometime, huh? Show me what that car can do."

"Ah," Buddy said, understanding. But he'd just as soon nobody knew what he'd put under the hood. If he had to go after somebody fast, he wanted it to be a surprise. He said, "We were probably better than halfway out here when the warden put in that call." He paused. The prison farm usually took care of its problems on its own. He couldn't remember a time when the warden had telephoned the sheriff's office. "What was Burford calling about?"

"Dunno," Leonard said. "All I heard was that somebody got shot. Anyway, he'll tell you about it. I reckon you better go on over there."

Wayne leaned forward. "Over where?" he asked.

Leonard stepped back, pointing. "Try the warden's office first. If he ain't there, somebody can tell you where he is. Fifty yards down this road, second building on your right." He added, "Don't park in the warden's space. Good way to get your tail kicked."

"Thanks," Buddy said, and shifted into gear.

The prison offices were in the middle building in a row of wood-frame single-story buildings on one side of a neatly mowed grassy quadrangle. Other buildings, all painted the same drab green with brown trim, housed the mess hall and kitchen, a hospital and dispensary, and prisoners' barracks segregated by race, with additional separate barracks for white and black trusties. On the opposite side of the quad were sheds for shops, equipment repair, and maintenance. Floodlights cast a pale light over the grassy space and along the perimeter fence.

Buddy pulled up and parked on the gravel apron in front of the office building, careful to avoid the space designated as the warden's with a wooden sign. Most of the windows were dark, but there was a bare bulb over the main door and lights on in a couple of the windows nearest the door.

"What's the plan?" Wayne asked.

Buddy had been puzzling over that, but he still hadn't come up with anything. "Don't have one, exactly," he said. "I figure we'll just tell the warden what we've got on Bragg and that we're fixin' to impound the car he was driving last night and take him into town for questioning. I reckon we'll also have to deal with whatever it was he called us about." Which Buddy still didn't understand. The prison farm had its own justice system. What was important enough to call out the sheriff after nine on a weekday night?

"What if he won't give Bragg up?" Wayne asked. "Or refuses to let us have that car?"

Buddy didn't like either question very much, especially when he remembered what Bodeen had said about Bragg being the warden's fair-haired boy.

He sighed. "Well, the warden's a law enforcement officer, just like you and me. What goes on out here is his business and he can handle it pretty much any way he sees fit. But what happened on Spook Hill is in *our* jurisdiction, and a man was killed — a citizen of Darling. Bragg may be a state employee, but that doesn't exempt him from being questioned. Or from being arrested and charged, if we figure we've got cause. Or from being indicted and tried and convicted." Which was true, although it didn't exactly answer Wayne's question.

"I get that." Wayne's voice was hard and flat. "But this isn't friendly territory, you know. There are folks out here who don't have a lot of good feeling toward the law."

"I know," Buddy said, and sighed again. He opened the car door. "Let's go."

The building's front door opened into a small lobby and then intersected with a hall — recently painted a particularly bilious color of green — that ran the length of the building. Under the smell of fresh paint and turpentine, Buddy caught the smell of mold and damp wood. As close to the river and the swamp as these buildings were, it was a challenge to keep them from rotting, he reckoned.

A sign on the wall announced the Warden's Office, with an arrow pointing to the right. Leading the way, Buddy went down the hall in that direction. His revolver felt heavy and uncomfortable on his hip, and he was more than usually aware of the badge on his shirt. Wayne was right. They were in hostile territory, where not even the guards could be counted on for help, if they needed it. He was glad for his deputy, a couple of steps behind him. But it was moments like this when he wished he'd been smart enough to look for some other line of work.

The door to the warden's outer office was open and two uniformed guards and a couple of trusties were standing around, talking. They turned when Buddy and Wayne came in, and one of the guards — an overweight, balding man with a scar across his chin — came forward. His badge identified him as Lamar Puckett.

"Hey, Sheriff, kinda surprised to see you," he said, thrusting a fat hand forward. "That girl just called back and said she couldn't find you. How'd you get the word?"

Buddy shook his hand. "What girl?" He nodded toward Wayne. "This is Deputy Springer."

"Good to meet you, Springer." The guard shook the deputy's hand. "You know, the girl who runs the Exchange," he said, turning back to Buddy. "The pretty one. Violet. When nobody answered at your office, she said she'd try to track you down and get a message to you. Where'd she locate you?"

"She didn't," Buddy said, not bothering to explain. "Where's the warden?"

"At the hospital," Puckett said. "With the body. Come on. He told me to take you over there when you showed up."

"The body?" Wayne asked curiously. "You got somebody dead?"

"Yeah." Puckett showed a toothy grin. "You know how it goes. The boys get mad, get in fights, cut each other up. Or sometimes they kill themselves, one way or another. Tell you the truth, I was kinda surprised that the warden called you about it. But I guess since he wasn't a prisoner —" He broke off, making a motion with his head. "Come on. Let's get on over there before it rains."

Wayne gave Buddy an eyebrows-up glance, but Buddy shook his head. They'd go along with whatever was happening until it played out, and then they'd tell the warden that they were looking for Bragg.

It wasn't raining yet, but the lightning was flickering with greater intensity, thunder was rumbling to the south, and the wind had picked up. The prison hospital was forty yards away, a narrow building with a door at either end and bars over the windows. Inside, the hallway was dimly lit by a couple of bulbs hanging from the ceiling. Ten yards down the hall, Warden Burford was standing in front of a closed door, talking to a uniformed guard. A large black dog with muscular shoulders, restrained by a leash and a heavy choker chain collar, stood at his knee.

The warden turned when he saw Buddy and Wayne and stepped forward. The dog growled low in its throat.

"Sheriff Norris," he exclaimed, his round face beaming. "So the girl at the Exchange was able to locate you. Good of you to come all the way out here so late. Thank you." Buddy started to explain but the warden didn't give him a chance. "I thought you'd prefer to see for yourself what's happened, since it involves that tragic business with Mr. Whitworth. I can't tell you how shocked I am about this whole affair. To think that one of our men —"

He broke off. The dog was pushing forward, ears laid back, growling louder and baring its teeth. "Stop it, Jingo," he said sharply. "Behave yourself." To Buddy, he added, in a conciliatory tone, "He doesn't bite unless he feels threatened."

Buddy didn't like the sound of that, since he didn't know what Jingo might consider threatening. But he only said, "I'm not sure I understand, Warden. What exactly are we talking about here?"

The warden's face momentarily darkened. "I thought you got the word, but perhaps not. We're talking about Bragg. Jimmie Bragg." He turned to Wayne. "You met him this morning, Deputy. The man who was with me at the site of the wreck. My assistant."

"Ah," Buddy said, relieved that he was finally hearing something he could pin down. "Jimmie Bragg. Actually, he's the reason we're here, Warden. We need to talk —"

"Good, then," the warden said briskly. "You *did* get the word. Well, you'll find him in there." He nodded toward the door. "You two just go on in. Take all the time you need for whatever you have to do — don't feel you've got to hurry."

"That's fine," Buddy said. "But I was thinking that you and I need to talk first, and get a few things straight. We —"

"Thanks again for coming." The warden opened the door to the room and stood back. "I'm going to my residence. Sergeant Richards here will answer your questions." He gestured to the guard leaning against the wall, hands in his pockets. "Richards knows as much as I do about this unfortunate situation. He'll also take you out and show you the damage to the car." He stepped back. "And now, if you'll excuse me, I'll be on my way." He tugged on the leash. "Let's go, Jingo."

The dog cast a baleful look over his shoulder, gave one last growl, and followed the warden. If asked, Buddy would have said that *he* was the one who felt threatened, but nobody asked, so he kept it to himself.

"Guess we'd better get to it, Wayne," he said. "I want to hear his story."

He stepped through the door the warden had opened, Wayne on his heels. But they weren't going to hear Bragg's story, at least not from Bragg.

Stretched out on the porcelain-topped table in the center of the room was a man's body, fully clothed. The front of his blue work shirt was soaked with blood, and there

383

was a single bullet hole in his left shirt pocket. An old Colt single-action six-shot revolver lay on the table between his feet.

"Jimmie Bragg," Wayne said, under his breath.

"Blast and damnation," Buddy said fervently.

They stood staring for a moment, then Buddy stepped forward and unbuttoned Bragg's shirt. The man's skin was cold to the touch, and the blood was dried. Buddy raised one arm, feeling the resistance. He'd been dead several hours, Buddy guessed. To Wayne, he said, "Get Richards."

The sergeant was a swarthy man, barrel-chested, with dark hair and a bushy black moustache. The story, as he told it, was a simple one. He'd been on his way back to the cabin where he stayed weeknights. He took a shortcut around the automotive maintenance barn and stumbled over Bragg's body. The man was dead, obviously of a self-inflicted gunshot. The gun, a revolver, lay on the ground beside him. Richards had found a typewritten note in his pants pocket. He handed it over. It read:

To whom it may concern, I caused the accident that killed Mr. Whitworth. I was driving behind him last night and I got to going a little too fast on the downhill and hit his car in the rear. It was an accident and I thought maybe I could get away without anybody knowing it, but my conscience won't let me off the hook. Tell the widow I'm sorry. I'm really not that bad of a guy, just a little careless is all.

The note was signed with a rough scrawl: "J. Bragg."

There was a long silence. "So," Buddy said finally, "Nobody saw him shoot himself?"

The sergeant shook his head. "Nobody we could find. Happened just like I said. He was dead when I stumbled over him. I went and got the warden and we brought him here. The trusty who works as a medic — we don't have a reg'lar doc out here — pronounced him dead."

"I suppose you picked up the gun," Buddy said, thinking about fingerprints.

"Well, I wasn't going to just let it lay out there on the ground, was I?" the sergeant said stiffly. "Warden said you could take it if you want."

"I will, then," Buddy said, although if the warden was giving them the gun, it wasn't likely to be of much use. He added, "Does Bragg have family around here? Where's he from?"

"Warden said his mother lives in Monroeville," the sergeant replied. "Reckon we'll send him over there."

Buddy looked back down at the body. "Tell the warden we'll take that little job off his hands. I'll call Noonan to come out here and pick him up tonight." He fielded Wayne's quizzical look with a short nod. "That way, his mother won't have cause to complain that it's not all done proper. I'll need her name. Address, if you've got it."

"Whatever you say, Sheriff," Richards said. "The warden will prob'ly be glad he don't have to fool with it."

Wayne cleared his throat. "Burford said you'd show us the damage to the car."

"Sure, I can take you out to the car, if you're done here." Richards nodded at the note in Buddy's hand. "Warden said to tell you to keep that, too. Kinda wraps everything up for you, don't it?"

"I reckon it does." Regretfully, Buddy glanced down at the note, then took one last look at Jimmie Bragg, who wasn't ever going to tell *his* side of the story — if it was different from the story in the note, that is, and from Sergeant Richards' story.

He sighed. "I reckon we're done here. Let's go get a look at that car."

Back at the sheriff's office an hour or so later, Buddy watched while Wayne chopped an onion and cooked it with some other stuff in a skillet, then stirred in four sliced hot dogs and a can of beans. He got a couple of bottles of Jax beer out of the icebox, and the two of them sat down to a late supper. On the table in front of them: their plates, the beer, the note, the rusty old Colt, and the Beast, who watched with attention as they dug into their food.

"This thing doesn't seem right to me," Wayne said around a mouthful of beans. "I was out there this morning when we hauled that Pierce-Arrow up the hill, and Bragg was as chipper as a kid at a baseball game. If his conscience was giving him trouble, he sure didn't show any sign of it."

Buddy forked up a big bite of beans and hot dog chunks. "I'm with you. This whole thing smells fishy to me. That's why I wanted Noonan to — *Whoa!*" He spit his mouthful of beans back onto his plate and grabbed for the Jax.

"Too hot for you?" Wayne asked. He fished around in his bowl and held up a limp strip of something red. "It's this, I reckon. I got to liking chili peppers when I was out in Texas, and I put 'em in just about everything. The hotter they are, the better I like 'em. I got these from those garden club ladies. They're growing 'em in that garden at the corner of Camellia and Rosemont. Fish 'em out if you don't like 'em."

Buddy had never in his life tasted anything with the firepower of those peppers. He cooled off his burning tongue with another swallow or two of beer, then forked out all the hot pieces he could find and dropped them onto a saucer. Other than that, he thought, the beans were just fine — certainly better than the cheese and baloney sandwich he would have had on his own.

When he'd finished eating, he pushed back his bowl and said, "I'm feeling like we've gone about as far as we can go with this Whitworth thing, Wayne. We've got an eyewitness who identifies the car and the driver and says it was a deliberate hit, twice. We've got the car — the warden's car — with a dented front bumper and cream-colored paint flecks on one fender. Plus, we've got a dead body and a suicide note." He paused. "Am I leaving anything out?"

"Nope." Wayne took out his cigarette makings. "Neat little package, I'd say. Want me to wrap it up that way on the report?"

Buddy thought for a minute. "Before you do that, why don't you see if you can pull any fingerprints off the gun and the note. If there's anything recognizable, I want you to go to the funeral parlor in the morning and get Bragg's prints, then go back out to the prison farm and get prints from Richards, Burford, and anybody else who might have handled either the gun or the note. You'll want mine, too. I had my hands on both."

"Sounds right," Wayne said, filling his cigarette paper with tobacco. "We might also ask Doc Roberts to dig out that bullet before we send Bragg's body to his mother."

Buddy drained his Jax. "You're thinking that maybe —"

"I don't know what I'm thinking," Wayne said flatly. "Let's just get it and see what we've got."

Buddy nodded. "I'll finish it myself. I'll use what you have and add whatever we learn tomorrow. We can call the case closed — for now, anyway."

"For now?"

"For now." Buddy turned his empty beer bottle in his hands. "We know how Whitworth died and who was involved, but we don't know why. *Why* did Bragg ram that car? Ram it twice, according to Hawkins. And what was Whitworth doing out there on the Jericho Road on a Sunday night, anyway? Bodeen Pyle swears he wasn't on his way out to the moonshine camp. Was it just bad luck — wrong place, wrong time?"

Wayne rolled his cigarette between his thumbs and middle fingers. "And that business out at the prison farm was a little too pat for me," he said. "My gut tells me something is going on out there. I'd like to know what."

Buddy looked at the clock on the wall. It was after ten. "Well, it's too late to bother Mrs. Whitworth tonight. I'll go over to her house in the morning and let her know what we've found out so far. You talk to Doc Roberts and get those prints, and we'll see where we are. You okay with that?"

"Yeah," Wayne said. He finished rolling and licked the paper to seal it. "There are a couple of rounds in that Colt. I'll test-fire it. Maybe we can check it against the slug Doc Roberts digs out. See if it matches." He lit his cigarette.

Buddy stared at him. He had never heard of such a thing. "You can *do* that?"

"Dunno whether I can or not." Wayne reached up to the shelf over the table and took down the copy of *Popular Science* he'd been reading at lunch. "Some people can." He flipped to a page headed "Who Did the

Shooting?" and pushed the magazine toward Buddy. "In fact, the guy who wrote this article — Calvin Goddard — claims *he* can. He says every gun leaves a fingerprint on a bullet. Some people don't believe him, but it kinda intrigues me, you know?"

Buddy looked down at the magazine. The caption declared *New Scientific Methods "Fingerprint" Bullets and Firearms.* "Do we have the right equipment?" he asked.

"No, but I've got a microscope," Wayne said. "That'll get us started. If we find anything interesting, maybe we can get some help from Goddard. He's running a crime lab up in Chicago." He pulled a fleck of loose tobacco off his lower lip. "Something to consider, anyway."

Buddy gave him an approving glance, once more congratulating himself for having the sense to hire Wayne Springer. Personally, he doubted that matching a bullet could be done, but if it was the kind of thing they were doing in big-city police departments, he was willing.

"Sure," he said. "Give it a try, Wayne. Can't hurt, you know."

"Thanks." Wayne looked at the saucer of chili peppers bits that Buddy had fished out of his beans. "If you're not going to eat these, can I have them?"

Buddy pushed the saucer toward him. "Oh, you bet. What are you going to do with them? Put them in your eggs in the morning?"

"Nah." Wayne shook his head. "The Beast likes peppers. Gobbles 'em up like they're candy or something." He put the saucer on the floor. "It's all yours, Beastly, my friend."

Buddy, watched, disbelieving, as the cat cleaned up the saucer — with no smoke coming out of his ears.

Chapter Twenty-Two:
The Dahlias and the
Lucky Four Clovers

Friday, October 26, 1934

"Is this our table?" Ophelia asked, looking around the large dining hall at the Academy.

People were lining up in the hall for the pie supper that followed the Dixie Regional Barbershop Competition, and the Dahlias were hurrying to set up their table, one of several arranged around the room. The ticket table was beside the door, with Miss Rogers seated behind the cash box. Pie was fifteen cents a slice and coffee was a nickel a cup. And yes, people could buy as many tickets as they pleased — until the pie ran out. The proceeds from tonight's event would go to the Darling Blessing Box.

"This is it," Lizzy replied, smoothing the white tablecloth she had brought. "Aunt Hetty is bringing some chrysanthemums and asters for a centerpiece. We have thirteen pies coming, already sliced into eight

393

pieces and ready to serve. Fannie Champaign is still in New York, but all our other members contributed." She set her green tomato pie on the table, with a small white card that included the name of the pie and her own name.

"Well, I'm sure the Clovers appreciated the turnout," Ophelia said. "It looked like a full house tonight — every seat was taken. I'm so glad they won!"

For they *had* won! The Lucky Four Clovers had charmed the panel of judges, as well as the entire audience. At the end of the evening, they were named the top men's barbershop quartet in the entire Dixie region.

Ophelia was looking around the table, where several pies were already in place. "Liz, where do you want me to put this buttermilk pie? Anywhere special?"

"You could put it there, Opie," Liz suggested, "between Alice Ann's sweet potato pie and Miss Rogers' vinegar pie. Be sure your card is with it."

"Wasn't that a wonderful evening?" Bessie Bloodworth said, hurrying up with her pineapple pumpkin pie. She set it down next to Liz's green tomato pie. "Our Clovers did us proud, didn't they?"

"Oh, they did!" Aunt Hetty Little exclaimed, putting a vase of flowers on the table, along with her pecan pie. "And it's a marvel, too, considering how *unlucky* they've been in the past couple of weeks."

Liz glanced at Aunt Hetty's card. "You didn't mention that you added your secret ingredient?" she asked with a chuckle.

Aunt Hetty twinkled at her. "No, dear. But I'll be right here, if anybody wants to ask. And after all that time in the oven, nobody's going to get tipsy, no matter how many pieces they eat. The only thing left of Cousin Rondell's brandy is the flavor."

"I'll say they've been unlucky!" It was Earlynne Biddle, with her cherry pie. "Can you imagine — losing Mr. Ewing *and* Mr. Whitworth, both, in one weekend? Why, that's fifty percent of the whole quartet! Replacing them both took a miracle, if you ask me."

"Half of the miracle was my Hank," Beulah Trivette said proudly, and a murmur of agreement went through the group around the table. Hank Trivette had replaced Mr. Ewing, after Dr. Roberts had told him that the pimples in his throat would never heal if he continued to sing. Hank had stepped right in and sang lead just as if he had done it forever. He had even acted as the group's master of ceremonies, as well. He wasn't as funny as Mr. Ewing, but he was good in his own way.

"Hank did a wonderful job, Beulah," Mildred Kilgore said. She moved Earlynne's cherry pie to make room for her lemon icebox pie, and a few graham cracker crumbs fell onto the tablecloth. "You would never in the world guess that he was new."

"The other half of the miracle was Deputy Springer," Lucy Murphy said, holding up her contribution. "Peach pie, Liz, with the peaches we canned last June from Bessie's tree. Where does it go?"

"Right there," Lizzy said, pointing. She added, "Deputy Springer was a wonderful surprise, don't you think?"

Verna Tidwell nodded enthusiastically. "Amazing, really. Nobody had a clue that he had such a fine voice. Everybody's talking about him — and about everything that's happened."

Verna was right. Darling was still buzzing over the remarkable events that had occurred in the past two weeks. Mr. Whitworth (a very *unlucky* Clover, some said) had been killed in that freak automobile accident on Spook Hill, when he was hit from behind by Mr. Bragg, who worked for Warden Burford at the prison farm. And then poor Mr. Bragg had been so overwhelmed by anguish for what he had done that he had *shot* himself!

Everybody said this was a double tragedy and of course simply heartbreaking for both men's families. Darling had talked of nothing else for a whole week, and the whole town had turned out for Mr. Whitworth's funeral. Mr. Noonan did a stellar job with the service, which was just beautiful, and Mrs. Whitworth was deluged with condolence cards — so many, DessaRae said, that she had to get a bushel basket out of the garage to keep them in.

Unfortunately, the only people in Darling who knew Mr. Bragg were the ones who had run into him at Pete's Pool Parlor. But Darling folk were always generous with their sympathies, extending them even to neighboring towns. They had nodded approvingly when they heard that Warden Burford had sent an enormous spray of calla lilies to Mr. Bragg's funeral in Monroeville, and had written a letter expressing his sorrow to the *Monroe Journal.*

But Darling's grief at this double loss had turned to pleased surprise when it was learned that the new deputy, Wayne Springer, would be taking Mr. Whitworth's place among the Clovers. It was said that the suggestion was made to the other members of the quartet by Sheriff Norris, who had heard his new deputy singing "Old Man River" and thought he had quite a remarkable bass voice. The three Clovers had auditioned him and approved his selection on the spot, then got down to business practicing for the Dixie Regional.

"I hope I'm not being disloyal to poor, unlucky Mr. Whitworth," Verna went on, "but I honestly believe that Deputy Springer — and Hank, too, of course — has given the Clovers a new lease on life." She set down the shoofly pie she had made. "This is Bettina's recipe," she added.

"Speaking of Mr. Whitworth," Ophelia said in a low voice to Lizzy, "I saw the new Widow Whitworth out driving with Frank Harwood last night. You don't suppose . . ."

"Ophelia," Lizzy said in a warning tone.

"I know," Ophelia sighed. "None of my business. Still —"

"Ladies, I have wonderful news!" Myra May Mosswell hurried up with a pie in each hand. "I've just been talking to Mrs. Whitworth. She has inherited her husband's share of the Exchange — and she says she's willing to put in the money to help us buy a new switchboard. Our telephone problems will be solved! Isn't that swell?"

"That is terrific!" Lizzy exclaimed, and

pointed. "Your banana cream pie goes here, and your mom's lemon meringue over there."

Myra May put the pies where Liz directed. "She says she's also going to help Mr. Dunlap get a new heater for the Five and Dime, so we won't all freeze to death in the winter, while we're shopping."

Lizzy nodded. She had already heard that news from her mother, who was delirious with joy over this development. And from Mr. Moseley, she had learned that Mr. Whitworth had moved some of his wife's inheritance to a bank in Mobile, so not all of her money had disappeared. She had a generous spirit and seemed eager to help out the two businesses in Darling in which her husband had invested — but *not,* she said, Bodeen Pyle's bootlegging business. Mr. Pyle would have to get along without her money.

At the same time he told her this, Mr. Moseley had also shared something rather unsettling about the death of Jimmie Bragg. "The sheriff seems to believe that there's reason to believe that Bragg didn't kill himself."

"Didn't kill — oh, my goodness!" Lizzy had gasped. "But that means . . ."

"Yes," Mr. Moseley said. "But don't say

anything about it, Liz. Buddy is keeping the case open — quietly — and he and Deputy Springer are taking a closer look at some of the physical evidence. I suspect there may be some further developments."

But that disturbing news had been balanced by something a little more comforting. Lizzy and Mr. Moseley had gone through the office accounts together, and he had decided that it wouldn't be necessary to cut her hours.

"At least not for the rest of this year," Mr. Moseley had said. "To tell the truth, I don't know how I'd get along without you, Liz. You're an essential part of this office. I want you to know that."

"Thank you," Lizzy had said gratefully. She was very glad to hear this, although after her talk with Mr. Nichols (the man from the WPA), she had received a very nice note from him, letting her know that her name was at the top of his list of people he would contact as soon as Federal Project One was funded. She would prefer to stay with Mr. Moseley, of course. But it felt good to have an alternative, if she needed it.

"That's wonderful news — about the Exchange, I mean," Ophelia said excitedly. "Say, do you think I could do a story on that for the *Dispatch*? People will be so glad to hear that they can stop worrying about their telephone service. I could interview Mrs. Whitworth, too."

"Sure," Myra May said. "That would be great, Opie." She grinned. "I really think things are looking up for Darling, don't you?"

"Hey, Liz!"

Lizzy turned at the sound of a familiar voice. It was Grady Alexander, holding up two tickets.

"I've been waiting all day for a piece of that green tomato pie," he said warmly. "How about choosing one for yourself and eating it with me?"

Lizzy looked around doubtfully. "I'm supposed to be responsible for this table," she said. "I don't think I should —"

"Oh, for pity's sake, Liz," Bessie said firmly. "Of course you should. There are plenty of Dahlias here to take care of things." She put a piece of Lizzy's pie on a plate and handed it to Grady.

Lizzy couldn't help feeling a little cornered. But Bessie was so insistent and Grady looked so happy that she smiled and pretended to deliberate over the pies. "I think I'll have that one," she said finally, pointing to Myra May's banana cream pie.

"Coming right up," Bessie said, sliding a

piece onto a china plate. She handed it to Lizzy but her smile was for both of them. "You two young people go and have a good time. You hear?"

"Yes, ma'am," Grady said emphatically, and slid his arm around Lizzy's waist. "We will do that. We will *certainly* do that."

Lizzy had to admit that his arm felt right, somehow, and to her surprise, she found herself leaning against him. Then, a little later, the Four Lucky Clovers came in for *their* pieces of pie and sang a final encore for their Darling friends and supporters.

And as Grady smiled and reached for her hand under the table, Liz couldn't help wondering whether fate or luck or fortune or perhaps even destiny was holding out another opportunity for her — another chance to choose.

I'm looking over a four-leaf clover
I overlooked before.
One leaf is sunshine, the second is rain,
Third is the roses that grow in the lane.

No need explaining
The one remaining is somebody I adore.
I'm looking over a four-leaf clover
That I overlooked before.

THE DAHLIAS' PIE
SUPPER RECIPES

If there were no other reason to live in the
South,
Southern cooking would be enough.
Michael Andrew Grissom
Southern by the Grace of God

The old-fashioned pie supper is a favorite Southern tradition. In communities where money was fairly easy to come by, each pie would be auctioned off to the highest bidder in an entertaining competition. But in many communities, it was common to sell the pies by the slice, since almost everybody could afford at least one slice.

It's easy to find recipes for apple, cherry, and peach pie. Recipes for heritage pies are a little harder to locate. Here are five of the Dahlias' favorites.

AUNT HETTY LITTLE'S PECAN PIE

The first recipe for what we know as pecan pie was published in *Harper's Bazaar,* February 6, 1886, with the comment that it could be "a real state pie." There was no clue to the state, but Alabama would have been glad to claim it. Early pecan pies were made with sorghum molasses, cane syrup, or molasses, purchased out of a barrel at the general store. The pie gained national popularity in the 1920s, when the manufacturer of Karo corn syrup (which had been around since 1902) began printing the recipe on Karo cans. There is an old Southern saying that a pie should be "sweet enough to make the fillings in your teeth ache." The true Southern version of pecan pie certainly qualifies.

1 unbaked 9″ pastry shell
1 cup brown sugar
1 1/2 cups light corn syrup, or a mix of light and dark
4 eggs
1/4 cup butter
1/4 cup peach brandy
2 teaspoons vanilla
2 cups pecans, coarsely broken

In a saucepan over medium heat, boil sugar

and corn syrup together for 2 to 3 minutes; set aside to cool slightly. In a large bowl, beat eggs lightly. Slowly pour the syrup mixture into the eggs, continuing to beat. Stir in butter, vanilla, and pecans. Pour into crust. Bake at 350° F for 45 to 50 minutes, or until just set.

MILDRED KILGORE'S LEMON ICEBOX PIE

Icebox pies and other no-bake desserts became popular in the 1920s, when electric refrigeration made its way into the kitchen. (Electric refrigerators were still called "iceboxes" in the 1950s and 60s.) Lemon is only one of a dozen variations, including pineapple, lime, and orange. Crusts were often made of crushed graham cracker, vanilla wafer, or gingersnap crumbs. This filling is made with sweetened condensed milk and eggs; others were made with gelatin. Evaporated milk (also called condensed milk) was a popular product before refrigerators were common in homes; sweetened condensed milk was manufactured as early as the 1850s and was very popular.

9″ graham cracker or cookie shell
2 14-ounce cans sweetened condensed milk
1 1/4 cups fresh lemon juice

2 tablespoons finely grated lemon zest
8 large egg yolks
Sweetened whipped cream for topping
Lemon slices for garnish

In a medium bowl, whisk the condensed milk with the lemon juice. In a separate medium bowl, beat the egg yolks and lemon zest until pale. Gradually add the condensed milk mixture, beating until smooth. Pour the filling into the shell. Bake at 325° for 25 minutes, until the edges are set and the center jiggles only slightly. Chill for at least six hours, preferably overnight. Top with sweetened whipped cream and garnish with lemon slices. For easy cutting, use a hot knife.

VERNA TIDWELL'S SHOOFLY PIE

While pie for breakfast was a New England tradition, folks in the rural South enjoyed it too. Food historians tell us that Shoofly Pie began as a cake and was later baked in a pie shell so it could be eaten without a plate and fork. The pie had two versions: "wet bottom" and "dry bottom." In the dry-bottom pie, the crumb topping is mixed into the filling and baked until the filling is firm and cake-like. In the wet-bottom pie, the filling is layered on top and the bottom is gooey, like British treacle custard. Some say the name comes from the need to shoo flies off the sweet treat, but food historian William Woys Weaver speculates that it originated with a popular 1830s circus mule named Shoofly, whose name later appeared on Shoofly Molasses. It's also possible that the word is a corruption of "soufflé," for there is an 1837 recipe for molasses pie that is made like a soufflé, with the addition of beaten egg whites to the filling. The recipe Verna got from Bettina produces a "wet-bottom" pie.

9″ unbaked pie shell
Crumb topping
1 1/2 cups flour
1/2 cup dark brown sugar
1 teaspoon cinnamon
1/2 teaspoon nutmeg
1/8 teaspoon salt
1/2 cup cold unsalted butter
Filling
1 egg yolk
3/4 cup molasses
3/4 cup strong coffee
1/2 teaspoon baking soda

Heat oven to 375°. Make the crumb topping: In a bowl, mix flour, sugar, cinnamon, nutmeg, and salt together in a bowl. Cut in the butter with a pastry cutter until the mixture looks like cornmeal. Make the filling: in a medium bowl, beat egg yolk with the molasses. In a saucepan, bring coffee to a boil and stir in baking soda. Beat hot mixture into molasses mixture and pour into pastry shell. Spoon the crumb mixture evenly over the top. Bake 15 minutes at 375°, lower temperature to 350°, and bake until set.

MISS ROGERS' VINEGAR PIE

This recipe comes from the *Pure Food Cook Book,* compiled and published by the Women's Progressive Farmers' Association of Missouri in 1935. Vinegar pie was a Depression-era favorite because it required only inexpensive ingredients that were likely to be already on hand. Another version (meant to taste something like apple pie) includes familiar pie spices: cinnamon, ginger, nutmeg. Lemon, maple, and vanilla extract were also commonly used.

1 baked 8″ pie shell
1 cup sugar
2 eggs
2 tablespoons cider vinegar
1 cup water

2 tablespoons flour or corn starch
Sweetened whipped cream for garnish

Mix all ingredients. Cook and stir in double boiler, then pour into baked pie shell. Chill. Garnish with sweetened whipped cream.

LIZ LACY'S GREEN TOMATO PIE

An early version of green tomato pie was contributed by a housewife identified only as Mrs. S. T. to the early cookbook *Housekeeping in Old Virginia* (1878):

> Slice green tomatoes and stew in a thick syrup of sugar and lemon juice. Grate in the yellow rind of a lemon. When transparent, spread evenly over the bottom of a pie-plate that has been lined with paste [crust]. Spread strips of pastry across or cut into ornamental leaves with a cake-cutter, place over the fruit and bake.

During the Southern summer or whenever apples were not available, green tomatoes were a popular substitute. Here is Liz's 1934 version of this traditional pie.

2 9″ unbaked pie crusts for top and bottom
3/4 cup sugar
1/2 teaspoon cinnamon

1/8 teaspoon nutmeg
1/4 teaspoon salt
3 tablespoons cornstarch
Zest of 1 lemon
2 pounds green tomatoes, sliced 1/4" thick
1/2 cup golden raisins
2 tablespoons lemon juice
4 tablespoons butter

In a large bowl, mix sugar, cinnamon, nutmeg, salt, cornstarch, and lemon zest. Dredge tomato slices in the sugar mixture. Arrange in pie shell, adding raisins as you layer. Drizzle with lemon juice and dot with butter. This pie can be made with a top and bottom crust, or with a bottom crust and a lattice-work top. Bake at 400° for 25–30 minutes, until golden brown.

RESOURCES

Here are some resources (print and online) that I found helpful in creating *The Darling Dahlias and the Unlucky Clover.*

Books and Periodicals

Daily Life in the United States 1920–1940, by David E. Kyvig. How Americans lived in the Roaring Twenties and the Depression era. Helpful period background.

Driving with the Devil: Southern Moonshine, Detroit Wheels, and the Birth of NASCAR, by Neal Thompson. Moonshine, moonshiners, and fast cars.

The Foxfire Book: Hog Dressing, Log Cabin Building, Mountain Crafts and Foods, Planting by the Signs, Snake Lore, Hunting Tales, Faith Healing, Moonshining, and Other Affairs of Plain Living, edited by Elliott Wiggington. An oral history collection of traditional crafts.

411

Month-by-Month Gardening in Alabama, by Bob Polomski. What Alabama gardeners might be doing at different seasons of the year.

Mountain Spirits: A Chronicle of Corn Whiskey from King James' Ulster Plantation to America's Appalachians and the Moonshine Life, by Joseph Earl Dabney. Informative, readable history, with many anecdotes but no recipes.

Popular Science Monthly, November 1927. The article that Deputy Springer has read is titled "Who Did the Shooting?" by Calvin H. Goddard. It begins on p. 21.

Sears and Roebuck Spring Catalog, 1932. General merchandise catalog. What people were wearing and using during the early 1930s.

To Kill a Mockingbird, by Harper Lee. Harper Lee grew up in Monroeville (the source for her descriptions of Maycomb, where *To Kill a Mockingbird* is set). Monroeville is a real town, only fifteen miles from the fictional Darling.

Websites

"Betty Crocker Radio Show: Cooking School of the Air." https://www.otrcat .com/p/betty-crocker. Information on the show where Liz Lacy heard about the Chocolate Crunch cookies.

"Federal Writers' Project." https://en.wiki pedia.org/wiki/Federal_Writers%27_Proj ect. A New Deal program designed to support out-of-work writers and document local history and culture.

"Newspaper Archives." http://www.news paperarchive.com/. A subscription website that allows you to search, read, clip, save newspapers from the U.S. and around the world.

"The Accidental Invention of the Chocolate Chip Cookie." http://www.todayifoundout .com/index.php/2013/03/ the-accidental-invention-of-the-chocolate-chip-cookie/. More about that cookie.

Discover More About the Dahlias and Find a Reading Group Guide

http://www.DarlingDahlias.com
Subscribe to Susan's free monthly eletter, All About Thyme
http://www.abouthyme.com/dayletters/

ABOUT THE AUTHOR

Growing up on a farm on the Illinois prairie, **Susan Wittig Albert** learned that books could take her anywhere, and reading and writing became passions that have accompanied her throughout her life. She earned an undergraduate degree in English from the University of Illinois at Urbana and a PhD in medieval studies from the University of California at Berkeley, then turned to teaching. After faculty and administrative appointments at the University of Texas, Tulane University, and Texas State University, she left her academic career and began writing full time. Her bestselling fiction includes mysteries in the China Bayles series, the Darling Dahlias, the Cottage Tales of Beatrix Potter, and (under the pseudonym of Robin Paige) a series of Victorian-Edwardian mysteries with her husband, Bill Albert.

The General's Women (2017), a novel

about the World War II romantic triangle of Dwight Eisenhower, his wife Mamie, and his driver and secretary Kay Summersby, is Albert's third work of biographical-historical fiction. It follows *Loving Eleanor,* a fictional account of the friendship of Lorena Hickok and Eleanor Roosevelt, and *A Wilder Rose,* the story of Rose Wilder Lane and the writing of the Little House books. Albert is also the author of two memoirs: *An Extraordinary Year of Ordinary Days* and *Together, Alone: A Memoir of Marriage and Place.* Other nonfiction titles include *What Wildness Is This: Women Write about the Southwest* (winner of the 2009 Willa Award for Creative Nonfiction); *Writing from Life: Telling the Soul's Story;* and *Work of Her Own: A Woman's Guide to Success off the Career Track.* She is the founder of the Story Circle Network, a nonprofit organization for women writers, and a member of the Texas Institute of Letters. She and her husband Bill live on thirty-one acres in the Texas Hill Country, where she gardens, tends chickens and geese, and indulges her passions for needlework and (of course) reading.